86'd

Also by Dan Fante

Chump Change

Mooch

Spitting Off Tall Buildings

A Gin-Pissing-Raw-Meat-Dual-Carburetor-V8-Son-of-a-Bitch from Los Angeles: Collected Poems, 1983–2002

Don Giovanni: A Play

Short Dog: Cab Driver Stories from the L.A. Streets

Kissed by a Fat Waitress: New Poems

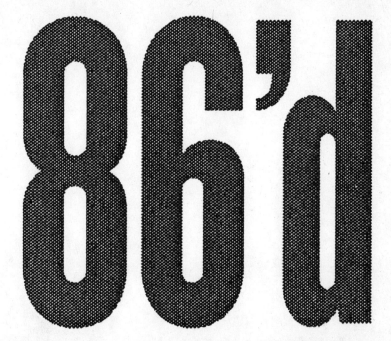

86'd

A NOVEL

DAN FANTE

HARPER ⬤ PERENNIAL

NEW YORK • LONDON • TORONTO • SYDNEY • NEW DELHI • AUCKLAND

HARPER ● PERENNIAL

HarperCollins books may be purchased for educational, business, or sales promotional use. For information please write: Special Markets Department, HarperCollins Publishers, 10 East 53rd Street, New York, NY 10022.

FIRST EDITION

Designed by Sunil Manchikanti

Library of Congress Cataloging-in-Publication Data is available upon request.

ISBN 978-0-06-177922-0

09 10 11 12 13 OV/RRD 10 9 8 7 6 5 4 3 2 1

For Hubert Selby, Jr. Without your heart and your truth, Cubby, I'd still be bumping into walls and trying to make bail. *A mouth in search of a scream.*

You think you know but you really don't know.
Eventually—finally—you find out that
what you think you know is nothing. What you
really know amounts to shit.

A. L. CATLETT

Nice to see that you've finally gotten the monkey
off your back . . . although, apparently, the circus
has not yet left town.

KEN O'BRIEN

one

Sorry to be the bearer of bad news, Bruno. Our new projects team met on Friday. Second quarter numbers for all Canonball Press editions are down. The decision was out of my hands, unfortunately. They are rescheduling your book and all new short story anthologies for next year at the earliest.

My best advice is for you to look on this as a temporary setback and nothing more. I know we'll publish UNTIL THE FAT LADY SINGS . . . eventually."

Evanston Wright, Senior Editor

A fucking cosmic shit shower.

Up to the minute I opened the e-mail from Canonball Press I'd thought the five years and three hundred pages it had taken to put my book together had been worth it. Only three months before the pricks had sent me their acceptance letter and a token five-hundred-dollar advance. I would finally be a published short story writer.

Wrong.

I printed out Canonball's e-mail, underlined the word *eventually* in black marker, then taped the goddamn thing to the wall in my room, above my desk. *Eventually* I'd start fucking dead chimpanzee corpses too—*eventually*.

Suddenly I realized how much I hated my goddamn computer and all computers for the ease with which they delivered such terrible news. Slamming my fist on my writing desk I cursed the day a year before that I'd allowed my friend Eddy Dorobek to flimflam me into buying a used laptop from him and giving up my dead father's rickety old Underwood portable. Fuck Eddy Dorobek! and all software and DVDs and e-mail and instant messages that *instantly* ruined people's lives. Fuck Google and *MySpace* too. And fuck fucking Evanston Wright at Canonball Press for not even conceding to me the courtesy of a goddamn stamp and a signature on a signed piece of paper.

Still left on my telephone's answering machine was a two-year-old message from Hubert Selby, Jr., my literary mentor, my favorite writer. Still un-erased. A thirty-second crack in time that had altered everything and changed my life.

To heal myself and interrupt my brain's fury I pressed the "Saved Messages" button on my phone.

I'd heard his words a thousand times now, listened to them over and over like a hit song—from my writing table while eating dinner or reading the newspaper, or posing in the mirror or getting in and out of the shower. While jerking off or listening to a Van Morrison CD or doing leg-lifts on the floor. I'd even played the message for the old guy I rented my room from, Uncle Bill, and for my sister, Lucia. Selby's words had saved my sanity.

I pressed play.

. . . Dante? Bruno Dante? Cubby Selby here. You gave me your manuscript a few weeks ago . . . and the other day I finally had a chance to look it over. So, okay, first, let me say that I like your stories. As you might guess I get many requests from people to read their stuff. And most of it, truthfully, regretfully, is crap. Plain and simple. Just crap. But Until the Fat Lady Sings *is the real thing. Stories from the gut and from the heart. I was moved—more than once. You can be proud of your manuscript, Bruno. I remember you saying that you got discouraged. Well don't! You're good and you've got what it takes. Keep writing no matter what. Never stop. Never give up.*

I hope we bump into each other again sometime soon.

Thank Christ. Thank God for the miracle of Hubert Selby, Jr.

I'd followed Selby around Los Angeles for months—stalked him even—gone to half a dozen of his readings and appearances—and finally, sober that night, I'd worked up the courage to ask the great writer to have a look at my story collection.

After his reading that night, behind Midnight Special Bookstore, in the parking lot as he was getting into his car, I'd approached Selby with my manuscript and asked if he would mind taking a look. He recognized me from the audience that night. I'd been the guy who'd hogged the Q & A time, asking more than my share of questions.

The thin old cynic smiled, patted my shoulder, then wheezing in a drag from his black Sherman. "Sure kid, I'll read it over and get back to you. Don't worry. Your stuff's in good hands."

Again I pressed the save button on my phone. Selby's message was all that I had now, all that was keeping me from black madness.

two

I have no idea why I am crazy and angry and edged-out most of the time and why alcohol and painkiller pills and Xanax-type stuff are the only things that help to keep me remotely calm. I have no idea why I experience life as pointless and screwed and I know that most people don't pour a cup of bourbon into their milk and oatmeal in the morning. That's just how it is.

After the publication of *Until the Fat Lady Sings* was postponed indefinitely I decided that I needed a change from the telemarketing industry. For months I had been hawking risk-free Pinkerton burglar alarm installs out of a cave: a windowless, industrial, cinderblock office in Manhattan Beach. A hundred calls a day to set five realistic sales appointments. Torturous, brutal shit.

Behind the workload quota and hitting the juice too hard I'd developed attitude problems and begun showing up late for my 5:30 a.m. shift.

Me and Kassim, my boss, had disliked each other from jump street. The prick was a former math professor from Tehran with a Godzilla ego. He spoke three or four Middle Eastern tongues but his combined English syntax and cultural grasp of anything American equaled shit. Each time—especially with other people around—when I'd ask the jerk if he wouldn't mind speaking more slowly, or repeating what he'd just said, Kassim would consider that I'd challenged his authority or was somehow mocking him. His expression would blacken and he would glare at me murderously.

Things came to a head near quitting time one Friday afternoon. The office's ceiling intercom blasted: *Bruno Dante—Bruno Dante—to Kassim's office. Now.* Strike one.

Once there, I was ordered to sit in the outer waiting room for half an hour and watch as the rest of the staff came and went, picking up their paychecks. Strike two.

Finally, in front of Kassim's desk, his henchman, the telemarketing manager, Gretchen—the hugest deep-fried, ass-kissing, hogface, grease-soaked twat to ever sit in an office chair in Los Angeles—handed me my call records as evidence. Turns out that Professor Kassim and blubbergirl had been monitoring my phone work over the last several shifts.

Kassim began waving his copy of my stats. "*Dree bersonal kallz ober de lass doooo daze. Und fourrr dimez,* diss sheeeef alone, jou hab *borgodden do hoffer de flee Dizzylannn teekets ah de enn off your prezendadion.*

Gretchen stood by wheezing, nodding sycophantically at whatever additional unpronounceable broken English mumbo jumbo snot came from her boss's mouth.

I looked at her for a clarification. "So I'm fired, right?" I said. "Is that it?"

"Correct," she oozed. "Terminated, as of today."

Strike three.

Refusing any more eye contact, Kassim handed pigass a sealed envelope. My paycheck. Blubbergirl passed it to me.

Before leaving, I stuffed the check into my pants pocket then tossed my headset on to his desk. Then I leaned in close to his ear. "You and big Gretchen here must be having some pretty hot sex," I hissed. "No kidding, I'd pay good money to watch you hump that shit."

Once outside in the parking lot, after hearing the steel building door hiss closed then latch behind me, I lit a cigarette and sucked the smoke in.

The voice, the one always screaming in my head, telling me what a fool and an asshole I was, was getting louder. Worse all the time. Sometimes, like now, when I had quit or left a job or woke up drunk not knowing where I was, the goddamn thing was maddening—unstoppable. I decided that from now on I would give it a name. From now on I'd call the prick *Jimmy*.

At least I was free and reeligible for unemployment. I'd already paid my rent two weeks before so I decided to splurge on a few extras over the weekend: A paperback or two. A couple of bottles of decent wine. Maybe a movie. So I tore open my pay envelope to verify the amount: Five hundred and eleven dollars.

That's when the real curveball cracked me in the center of my forehead. The goddamn thing was unsigned.

Now, completely out of money, with the sun beating in through the window of my ratbox room in the Venice house

I shared with my ex-girlfriend's eighty-five-year-old uncle, hoping to counteract last night's excessive gin and tonic with gulps of milk and spoonfuls of peanut butter, I sat at my writing desk staring at the computer keys.

Through money worries and too much down time and the almost constant boozing that'd been assaulting my health and sanity, I'd taken Hubert Selby's advice to heart and kept my commitment to "keep going." I had written one good page a day—no matter what—do or die. For the last few weeks I'd scribbled in my notebook while in my car or in a bar or a coffee shop, then transposed them to my laptop. But there they were. All there in front of me. I'd done it. I'd kept my promise to myself.

So what if I couldn't pay my rent. So what if I had to go back to another boiler room gig or even the taxi business. So what if Canonball Press didn't publish *Until the Fat Lady Sings* for another two years or another five even. So fucking what! Through my madness and boozing and the pain pills I'd kept my promise to myself. I was writing.

But with the loss of my job I was beginning to be scared. Afraid of a bad crash. Over the last year or so I had been working five different doctors to get my pills; my Vicodin, my Halcion, and my Xanax. When I needed the stuff or when I would overdo the booze for days or weeks at a time, I offset my alcohol use with the pills to get relief. But that option was running out. I could no longer afford my scripts and I was scared.

Shutting down my computer I flipped open the Sunday *L.A. Times* to the employment section. When I got to "Drivers Wanted," I stopped. The company name at the bottom of the box surprised me. Dav-Ko.

David Koffman picked up the phone when I called in and remembered me right away. I had worked for Dav-Ko in New York five years before as a chauffeur and part-time night dispatcher. In those days his company was in its infancy and little more than a gypsy cab car service that did periodic chauffeur jobs. Koffman really only had two limos. One was an eight-year-old dented, black, stretch Caddy with over a hundred thousand miles on the odometer and the other was a big blue Lincoln sedan that was more for personal use than the livery business. We stored them both and a half dozen beat-up airport vans and station wagons behind a gas station and ran the whole deal out of a three-bedroom brownstone apartment on Sixty-fourth Street and Second Avenue.

Koffman was a speed-talker, an ace business guy, almost seven feet tall, and an unashamed homosexual. For a year when I lived in Manhattan me and David's cousin Stewie split dispatch duty while he spent his days taking people to lunch and drumming up new clients. Stewie and me wore the same size chauffeur jacket, so at night we'd take turns playing chauffeur, putting on a black cap and clip-on bow tie, jumping out of the car to open and close the back door for David while he passed out business cards and acted the role of the big shot limo owner in front of the gay after-hours clubs below Fourteenth Street. But as the company grew so did my personal clientele. In the end I had no life other than the East Side Saloon on First Avenue and spending twelve hours a day behind the wheel. My writing was out of the question. I'd return home only to sleep and shower, then take the IRT subway uptown back to the office. The money was decent and in those days I was less insane. So eventually I packed it in, leaving on good terms to take a four-hour-a-day bootleg DVD phone sales gig at an office building in Times Square. There were no hard feelings.

Koffman hadn't changed. He'd never been much for tele-phone chitchat so he came right to the point and wanted to know my work history since I'd been with Dav-Ko. Had I, over the last few years, had any experience managing people, over-seeing a staff? Work other than chauffeuring?

Without hesitation my lips composed the necessary lies. "Sure. Absolutely," I said. "It's right on my résumé. I can show you."

My reply caused him to shift gears. He immediately began "selling" me, reciting the statistics of how successful and hip Dav-Ko had become since I'd left. The company now oper-ated ten new stretch limos and another half dozen town cars out of a three-story Midtown New York garage. They had a full-time mechanic, fifteen drivers, and an in-house train-ing manual. All the chauffeurs wore Greek seaman's caps and vested blue suits as a uniform. Dav-Ko's "hip" trademark was a red hankie in the breast pocket of each chauffeur's suit jacket. Koffman bragged that his current customer base con-sisted mainly of celebrities and rock stars and New York–L.A. entertainment big shots.

For the last week he'd been renting a bungalow at the Bev-erly Hills Hotel and intended to be in town for as long as it took to make Dav-Ko Hollywood a turnkey operation.

Trust was important to Koffman. I could tell that he liked the idea of having a known quantity—a former dispatcher-driver like myself—working with him again. For David, us having refound each other after so long was a kind of *sign*. A good omen. He had been a heavy social drinker with his gay buddies when we had worked together. I assumed that was still the case.

I'd gotten lucky and I knew it. The longer we stayed on the phone the closer I was to being offered a job. Before hanging up he and I set up a breakfast meeting for the next morning at the Formosa Café on Santa Monica Boulevard in Hollywood.

I arrived at the restaurant early and headed for the men's room. Once inside with the door locked, I set the manila envelope containing my fictitious job résumé down under the paper towel rack then finished off one of two half-pint bracers I'd picked up on the way, tossing the empty into the trash.

Then I took a minute to focus in on the face in the mirror. I looked okay. Eyes clear. Good close shave. I'd been sweating through my shirt as usual and my tie had a stain—snot or food or something—but it wasn't that noticeable. I smoothed my hair down with my fingers and that was that.

To quiz myself on my bogus work history I unclamped the envelope and took a last look at my résumé. If Koffman required a document that showed management in addition to straight chauffeuring, no problem, I was ready. I had one.

It was ten-thirty and after the breakfast rush, so the Formosa wasn't busy and I was able to find a booth with a window.

The owner of Dav-Ko Hollywood made his appearance as I was finishing my second cup of coffee. I watched as his hired-by-the-hour chauffeured blue stretch Lincoln pulled up in front of the restaurant blocking the Santa Monica Boulevard crosswalk. Before entering, David Koffman, all six foot seven inches and three hundred pounds of him, now with shoulder-length gray hair, stood outside the restaurant's glass door, a spring fashion statement in his Tom Wolfe, open-collared, white-on-white linen suit. Posing there, half man, half tent, he chatted amiably with his driver long enough to make sure everyone inside the place had a good opportunity to check him out.

He shook my hand, flashed me his million-peso grin, then flopped his long body into the booth. He looked older. The night life and years with the booze had taken their toll.

"Is that for me?" he asked, pointing at the brown envelope on the table.

I nodded and pushed it toward him. I couldn't help but notice that this guy and his Buffalo Bill act were ideally suited to a city composed mainly of status junkies and now-you-see-it-now-you-don't flimflam sincerity.

After ordering eggs and green tea and taking a quick cell phone call, Koffman gave my résumé a ten-second once over then looked up. "Soooo . . . you drove a yellow cab here in Los Angeles for over a year?"

"Yeah. Correct," I said. "Long hours. Lousy pay." Then I went on. "There's a limo job there too—underneath the taxi job."

"Right, okay, here it is. A private-party chauffeur position. Part-time. You drove for an ex-CEO?"

This of course was a lie. From here down everything I had written on the résumé was an exaggeration or outright bullshit. For me it had always been easier to make stuff up than to remember the sequence of an unimportant and ridiculous job or its dates in history.

"A retired guy," I said. "He traveled with a large, stinky, fifteen-year-old Irish setter. The dog had a bladder problem and the old guy never bathed him. He died—I mean the guy died—probably the dog too. Anyway, I'm not a big Irish setter fan."

Koffman seemed amused. "The important thing is that you know the L.A. streets."

"Hey, I know the streets. No problem."

"Okay, okay—here we go; you managed a staff of three to five at Kassim's Worldwide Precious Metals and Rare Coin Consortium in . . . in Manhattan Beach."

"Right. Correct."

"Long name. What sort of consortium?"

"It wasn't a consortium at all. This is L.A. I guess the guy just needed a flash title for his telemarketing boiler room."

"Reason for leaving?"

"Reorganization, I guess you'd call it."

"Reorganization? Ha-ha. You mean the place went tits up?"

Suddenly I had an overwhelming need for a drink. For the last thirty seconds I'd been controlling the onset of leg tremors by tightly crossing the fuckers at my ankles. Even now the heebie-jeebies appeared to be traveling their way up my body to my upper torso. Maybe I was about to get a sudden spell of the flyaways because my left hand had just begun to shake—my coffee cup hand. I slid it under the table then pinned the prick beneath my thigh. "Right," I said. "Bad management."

"I see," said Koffman, whose hands never seemed to shake at all.

Now I was dizzy. My throat was dry and I needed air. My heart began slamming itself against the inside of my rib cage. The guy in the polar bear uniform leaned closer. "Are you okay?" he whispered. "You're trembling."

My mouth formed words but the lips refused the marching orders. I had to settle for wagging my head up and down. My full attention was fixed on the glove compartment of my Pontiac—parked at a meter fifty feet away—where I'd left my backup half-pint of vodka. I was now acutely aware that I'd be unable to endure another four seconds of this moron interview. I needed an excuse—any excuse—to get up and leave the booth.

"Bruno, what's up? What's going on? Are you . . . hungover?"

Unlike me David Koffman was an excessive episodic drinker and not a day-to-day juicer. There was no way he could not *get* what was going on with me. I thrust a trembling thumb down on top of the résumé and was finally able to blurt some words. "Bottom line," I said, "that company was a total Chinese fire drill. If you want to know, the guy . . . the owner, was a foreigner. He spoke about five words in American. He wouldn't know a cold call from the goddamn La Brea Tar Pits."

"I see. I understand."

"Swell. Can we move on?"

"Okay, but just below that in your job description you write that you ran a staff of three to five people? I'm confused. Was it three or was it five, or what?"

Sweat was now soaking my hair, forehead, and armpits. For some reason—beyond my control—my voice was getting steadily louder. I pointed back down at the page. "Confused! I was a supervisor," I barked. "I managed trainees. Some weeks there were three and some weeks there were more than three—sometimes five. Sometimes more. Sometimes two. Sometimes one. Sometimes seven. Okay? Jesus Christ!"

"Okay, fabulous. And you did this supervisor job for how long?"

"It's there in front of you typed out in bold New Courier twelve-point font!"

"Right, I see it. Two years. And what products did you sell?"

"Rare coins! Valuable! Rare! Coins!"

"Why are you so nervous?"

"You're mistaken, David. You've misconstrued my enthusiasm as a sign of tension. I get warm sometimes. Sometimes I sweat. What's the big deal?"

Koffman took a sip of tea. "May I suggest that we keep our voices down? We appear to be attracting attention."

"Sure, no problem. Fine with me. *Fabulous.*"

"Okay, let's move on. Tell me about the precious metals aspect of the company?"

I sucked in air. I could feel my face reddening and I was beginning to experience the onset of two simultaneous physical sensations: Either (a) I was going to pass out or (b) I was going to shit in my pants. "That's just more hyperbole, prevarication, and cocksnot," I snarled. "Like calling the company a *consortium.* We didn't sell precious metals. No such thing. We sold coins. You know, uncalculated old silver dollars and Buffalo nickels 'n' shit. Krugerrands. Stuff like that."

Setting my résumé on the table Koffman folded his arms. "What's bothering you, Bruno? Is it a hangover or what? Just tell me what's going on."

It became apparent to me that I needed to murder this huge, tea-slurping faggot.

Leaning across the table I was an inch from his face. "Okay look, here's the deal," I blurted. "My Pontiac is parked down the street at a meter. Okay. That meter is about to expire. I've been here over an hour. Okay. This is Hollywood. Okay. Expired meter parking tickets here are forty-nine fucking dollars. Okay. And I'm about to get one. Okay! And additionally, I think I'm coming down with something. It isn't a hangover. Possibly it's the flu."

Koffman rolled his eyes. "We're almost done. Can't you just calm down. I'll pay the ticket. Your car will be fine. We were discussing your last job."

"I know what we were discussing, David. I'm not a mongoloid imbecile."

"Will you be straight with me about something: Have you been drinking this morning? Be completely candid, please."

"Here's what I'm saying, okay?" I whisper-yelled. "I'm saying that the owner of that company—the main guy—the prick that ran the coin place—was a Middle Eastern anal-retentive Taliban fuck. I lied, okay? They didn't reorganize the company. I quit. I quit because I became aware that they were recording all our phone calls. Believe that shit? Recording calls! Every goddamn call!"

Koffman inclined his lanky body away from me, pressing his back against the red Naugahyde. He looked scared. "Soooo, you're saying that you left that position voluntarily."

"Yes, I did. I quit. Know w'amsayin'?"

"Okay, fine, but as far as I know there's really nothing illegal about a company recording calls."

"Hey, this is the United States of America if I'm not mistaken! Okay. We have laws relating to espionage and wiretapping here. The particular rectumshitbreath jerkoff I'm referring to was a vindictive Persian prick. A pernicious towelhead un-American alien pompous shitsucking dorf. And the sonofabitch beat me out of my final paycheck. Okay! Five hundred and eleven bucks. If that's not the definition of a card-carrying cocksucker then I don't know what the hell is?"

"I can see that we're not on the same page here."

"The page you're on is the page I'm on. Ten thousand percent the same page. I promise you."

"So, is it your car? Or the flu? Or are you upset about your last boss?"

"Okay, look, I'm sorry about the cocksucker remark, David. I apologize. Okay. It was uncalled for and off-the-cuff, completely out of context and inappropriate to our discussion. I'll just say this: In my book a cocksucker can be male or female, anatomically. Cocksuckers are—let's say—potentially interchangeable. That doesn't make 'em right or wrong. I think we can both agree on the definition of the word cocksucker as sort of neutral. Okay. I mean you yourself may or may not suck cock. That's none of my concern. It's a private matter between you and your conscience and any other consenting adult whose cock you might be sucking. What I'm saying is that it doesn't necessarily follow that all homos must ipso facto be cocksuckers. Perhaps most are but who says we should throw the baby out with the bathwater. Right?"

On the table by the menus and the sugar shaker Koffman's cell phone began to chime to the tune of "Dancing in the Dark."

"Go ahead," I said, still battling dizziness, gulping in as much air as possible, pointing at the chrome-colored chiming turd on the table, "answer your phone. I'll go put some quarters in my meter."

Big David was staring at me—ignoring his phone. He sighed deeply. Then, extending his thick arms, a benign expression infecting his face, he covered my hands with his massive paws in a misguided dumbfuck homosexual attempt to soothe me. "I know you're upset, Bruno," he whispered. "It's okay."

Now I was impaled, pinned to the formica by a gay Hulk Hogan in a milkman's uniform. "Okay, Jesus," I howled. "Yes I am. I'm upset. I admit it."

"Please listen carefully, Bruno. Just try to let in what I'm saying. I'm offering you an excellent opportunity—a live-in chauffeur manager position. Are you interested?"

"Jesus—of course I'm fuckin' interested! I want the job."

"Good."

A minute or two later, as I was sliding across the booth's fake-leather bench seat to get to my feet, somehow the trembling butt of my hand came down on the outer rim of my coffee cup. Its contents were launched across the table and landed on the sleeve of David Koffman's white jacket. It didn't help seal the deal. It just happened.

I was half-sure I'd blown it until he phoned me the next day. One of his ex-lovers had been an active New York City AA guy. Based on that, in the end, Koffman must've decided he'd take a chance. His one condition was simple and straightforward: He knew I'd been drinking. He insisted that I attend twelve-step meetings.

"You and I have worked together before with good results," he said. "I realize I'm taking a big chance but I'm betting with an opportunity like this one, you'll clean up your act."

"You won't be sorry," I said.

"Will you do it?" he asked. "Will you cut down on your alcohol consumption and go to meetings?"

"Absolutely. One thousand percent!" I shot back. "You can count on it. You have my word. And I'll pay the cleaning bill for your jacket too."

My new boss told me that we would sign a contract for the job. It would include medical insurance and a paid vacation and a 25 percent partnership after six months if I managed not to screw the pooch. Also, because of Koffman's kinkiness for honesty, if I was somehow arrested and convicted of a crime, other than a traffic ticket, for any reason, the deal would be void.

That afternoon when I opened my e-mail, I saw something that drove me to my keyboard. I'd been receiving more than my share of crazy spam solicitations from Africa. People telling me I'd won some fucking lottery or another, or that they wanted to split some inheritance or annuity or some goddamn thing. This one was from some conniving bitch impersonating a princess. Here's the letter I wrote. After I finished it I bummed four stamps from Uncle Bill then took it to the post office:

Crown Princess Makeba Urabe (Deposed)
18 Rue Marselles
Zimbabwe—AFRICA

Hello Dearest Princess:

I have no idea how you got my e-mail address but I consider it a treasured blessing to have received your vital correspondence. How gracious and kind you are, dear one, to make me such a generous, even dare I say, unselfish, offer. Your description of your plight and your efforts to recover your stolen family fortune from the evil and tyrannous political opportunists who have betrayed you brought me to tears and opened my heart to you big-time.

You mention that all you require is $50,000 to travel to Europe and recover the 3,000,000 pounds sterling awaiting you at the Royal Bank of England. Then you will reclaim your fortune. And, let me make sure that I get this down correctly; you are offering me $500,000 in return!! I am breathless! I cannot believe your kindness! Dear and gracious Princess, how giving and momentous can one person be? All I can say is, thank you, and gee whiz!

Our local prayer circle meets the day after tomorrow. We will hold your success and well-being and the restoration of your title and fortune in our hearts from then on, with HE who presides over us all.

I am confident that I can speak for my fellow parishioners when I tell you that we will vote to put ourselves at your immediate disposal. This is your hour of need and I'm quite sure everyone will be in agreement. Therefore, I am confident that you can expect our check for <u>not</u> $50,000 but <u>$60,000</u>—almost immediately. Also, as you astutely suggest, we will include our church's wire-routing checking-account number, should there be any confusion regarding the cashing of our check.

Dearest one, please wait at your mailbox daily for the funds to arrive.

Your newest and most ardent admirer,

Bruno Dante
666 Ohsureur Drive
Gulfport, MS 39501

three

The next morning, wearing the same puked-on tie from my interview, after paying the parking valet guy at the Beverly Hills Hotel almost ten bucks to relocate my Pontiac, I found the path to the bungalows and knocked on Number 104. I was sober except for slamming three Vicodin with my morning coffee on my way driving down Venice Boulevard.

A gray-haired giant wearing a monogrammed blue robe opened the door, yawning and rubbing his eyes. "Well, Bruno Dante. This is a surprise."

"At your service," I said, feeling the *vike* buzz kicking in. "I'm ready for my first day."

"I wasn't sure that I'd be seeing you today."

"I'm better," I said. "Ninety-nine percent. Fact is I had an excellent bowel movement this morning."

Standing on the steps outside the bungalow, it was hard not to notice that my new employer's robe wasn't tied all the way closed. I caught a glimpse of what might roughly approximate the genitalia of a pastured rhino behind the terry cloth.

"Wait here," Koffman said, then disappeared into the darkness. A moment later he was back with a wad of money-clipped bills in his hand and the robe cinched closed.

After peeling off several fifties Koffman held them out toward me. "There's a men's store on Hollywood Boulevard," he said. "The Manhattan Tie Shop. At the corner of Cahuenga. Ask for the manager. His name is Octavio. He's a doll. The store sells a three-piece polyester blue business suit—the perfect chauffeur's uniform. They charge a hundred and seventy-nine dollars. Buy two. Have the store do the alterations while you wait. Then come back here dressed for work."

"Ten-four," I said, half-snatching the money from his hand, wanting to appear eager and confident. "I'll be dressed for success."

Again Buffalo Bill eyed me up and down. "Sooo, you're okay, ready to start your new career?"

"Nothing equals a good dump. To my way of thinking taking a decent shit is a life-affirming experience."

"How delightful."

"So I'll be driving you around after I get back with my new duds?"

"I've got a full to-do list."

"Swell. Have you rented another limo?"

Somewhere in the room behind my boss a curtain came open and a sudden shaft of light illuminated a person—a young Latino guy—naked from the waist up, a foot shorter than Koffman and twenty-five years younger. The kid continued moving around and getting dressed for the rest of the time me and my boss stood shooting the breeze.

"I'm picking up a Lincoln Town Car," Koffman went on. "You'll drive me—us—around for the rest of the day and I'll begin your indoctrination as the first Dav-Ko employee at the

California branch. Dav-Ko Hollywood. You'll be paid in cash for the day."

"Sounds good," I said.

Koffman was never less than a hundred percent business. "I've been working with a Realtor," he went on. "We've found a furnished duplex on Selma Avenue, near Highland, near Hollywood High. It's the perfect launch pad for the new company. The bottom floor is commercial space—a former doctor's office—and the second floor has two bedrooms and there's a full kitchen. Granted, it's not the most elite neighborhood in Los Angeles, but the property has a fenced yard and it's clean and close to the freeway. And there's off-street parking for a dozen limos . . . and the rent is fabulously reasonable."

I knew the area. Years before, as a kid, I'd frequented the Baroque Bookstore, a block away on Las Palmas. Hank Chinaski and Jonathan Dante's books were well represented at the Baroque. Red, the owner, had been a nice old guy too. But, aside from the Baroque Bookstore and Miceli's restaurant across the street, most of the rest of the neighborhood was seedy and transient. A near slum in fact.

Koffman beamed. "I'm signing the lease this afternoon."

"Ba-da-bing-ba-da-boom," I said. "So I guess that's that. Hollywood here we come!"

Koffman eyed me. "Are you okay, Bruno?"

"Clean and sober. Very okay."

"You're sure?"

"Absolutely. I'm completely committed."

"I have your word on that?"

"Five thousand percent."

"Okay then. Selma Avenue will be our first stop after you get back here and pick us up. I'm excited, Bruno."

"You bet, David. So am I."

"My New York astrologer says I'm coming into a Mars trine aspect. Excellent for business."

"So, I guess that means I'll be relocating sooner than later," I said. "So I guess you'll want me living there?"

Koffman was smiling. "Ten-four," he said, imitating me. "When I leave Los Angeles you'll be in charge. I'll be entrusting Dav-Ko L.A. to you . . . if you prove yourself."

"You have my commitment," I said.

"We're on our way, Bruno," he grinned. "I can feel it."

Then Koffman swung the door open. "I want you to meet Francisco, my lover. He's from Guatemala. Say *hola*, Francisco."

There was the kid across the room waving shyly and mouthing the word "hi," now with his shirt on. About twenty-five. Black hair combed straight back and copper skin with the miniature body of a gymnast. Nice even teeth too.

But, as promised, I went to AA. My first meeting the next day was at a place called Architects of Adversity in West Hollywood. I looked it up on Google.

Five minutes into the deal while the leader is reading from the meeting format, two guys started screaming at each other. Guy #1 was mad. He appeared to be about eighteen minutes off crack and the leader made the mistake of read something about God in the format. #1 stood up and stopped the leader to protest.

Then Guy #2 told Guy #1 that if he didn't like what he was hearing then he should find another meeting. So naturally now Guy #1 loses it. He picks up his folding chair and begins screaming fuck this and fuck that and knocks his coffee cup over on the table soaking some woman's purse. Turns out this is her best I. Magnin purse or some shit and now she's pissed too because of the coffee stain.

Enough was enough. I decided to leave.

Outside, in front of the meeting hall, there's a guy just lighting up a cigarette. He's wearing a wool cap and a heavy black suede coat in the eighty-degree heat. I asked him for a light.

"That was pretty crazy in there," I said. "Are all the meetings around here like this one?"

"Whatever, man. It's cool with me," he says back. "I'm just here to get my card signed."

"So," I ask, "what do you do when it gets like that? How do you handle it?"

The question amuses him. "Timing is the key," he snickers. "I do the same thing every day. I come out here and smoke right after they read chapter five at the beginning. Then the speaker starts. I wait about half an hour and when I hear people clapping I know he's done. I go back in. Then, after they sign the court cards and pass them out, I'm gone."

"You don't stay to hear what's going on?"

"Yo, sixteen more meetings and I'm done. Free. My AA sentence is completed."

"Okay. But what if someone like me shows up and doesn't like what's going on in the meeting?"

The guy scratched the top of his cap with the shiny end of his Bic lighter. "The key is, do you have a court card?"

"No. I'm just here."

"Whoa! Don't waste your time, bro. If I were you I'd go to the movies. Higher Power this and Higher Power that. It's a group therapy circle jerk with Jesus in the middle."

"C'mon, really?"

"No shit, dude. I've been to a hundred meetings. It's

always the same. Nothing changes. Go to therapy or whatever but don't waste your time here. I promise you."

I tried one more meeting the next day. It wasn't any better. I decided the guy was right. I took his advice. Every morning after that at eleven o'clock I'd tell David Koffman I was going to a meeting. I didn't say that the *meeting* was being held at one of the local movie theaters or a bookstore or at a Starbucks.

four

I t took three full carloads in my Pontiac to get my books and my computer and TV and boxed-up belongings from Uncle Bill's house on Twenty-seventh Place in Venice to Dav-Ko's new home on Selma Avenue in Hollywood. But I'd gone the entire day without a pill or a drink. Not easy because as it turned out eighty-year-old Uncle-fuckin'-Bill had a curveball to throw my way.

I was passing the living room hauling a heavy box of books out to my car on my shoulder when Uncle Bill clicked the sound down on his TV remote and stopped me by using a cop-like hand signal. He motioned for me to set my box down. "Step in here for half a second, will ya, busta?" he hissed.

I set the box down.

Uncle Bill is a fat, wrinkled old shit with an arthritic back. Uncle Bill has elected to spend his golden years in a filthy, battered recliner watching cop show reruns. And judging from his odor, apparently the use of soap and water is an alien idea to Uncle Bill.

So I waited and watched while he finished chewing his last bite of Pop-Tart and wiped his mouth with a rancid, overused paper towel from his shirt pocket. Then Bill looked at me and grinned. "You're aware that I'm withholding your security deposit until further notice," he said flatly.

"No Bill," says I. "I had no idea you were doing that."

"You're a smoker, busta. That bedroom'll need fumigation and a double coat of repaint. And me and Pauline gotta check for damage and excessive use."

"Excessive use, Bill? Is that a technical legal landlord term?"

"I'm talking about wear and tear, busta. Repairs. That kinda thing."

"So when will I get my deposit back?"

"How should I know?"

"How about tomorrow?"

"You can call me . . . first of next week," the old prick snorted. "I'll have Pauline cut you a check—less damages and wear and tear."

"Look Bill," I said. "I've been here eighteen months. I paid a five-hundred-dollar deposit. In cash. I want my money back. Go check the room out for yourself. Right now. There are no *damages*."

Bill tore open the wrapper on a fresh Pop-Tart. Flakes of the hard sugar coating from the last two he'd eaten were still clinging to the front of his zip-up sweatshirt. "By law I have thirty days to return your deposit," he grinned. "I'm just makin' sure that I get a hundred percent what's coming to me, is all."

"If you got what's coming to you, Bill, that recliner you're sitting in would be resting in the center of a smoking crater half a mile wide."

"Huh?"

"Forget it."

The building at 6736 Selma Avenue was what I'd expected—a semi-dump. As I pulled the Lincoln Town Car into the driveway what I saw before me was a re-stuccoed, renovated, ninety-year-old shithole in the armpit of Hollywood. No wonder the doctor had closed his office and moved out. The only redeeming aspect to the location was the ten-foot-high security fence surrounding it.

Selma Avenue is the male hustler capital of the area and it was a warm day so the gay boys were out in force, populating the sidewalk. Crackhead skinny is a sexual fashion statement in Hollywood. Most of the hustlers still looked like teenagers and wore the uniform of the day, T-shirts and jeans. A few rode skateboards along the sidewalk while others—the fems in tight pants and eye makeup—hung together, leaning against parked cars, smoking cigarettes, posing for the passing traffic. But they all had that edgy, I'm-workin'-the-street look in their eyes.

It took four guys and a truck with a crane to install Dav-Ko's yellow and blue sign outside my bedroom above the second-floor balcony. That afternoon the male hustlers on Selma Avenue watched with fascination as workmen and moving trucks came and went.

In less than a week David Koffman and Francisco and a swish decorator friend who called himself Benecio had furnished both floors of the building with high-end used stuff from the second-hand shops on Western Avenue and Robertson Boulevard. Beds, desks, chairs, filing cabinets, paintings, a rebuilt stove, and a washer and dryer. The whole deal.

Upstairs in my room I took most of the afternoon to arrange my books by category and author on the freshly painted shelves, then I set up my desk. I had written my one page a day almost since I'd left my phone room burglar alarm gig with Kassim and I wanted to keep going. Now, in a new place, working a new job, I was sure I'd be able to continue. My life plan was simple: I would drive and write. Sleep and work. Make money. I'd give Dav-Ko my best shot. Just like I'd done with my short stories, through will power, I'd force myself to cut back on the booze and the vikes and do my best to hold my rages and mind stuff under control. I'd watch my mouth with my boss and his boyfriend and ride the horse in the direction he was going.

It was after sunset as I sat in the near darkness that first night, observing the male hustler action on Selma Avenue outside my window; the johns in their flash L.A. cars, the Benzs and BMWs and Porsches, pulling over to chat up the fresh curbside meat while a block away the bright street lights from Hollywood Boulevard began burning through the evening freeway smog.

I was a hundred yards walking distance from Musso and Frank Grill, where sixty years before my father would get drunk on a daily basis with his mean-spirited Hollywood screenwriter buddies. Everything in Los Angeles had changed but nothing was different. L.A. had become a perfect example of twenty-first-century America. A city of pay and play.

I lit a fresh Marlboro Light and in the fading light watched while a black kid down the block unzipped has pants to flash the merchandise for a guy in a red convertible.

Disgusted, I turned away and clicked on my computer to find my stories. I'm Bruno Dante, I thought, a writer of short fiction, a guy with a failed book, and a twelve-year-old Pontiac to his name. A forty-two-year-old wannabe. Swimming against the tide. Starting over one more time.

On the roof Dav-Ko's new neon sign clicked on. It began flashing every three seconds, alternately flooding my room with light, then blackening it. I was home.

five

I was beginning to see dead people. They were not really dead. They were people who I'd meet who looked like people I had known who were *now* dead. It seemed to be happening more and more. In bookstores or super-markets or liquor stores or bars. People who look like guys I used to know. For instance I saw Timmy Healy a month or so ago. The guy was a ringer for Timmy—except twenty years younger than the dead one. Then there was Bryan Mann. Bryan played jazz flute around town for years then got liver cancer—and ba-boom, he was dead in two months. And last week I saw KK Colberg. Bigger than shit. The KK look-alike sold me a pack of smokes at a liquor store. He reminded me exactly of him. I'd begun to think it might be an omen of my own death. A sign perhaps. And it happened enough that it was beginning to scare me.

But then the night after I saw the KK guy who sold me the cigarettes, I bet another guy—a baseball fan—twenty bucks at the Warm-Up Room bar. I'd bet him that Barry Bonds would homer for the Giants by the seventh inning.

Bonds cracked one in the fifth so I decided to set aside the omen curse idea.

Two of the first four limos arrived at the local Lincoln dealer in Hollywood several days after we moved in. These were new ones. Custom-built stretch limos. Both with tinted windows and chrome wheels. Black and sleek and elegant.

Our next two cars were trucked directly to Dav-Ko Hollywood from New York. These were David Koffman's pride and joy. Both only a few months old. Francisco had already christened the white one "Pearl" and the brown one "Cocoa."

While Cocoa was a state-of-the-art stretch limo, it was Pearl that was our company's most requested car in New York. Over-the-top glitz and piss elegance. Pearl actually had eight pounds of crushed pearl in the paint and a forty-eight-inch extension body panel in the center between the front and rear doors. The windows were smoked gray. It had a silk headliner, a stocked bar, a moonroof, two color TVs, and two phones. Pearl's inside trim was gaudy, gleaming burl wood and her seats were covered in maroon calfskin. Fabulous.

Because he'd chosen to move our office to Selma Avenue I'd pegged David Koffman as a business cheapskate. But I was wrong. When it came to publicity he spared no expense to jump-start Dav-Ko Hollywood, even hiring a top-shelf L.A. PR firm.

Unger & Lilly invaded our office. By mid-afternoon on Wednesday of the first week they'd begun making up fluff news stories and calling local celebrity TV gossip shows. Patricia Unger herself spent all day on the phone framing press releases about Dav-Ko Hollywood. Her staff photographer took a hundred photos of Buffalo Bill in his white linen suit getting in and out of Pearl and by week's end Unger had managed to get a local TV news program involved in doing a feature on Pearl's supposed one-year birthday.

Her brainstorm was to give a street party and parade for the limo to kick off the new office. By that weekend two local high school marching bands were recruited and a three-block stretch of Grand Avenue near the L.A. Music Center was closed off for the event. David Koffman contributed to the festivities by hiring three big-titted strippers in bikinis to ride on Pearl's roof and throw rose petals as the cameras rolled. Pure Hollywood. It took me five Vicodin—three before and two during the event—to get me through.

But Unger's gimmick worked and our phones began ringing. A record label booked two cars a day for a week to take an English rock band back and forth to their Staples Center concert gigs. Me and Francisco and Koffman himself did the driving.

By the third week our business had picked up to the point where David Koffman ran a new ad in the *L.A. Times*. *"DRIVE THE STARS!!! Elite limo cmpny seeks drvrs and day-line dsptchr. Drvrs ern $20 p.h. while wrkg. Gd DMV recrd req'd. Mst be cln cut and kno L.A. streets."*

The line of applicants went from our office door to around the corner on Highland Avenue. Even a couple of the local street hustlers, after quizzing the guys in the queue and finding out the pay rate, buttoned up their shirts, tucked them in, and invaded our waiting room wanting to fill out a job application.

Me and Koffman did the interviewing. It took most of the day but between us we hired four new drivers. All men. David wasn't looking for real chauffeurs. Dav-Ko didn't want middle-aged, cigar-smoking, fat-bellied, ex-cab-driver airport hustlers.

We ended up with a staff straight from central casting. All our guys were clean-cut L.A. locals—perfect for a young

Hollywood rock 'n' roll limo company. None had experience and not one arrived wearing a tie. All were twenty-five to thirty years old and needed a haircut.

These are the guys we hired: <u>Marty Humphrey</u>, a former rock band backup singer living on his girlfriend's couch. <u>Cal Berwick</u>, a skinny vegetarian from Whittier. <u>Robert Roller</u>, a shaved-headed 250-pound former security guard monster who had recently managed a Pizza Hut. And <u>Frank Tropper</u>, who, I later discovered through one of his ex-girlfriends, had once been a Hollywood escort.

My assignment was to take these guys to the Manhattan Tie Shop over on Cahuenga Boulevard and then to the ten-dollar Supercuts barbershop on La Brea. By mid-afternoon the next day Koffman's gay pal Octavio had outfitted all four of our new employees with vested blue polyester three-piece suits: $179.00 each. Two one-hundred-percent-synthetic drip-dry white long-sleeved dress shirts: $11.00 each. A Greek seaman's cap: $29.00. One black clip-on necktie: $8.00. And one red pocket hankie: $8.95. The hardest guy to fit was Robert Roller. Sixty-five bucks worth of alterations were required to get his bulging body to fit a suit.

My boss's plan was to keep the new company running for thirty days, then return to New York City. At that time he would turn the day-to-day running of Dav-Ko Hollywood over to me as resident manager.

When I began training the new drivers I was upgraded to the title of manager/chauffeur supervisor and given a weekly salary to augment my driving income.

Every day for a week the new guys took a turn at the wheel with me calling the shots from the backseat as we toured the L.A. streets, driving the half dozen best routes to the airports from the most popular West Side and Beverly Hills hotels. The freeway system in L.A. had become gridlock. From six in the morning until after ten at night most of them were impassable. Knowing the fastest ways to navigate the city streets was essential.

I continually emphasized to the guys how to anticipate the needs of our customers and I showed them how to behave like their professional New York City counterparts. I taught them little chauffeur tricks too, like how to wash out a shirt and leave it wrinkleless on a hanger after consecutive daily ten-hour gigs, and how to scrub stains off a polyester suit with just soap and a damp sponge. Also, because we lived in rainless Southern California, it was pretty much unnecessary to wash a car more than once per week, so I instructed my guys on how to clean the windows and exterior on a daily basis with just one damp terry-cloth towel straight from the spin cycle of our washing machine.

Koffman gave each of our new guys his own credit card. He also supplied them with a company cell phone, with strict instructions about personal use. But, after thinking about it, I decided to buy my own. I didn't want David up my ass and I wanted to keep my privacy.

Then one morning my boss had a brainstorm. Because limo parking in L.A. can sometimes be impossible, he came up with a scheme to make the rounds of the local old-age homes, offering free afternoon transportation to their clientele, to and from their doctor appointments. Mid-afternoons were always slow in the limo industry and this act of limited and manipulative charity allowed Dav-Ko to obtain half a dozen handicapped parking plaques from the State of California.

With these blue beauties hanging from the rearview mirrors of our cars we'd be able to park almost anywhere, anytime. Smart. Very smart.

Dav-Ko was ready to roll.

But the dispatcher we hired was a different story. A woman. To my annoyance I came to discover that David Koffman had developed an affinity for snotty British accents. I'd known him to be overly impressed by status and money and New York fashion but it had never clouded his good judgment before.

Her New York driver's license said that her name was Pat Waltz but on her job application she claimed to be Portia Darforth-Keats, and she confided that she was a distant relative of the British poet John Keats.

Waltz was thirty-two years old but her physical appearance was that of unearthed, well-scrubbed zombie with a pretty face. She was an ex-smoker turned nicotine gum chewer. Her constant chomping was endless and annoying and apparently unconscious.

Portia was my height, five foot six or seven, but weighed no more than a hundred pounds. She wore black horn-rimmed Gucci glasses and her boy's haircut was dyed Madonna white blond. Somewhere along the line she had surgically endowed herself with what appeared to be two NFL footballs for breasts. These two incongruous protrusions would arrive in a room long before the skeleton attached to them. When she sat down I noted that it would take three of her to fill one of our office swivel chairs—excluding her tits.

According to Ms. Darforth-Keats she was educated at Grafton College in London and during our interview she confided two things that told me all I needed to know about her lopsided personality: (a) As a teenager she'd developed an eating disorder (she said she was a recovering bulimic), and (b) she had a strong personal affinity for gay men. Her life-long best friends were all gay. Swell.

I learned that she'd obtained her green card and U.S. residency by marrying a New York City Times Square beat cop, Bernard Waltz. Her letters of reference testified that she was good with computers and had been a part-time nanny for ten years and then a dispatcher-bookkeeper for a Manhattan ambulance company. She'd recently slapped her ex Bernie with a restraining order then headed west on American Airlines.

Waltz's vocal manner made her sound more like Queen Elizabeth's personal assistant than a half-alive Biafra survivor. The woman was a yakky know-it-all and a snob and clearly held herself above all lesser humans. Looking across my desk at her the thought of having sex with this skeletal, nicotine-sucking phony made me want to reconsider my own sexual orientation. I immediately concluded that it would be impossible for someone with her uptight wiring to deal with our staff of homegrown L.A. beach-boy chauffeurs. Weekends in the limo business are made up of brutal hours and handling overworked drivers during the grind of back-to-back ten-hour shifts would take its toll. Her uptight attitude would do her in and the shit would fly. Bottom line: The woman was wrong for the job. And the notion that I'd have to spend some of my days at Dav-Ko cooped up in an office with her set me craving a handful of painkillers.

But David Koffman was the boss and his reality block was impossible to overcome. He'd wanted class for Dav-Ko and had somehow decided that Portia was it. He had interviewed her separately the day after I began training the drivers, then hired her on the spot. As it turned out my interview with Portia was a formality.

When Koffman arrived back at our office with Francisco I pulled him aside into our dispatch room and imparted my personal assessment of Pat Waltz. "Look, David, she's a puker and a whackjob," I said. "I don't like her. She's wrapped way too tight to deal with a staff of young drivers. And as far as I'm concerned that accent of hers is a ding—no plus whatever."

"Portia's hired, Bruno. That's that," he hissed, balancing his gargantuan frame on the edge of the dispatch desk after pouring himself a cup of coffee.

"Ouch! Thanks for not telling me."

"I think she's fabulous. I made a spontaneous decision."

"Well, it's a mistake, David. The woman's got emotional baggage up the wazoo. She looks like she hasn't taken solid nourishment in ten years. Bottom line, she doesn't know how to talk to people."

Koffman was now sorting through the day's mail. "That's your opinion," he said distractedly.

"It sure is. Apparently she's addicted to nicotine gum too."

"So . . . you're saying that I should steer clear of hiring a person because of how they look?"

"She says that all her best friends are pole smokers. She loves gay men."

"Does being around someone who likes gay men represent a problem for you?"

"Let's just say that I don't expect us to ever exchange Valentine's cards. Her only plus I can see is her knowledge of computers. Did you at least check her references?"

"I did not."

"Then I rest my case."

"I found her utterly charming," he sniffed. "She'll bring class to our company. And I see no reason why how she looks or her physical problems should disqualify her."

"Fine. Set that aside. How about that she's a pretentious, condescending asshole?"

"Now there's a solid professional assessment?"

"Just let me talk to her last employer—do some phone calling and some checking."

"Should I call your last employer?"

"Why would you?"

"The point is, I took a chance on you?"

"That's one hundred percent pigsnot. You and I worked together in New York. I proved myself. You know all about me."

"Correct. And I hired you again anyway."

"I think you'll be sorry."

"It's my decision. I'll live with it."

"You're the boss."

"How kind of you to concede that point."

Big Koffman began leafing through one of the two thick men's magazines that had arrived that morning and I went upstairs to shoot myself in the head.

six

As it turned out I was more than half wrong about Portia. That Friday afternoon a full staff meeting was called at Dav-Ko. The guys began showing up in their blue suits, white shirts, and Greek seaman's caps, ready for action. David wanted his drivers to meet their new night dispatcher, and as they filed passed the office on their way to the chauffeur's room, I watched Ms. Darforth-Keats checking out the talent.

We had a four-car job scheduled for six o'clock: A world premiere movie in Westwood.

As the meeting began Koffman and Portia positioned themselves in the front of the room, him wearing his best Tom Wolfe milkman getup, nervous about making a good impression that night with our newest account, the Beverly Hills GMA Agency. Koffman felt it necessary to reemphasize the fine points of opening and closing the rear door of a limo and greeting our clients and other stuff that they knew already, and there was Portia smiling, chomping her nicotine gum, eager to be every chauffeur's best pal. Watching her expression as the guys asked questions I quickly deduced that puking three times a day was most likely her second priority. Her lifelong best friends may have been gay, but she clearly had an affinity for California boys, as did her boss.

But Portia could be charming too. When David explained how he wanted the guys to each report in on the hour via cell phone she made a joke in her best snooty London accent about being there to serve their every need, *rain or shine*. "Think of me as your *'umble* servant," she crooned. The boys ate the shit up.

I felt better. She'd somehow left her arrogance at the door.

That night, clicking on my computer to write my page for the day, my mind gave me a reprieve, another needed perspective. Screw it, I thought. I'll make it work. In truth, on balance, Portia or no Portia, everything was going okay for me. I had a good job with paid medical insurance for the first time in years, a big upstairs bedroom with a newly swish-decorated john. I had a writing desk for my laptop and enough after-hours time to work on my new book of stories. For once I didn't have to worry about scuffling around for enough money to pay the rent. All I had to do was to show up and control my mind and my tongue. I even promised myself to cut back on the booze and try a few more AA meetings.

But it happened anyway. I woke up in bed from a blackout, still drunk, in a pool of blood with my neck slashed.

Koffman and Francisco were out for the night at the ballet and Portia was downstairs chomping on nicotine gum, man-ning the phones for her third full shift. I'd penciled in all the morning pickups for the drivers and set up the work schedule for the next day on the computer before going up to my room to work on my writing.

Ten minutes into it there was a sudden Hollywood power failure. My screen went blank. A minute or so later when the electricity was restored, I restarted the machine but everything was gone, all my writing, months of work.

I started the machine again. Nothing. I tried everything I knew. Anything I knew. But no luck. Sixty pages of work, all of it—my entire Word file—lost—down the shitter. No desktop, either. Complete death. I'd never had trouble with the goddamn laptop before so, out of laziness, I'd never bothered to backup my writing files. There I sat. SOL.

In my closet were two unopened fifths of Ten High. I turned off my computer then cracked the seal on one, pouring myself four fingers of dark blended whiskey. Fuck it. Fuck sobriety. Fuck the job. Fuck the writing. Fuck trying. Fuck breathing. Fuck it all.

By nine-thirty that night, driving my Pontiac with the bottle between my legs, I'd finished the jug and unsuccessfully negotiated for a blowjob from a Santa Monica Boulevard hooker. After that I stopped at a Latino bar on Western Avenue and ordered a double from a bartender whose only language was Spanish. But the weird omen was back. The guy sitting next to me turned out to be a dead ringer for my brother Rick who now had a house in Roseville up by Sacramento.

That was the last thing I remember.

It was Portia who found me. Koffman and Francisco were still out on the town making their usual stops at the gay bars on Santa Monica Boulevard. In my blackout I'd returned home and run my cutting knife across the base of my neck.

• • •

"Get the hell away from me!"

"You're bleeding. Oh my God!"

"I said get away—I mean it."

"There's blood all over your sheets—all over the bed."

"Who's that? What do you want?"

"It's Portia from downstairs."

"Who? Portia. Go away! Let me alone."

"I heard a crash. You must've knocked over your table lamp."

Something was in my eyes. Whatever it was prevented me from opening them. "What's wrong?" I yelled. "I can't see."

"It's the blood. Lie still. You have blood in your eyes and in your hair."

"Forget it. Just leave me alone. Get away."

Again the snooty British accent. "I'll be back in a jiff. Just stay calm."

The sounds of someone in the crapper opening, then rifling, then slamming my medicine cabinet shut. Then Portia's voice again: "I'll be right back. There's a first aid kit in the chauffeur's room downstairs—I'll go and get it. How did this happen?"

Struggling to get to my feet. "I have no idea. An accident maybe—bad luck maybe."

"Just please stay still. Stay where you are. Don't get up."

A minute or so later the voice was back. "Mission accomplished. I've got the first aid kit. Situation in hand."

"How bad is it?" I asked. "What the hell did I do?"

"You're drunk, aren't you?"

"Not drunk enough."

"Lie back. Please. Try to be still."

• • •

Running water in the bathroom sink then a warm wash cloth against my eyes and face then down across my belly.

"Can you see now?"

"Yeah, I can see."

"Excellent. Better already."

"Better? So why am I scared shitless?"

"Can you stand? Let's try to get you to the loo so I can wash you properly. I had some EMT training in New York. I know what I'm doing."

"Apparently my ass is in your hands."

On my feet shuffling toward the john I look down to discover that I am naked. For some unknown reason my cock is hard.

I looked at Portia then back down at my cock. "Sorry," I say.

Her face was stone. "Never mind. It happens."

I sit on the crapper while the pretty face further cleans the cut on my neck and washes my arms and begins cleaning the blood out of my hair.

"Help me up. I want to look in the mirror."

"Not yet. Remain quite still. Please."

"Then just tell me—how bad is it?"

"Apparently it's not fatal," the accent hisses, glancing back down at my cock. The damn thing is still thick and throbbing.

"Help me get up," I demand.

In the mirror I see it. The cut—the gash—is about four inches long, sloping down the side of my neck. The bleeding is slowed. "That doesn't look so bad," I say.

"You soaked your pillow and the sheets."

"Well, shit happens, right?"

"You're still drunk. No doubt it'll hurt tomorrow."

"I don't care."

"You missed the artery but you'll need immediate medical attention. A doctor. I'll telephone David on his mobile then transfer the phones to the answering service. I'll drive you to the hospital myself."

"No! No fucking way. You fix it. You just said you had training."

"That wound will require stitches. You're going to need a proper hospital."

"No hospitals. No goddamn doctors."

"That's absurd. Don't be a fool. Without treatment that cut could easily become infected."

"If Koffman finds out I'll lose my job. We had a deal. A no-more-drinking-or-you're-out-on-your-ass deal."

"There's nothing else I can do."

"The bleeding's almost stopped. Just help me back to bed."

"No it hasn't. Don't be an ass."

"Promise me—you won't tell Koffman. Promise me, god-damnit."

"I won't tell anyone. Why would I?"

"Okay, I'll go tomorrow. I'll do it on my lunch break. But don't tell David, okay?"

"Just tell me what happened?"

"I was drunk. I was in a bar. Then I came back here. I don't know. I guess I cut myself."

"Splendid."

"I said I can't remember."

"You drink too much, Bruno."

"Have I stopped bleeding?"

"No. Not yet."

• • •

Portia finished cleaning my cut. She put bacterial ointment on it, then a bandage and some tape to hold the gauze in place.

Standing up again I faced the mirror to examine her work. The bandage was right at my collar line. She'd done a good job. If I wore my shirts buttoned up, no one would be able to see what I'd done.

"You must promise you'll go to the doctor tomorrow? First thing."

"You have my one hundred percent guarantee. My personal commitment as a gentleman."

"Don't mock me. I'm deathly serious."

"So am I. No shit."

"Very well. Then I'll go back downstairs to my desk. You'll be okay for the time being."

"Wait," I said.

"Why? What's wrong?"

"Don't leave. I need you to help me back to bed."

"Certainly. Are you dizzy?"

"Yeah. I'm dizzy."

My arm around Portia's shoulder as we shuffle across the floor toward my bed.

When we reach my rack Portia throws a towel down over the bloodstains. She helps me sit, then lifts my legs up on to the mattress.

I glance down at my cock—amazingly the thing is still half hard. The skinny woman with the Madonna hair is standing above me, looking down. "I don't want to be alone," I say.

"Not to worry. I'll be right downstairs."

"Then—how about a nightcap before you go?"

"That's preposterous."

Nodding down at my cock. "What about . . . that? You could be a big help . . . with that."

"You're an evil pig."

"I'm attracted to you. Sexually. I love your tits."

"That's absurd. Tell the truth. You have an erection and I happen to be in the room."

"C'mon, Portia? One drink."

"Absolutely no. Good night."

"Okay, good night . . . Hey, what about this: You stand there and watch and I'll do the rest."

"Fuck off!"

I couldn't sleep. Two hours later, after the bleeding had finally stopped and I'd had a couple more drinks, and I was sure she'd fallen asleep, I went downstairs, tiptoed toward her snoring body, found her purse, then reached in and stole her supply of nicotine gum.

seven

efore dawn the next morning came the onset of the black dog. Madness. Shame. *Jimmy* screaming in my head. My eyes were not yet open but behind them the Voice was supplying my brain with poison. *Nice, asshole. Now you've done it. You're stuck with her. She's got a ream of shit on you now. What happens when she pisses you off and you try to bump her? What then? Smooth, jerkoff. Well done.*

I felt like puking while at the same time my body screamed its demand for a drink.

Ten minutes later, after half a bottle of Pepto, I was able to hold down two vikes and two fingers of whiskey. I could stand up.

The unshaven madman's face in the bathroom mirror told me everything I need to know: terror and humiliation.

Then the flash of truth that all of it, my months of work, all my short stories, were gone. Lost. As dead as my dead com-

puter. Then, over and over, the crazy rerun of the incident
with Portia and the knowledge that there was a good chance I
had permanently damaged myself with Dav-Ko. If the skinny
English girl decided to, if she saw fit to spill her guts to Koffman, I'd be jobless and homeless too. The damage would be
complete.

When I peeled the tape and gauze away from my cut I
discovered a quarter-inch-wide scab forming down the side
of my neck. There was no bleeding, so no medical attention
would be necessary. The hell with doctors.

After a shower I was able to hold down another half a glass
of whiskey. I could breathe again. The shakes were nearly
under control.

Pulling the sheets off the bed I discovered that a wide
blood stain had leaked through on to the new mattress.

Like a fumbling burglar covering his crime, I flipped
the mattress to the clean side then picked up the lamp and
broken glass, stuffing the pieces and all the bloody bedding
into three plastic supermarket bags I'd saved for trash. There
were a couple of bloody handprints on the wall above where
I slept that wouldn't come off. I scrubbed them as best as I
could then covered the stains with a throw pillow.

After dressing myself and putting on a new white limo-
driver shirt and tie for the day I discovered the only good
news in the last twenty-four hours; my collar actually did
cover the neck wound.

Downstairs in the kitchen it was almost six o'clock. Koffman and Francisco were not yet awake so I made a pot of
strong coffee.

Back in my room, sitting at the beast's blank screen, I tried
again in vain to recover my work. Nothing. Zip.

I phoned my biker pal Eddy Dorobek, the guy who'd sold
me his five-year-old laptop for a hundred bucks. Eddy was a

house painter. He was always up early slapping color on the walls of his upscale West Side customers' homes. He confirmed my computer's death then made a last-ditch recommendation: that I call the technical support 800 number at Microsoft.

After punching my way through their phone tree and ten minutes on hold, and another three fingers of whiskey, I got plugged in to Ramesh, a "second-tier specialist." "No problem, sir," Ramesh reassured me in his Hindyass-half-English accent: "Our rate is $3.95 per minute for service. How would you prefer to pay for this assistance: debit card or credit card?"

That afternoon the kindness of David Koffman prevailed. After I explained the loss of my work and my computer's death, he gave me a seven-hundred-dollar cash advance from the inch-thick bills on his money clip. An hour later I had a new PC.

The rage of losing my sixty pages of work, then being subjected to Microsoft's absurd "customer support" at the hands of Ramesh, twelve thousand miles away, had made me insane. I decided to put my PC to work. My first order of business was a letter to an asshole named Bill Gates.

> Mr. Bill Gates
> Microsoft Corporation
> 1 Microsoft Way
> Redmond, WA 98052
>
> Hiya Bill:
>
> Just a note to say atta boy and keep up the good work.
> I'm a believer in capitalism and I know you are too.
> As of today I've decided to sign up and join you in your

struggle for the rights of the bankers, Dubai oil sheiks, and instant payday advance broker shops everywhere. We both know that there are plenty of bloodsuckers and sniveling lowlife losers out there. Like you I've come to an inescapable conclusion: They get what they deserve.

Bill, there are two slogans that just this morning I taped to my bathroom mirror. I wanted to pass them on to you—words that I will try to live by day in and day out using your example. I was hoping that you and your guys up there smoking cigars in the THINK TANK just might get a kick out of them. #1: WHEN IN DOUBT CHARGE MORE. And #2: NEVER GIVE A CHUMP AN EVEN BREAK.

That brings me to reason number two for me sending you this letter. I've got to hand it you, Bill. In my book when it comes to wham, bam, thank you ma'am, most American companies shiver like drowned puppies compared to an outfit like Microsoft. When, just recently, I had occasion to speak with one of your offshore customer support techs regarding my computer's software collapse and death, I really learned a thing or two about the old *now you see it, now you don't*. After over an hour with your guy on the horn, at the end of a conversation, when nothing on my machine had changed, I actually discovered myself becoming physically sick when your trained tech—in his giddy and nearly inscrutable Hindi accent—presented me and my ATM card with the charges for his services: seventy-one minutes @ $3.95 per minute: two hundred and seventy-one bucks. That phone call left me speechless and I found myself contemplating a big sip of drain cleaner.

There are some people who would say that you
are to the computer industry what Idi Amin was to
population growth in Uganda. Let's not mince
words here. To me any man who will whimsically
crush a groveling call-in client or the tiniest software
competitor at the drop of a hat is a man to be reckoned
with. Personally, I'm hoping that someday your
company will expand to the publishing industry and
gobble up a firm like Random House. You and the guys
could put out a pamphlet on corporate beheading
or maybe a how-to chapbook on holding back a grin
while encountering an amputee. I read quite a bit
and I can pretty much guarantee you that there's an
untapped market for stuff like that.

Your comrade in arms,

Bruno Dante

eight

Working in the limo business in L.A. is a bizarre way to make a buck. Like licking up wet dog shit for God. The clientele for Dav-Ko in Los Angeles was mostly made up of night freaks and zombies. Rich, cranked-out movie producers, spoiled rock star punks, gangsta rappers with their black Glocks tucked into the belts of their pants, alkie ex-actors with too many DUIs, and a gazillion wannabe high rollers. Human beings who exhibited the most unpleasant personality characteristics common to L.A.: Too much ego and way too much money.

People come to L.A. hoping to discover something outpictured beyond themselves. Something they hope to name and believe in, some idea of satisfaction through success or accumulation or recognition. Of course it never comes. Then they buy a bigger house in Brentwood or another Benz or get more plastic surgery or smoke more amphetamine and marry someone they meet at the gym. Whatever's next. Whatever it takes to hold on to the fantasy and avoid a hard look at what's missing within. Here I was among them. Front and center. My ticket got punched at birth.

Three weeks after the madness of my *accident*, Koffman and Francisco left town and he turned the day-to-day running of Dav-Ko over to me. Portia had kept her word about the incident and managed to contain my folly. And wisely, to cover my ass, I'd cut back on the booze.

In effect Portia and I were now nearly partners in running the company. As planned her dispatcher hours were expanded. Her new schedule was six days a week. Twelve p.m. to ten p.m. except for our busy weekend twelve hour shifts.

After the few days of us working at close quarters it became apparent to me that Darforth-Keats's personality had two single overriding characteristics. The first one was the one I already knew about; a high-strung, gum-chewing, constantly talking, aristocratic weirdo, whose daily wardrobe consisted of nothing that wasn't black. Though Koffman had been right about her polished English style and its positive effect on our phone clients, it was personality number two in particular that, over time, was getting to me. Portia Number Two appeared to have a preponderant and unmanageable attraction to guys. All guys. I'd overhear her flirting on the telephone like an 800 number call-in hooker while taking bookings for agents and managers. And if she happened to be on the line with anyone whose life had ever included strumming an electric guitar, listening to her sycophantic cooing would often force me to take a bathroom break. And she never failed to sweet-talk her favorite chauffeurs as they came in to drop off cash payments or credit card slips—telling them how "splendid" they'd done on this or that airport run—or making a big deal and complimenting them for remembering ridiculous snot like emptying the ashtrays or vacuuming out the car, stuff that they were supposed to do anyway.

In particular she seemed to have taken a shine to Frank Tropper, our former male escort turned chauffeur. Frank was tall with red hair and blue eyes and nobody's fool when it came to manipulating any human who pissed sitting down, especially Dav-Ko's nicotine-gum-chewing dispatcher.

If a choice driving job came in from an e-mail or over the phone—an all-nighter with a rock star or a big money cash tipper—on too many occasions it was Frank who was somehow immediately available for the job, and got it. More than once I had to delete his name from the computer's dispatch screen and let her know that playing favorites with chauffeurs was a bad idea. The fact that Frank was an arrogant self-consumed pretty boy asshole and had a variety of woman picking him up after work every night was apparently the only thing keeping Portia from jumping his bones. This was in stark contrast to big Robert Roller. Robert could pass an entire afternoon sitting in our chauffeur's room with the TV on without so much as a glance from his *selective* dispatcher.

But, frighteningly, the other member of our company whom Portia appeared to have developed an attraction to, over time, was me. The closeness of us being stuck in the dispatch office together, when I wasn't out driving or supervising an on-site limo job, allowed her to yammer away by the hour. In the past she'd had a female cyst removed and two miscarriages and somehow had given herself permission to yammer away at me on the minutia of each procedure. I got to hear endless details about sedation and the three doctors in white coats staring at her coochie and her being treated like a lab animal. And on and on about other stuff. Her victory over her eating disorder and then jogging and her bad back and the right running shoes and how she'd once played the cello as a girl in some symphony in Glasgow. And her ex-husband's propensity for Times Square hookers. Tiresome, endlessly, vapid crap.

Every once in a while I'd try to interject stuff about work but the topics always seemed to come back to her and her physical ailments and how many times she used to puke per day or some male gynecologist pig or other.

After many nights of this I eventually found an opening. It turned out that Portia was an avid reader and a mystery novel buff and had consumed all the works of Agatha Christie and Lynda La Plante and Stephen King. Of course she'd known about my computer crash and the loss of my months of work and writing, so books and literature gratefully entered our topics of conversations.

I had mixed feelings about discussing my writing but sometimes in the late afternoon, after I'd had a few drinks following my shift, I didn't mind. Sometimes I even liked it. Talking about Kafka and Dostoyevsky and Henry Miller and Selby and Edward Lewis Wallant was a welcome relief.

One night when the dispatch desk was quiet, after half a bottle of Chianti and after her asking again and again, I did something I had never done before with anyone I had worked with: I showed Portia some of my work—a few poems and a short story I had just finished. The piece I gave her was about my working as an L.A. taxi driver. Over the last few days I had completed two stories on the idea and was deciding if I had enough to write a series. Maybe even a book.

Portia took my poems and one of the stories into the chauffeur's room to read. The yarn I gave her was called "Happy Birthday Tuesday." A true story. It happened on my first night as a cabbie in L.A. I had taken a radio call to go to Venice after a drop at LAX. My passengers turned out to be a pair of drunk and stoned out Latino drug dealers on their way to a section of Venice that is known to the locals as Ghost Town. Five square blocks of crack houses.

One of the guys was on his cell phone threatening his girl-friend in Spanish. Somehow after the call, after he had hung up, the two jerks began to fight, punching and ripping at each other. I had to pull the cab over on Rose Avenue and get out, to make them stop. Their whiskey bottle had spilled on the rear floor and a brown bag that contained a couple of dozen gram bottles of white powder got strewn across the backseat.

After they left my cab, after paying me, the two assholes continued up the street shoving each other and yelling curses in Spanish.

At a gas station nearby I got some paper towels from the men's room and began cleaning up the mess. That's when I found the ring in the corner of the back seat. A two-karat diamond pinkie. With the money I received from hocking it I paid my rent for the month in advance and took my girlfriend Stinky to Lake Tahoe for a weekend.

Portia came back to the dispatch room and flopped my pages down on the desk. She stuck a fresh piece of Nicorette gum into her mouth and began swooning over my poem, telling me how much she admired my directness and brevity and passion.

But when we got around to my short story her face changed. "This," she said, holding it up, "I truthfully found implausible and artificial. Unbelievable, actually."

The words stung and I was instantly sober. It felt like a kick in the balls. "In what way?" I said.

"Wellllllll," she whispered in her most melodious snooty drawl, "candidly, I found it's preposterous. Sort of a cab driv-er's old wives' tale. More of a fantasy, actually."

"The story's true," I said. "I found a two-karat diamond. It might not have belonged to one of the guys—it might have been stuck there in the crack of the backseat for days or months—but the story is true."

"Perhaps. But it didn't have the ring of truth. It rang of hyperbole. Exaggeration."

Before I could stop myself the words had leaped from my mouth like some fool on a bungee jump off the Grand Canyon. "You mean . . . *exaggeration* like those two fake fucking water balloons you have implanted in your bony chest?"

Thirty seconds later she was gone. She'd wordlessly scooped up her purse and her black coat and was out the door.

It took half of the following day, after threats of calls to David Koffman and accusations of a sexual harassment lawsuit, and a ten minute apology, to talk her down and get her to come back to work.

nine

I picked up the phone after midnight thinking it was one of the limo drivers calling in to report his hours at the end of a job. My sister, Liz, was crying softly. Whispering the words. Rick Dante, Jonathan Dante's firstborn son, his favorite son, a chess expert at ten years old and one of the precision toolmakers who designed and fabricated the landing feet of the Mars rover, was dead. He had boozed himself into the emergency room after his ulcer exploded onto the beige carpet of his bedroom in Roseville. His wife, Karin, found him there doubled over and moaning.

This time he and Karin had been separated for three weeks. When he failed to answer his phone for a couple of days she set her anger aside and drove to the house with their daughter.

Rick was forty-six years old and a 24-7 drinker from the age of thirty. A guy filled with demons and genius and bitterness and rage and isolation, tortured by his own failures, a man whose feet and spirit never really connected to solid land.

The news of his death hit me like a club. I'd seen his strange look-alike sitting at the bar the night I'd cut my throat. Another coincidence in a series of weird coincidences I'd been experiencing lately. An omen perhaps. But this time it turned out to be one that was real. The recollection sent a cold chill through my body.

The next day I left my limo office and took a plane from LAX to Sacramento airport, then drove the twenty miles to Roseville in a black sedan furnished by one of our Northern California affiliate limo companies. It was 103 degrees outside while I smoked and sipped from a pint bottle of Schenley, watching the Sacramento Valley go by.

For the last few years Ricardo Dante had been the general manager of a factory that manufactured shipping pallets, a grunt job he'd taken for money to support his family after drinking himself out of the aerospace business.

At Rick's home that afternoon I met a dozen people; friends and neighbors and a couple of my brother's coworkers. They sat in the living room while the air conditioner screamed, sipping wine and ice tea and eating from two prepared supermarket trays of cheese and salami and crackers. There were no televisions in my brother's house. All his life he'd detested their presence.

His best drinking buddy was an older guy named Cecil, a car collector and retired auto mechanic wearing overalls to a wake. He and Rick met at a Sacramento memorabilia trade show.

Cecil was working on a wine buzz and sported the red face of a lifelong juicer. He poured me a tall glass of the rosé then insisted we go outside to the shed behind the garage.

There it was. My brother's pal pulled the tarp away to

reveal a 1957 Studebaker Golden Hawk, complete with new paint and swooping fins and dripping with gaudy, replated chrome and a gleaming rebuilt motor. The two guys had spent the last eighteen months as partners working on weekends to restore the car. The only thing still left undone was to reupholster the seats.

Cecil located a small metal box hidden beneath the workbench, then grinning, tossed me the keys. "Start her up," he said.

I thought about it for a few seconds. "No thanks," I said finally, aware of the presence of my brother's bad-tempered ghost. "Maybe some other time."

The day of the dead tour continued. Back in the house Cecil directed me to a room on the ground floor at the end of a hall. Its door was made of thick wood and armed with a double lock denying access to his wife and daughter and any other uninvited meddler.

Inside was a sort of half museum, half shrine where Rick alone was boss. Everything in the room, even the stale cigarette smell, enforced the personality of its excessive, troubled occupant. I felt him there behind me—leering—furious with me for encroaching on his privacy.

Across the room in one corner was his large drawing board, its surface a disorganized collage of unfinished automobile sketches and clipped newspaper articles. From the age of eight, even before he could type a letter for himself, our Mom had sent his designs off to automobile makers. The practice had become a lifelong obsession with only rare acknowledgments.

One entire wall of the room was filled with Nazi biographies and World War II literature. Cecil told me something about my brother that I had not known: In the last few years he'd taught himself to read and speak German.

Another wall was filled with photographs of the Reich elite: Erich von Manstein, Heinrich Himmler, Erwin Rommel, and Martin Bormann. It felt like I was exploring my brother's decomposing asshole.

Cecil drained his glass then slid open a plastic closet door to show me Rick's two favorite German trophies: Von Ribbentrop's SS dinner jacket and his cap. They hung there in a thick, see-through plastic garment bag below the guy's scary WWII photograph. His son's uniforms were on either side. I was overcome by the need to get very very drunk.

We were about to leave the den when my guide stopped me at the door. "Wait. There's one more thing I want to show you," he half-whispered.

Cecil slid open the top drawer of a tall brown filing cabinet. "Here are the two things your brother loved more than anything."

I was handed two typed and bound manuscripts. My father Jonathan Dante's first-draft originals, yellowed by time. One was *Ask the Wind* and the other *Brotherhood of the Vine*.

It was like a punch in the face. Cecil had no way of knowing that our mother had guarded these manuscripts with her life and that she had never allowed them to leave the storage case in the basement of her home. Only a month before she'd given in and been persuaded to donate all Jonathan Dante's original work to a local university. Somehow, in a crack in time, these two manuscripts had been pirated away by Rick Dante and then tucked neatly into his Nazi time capsule.

I'd had enough. I dropped them back into the file cabinet then slid the door closed. I looked at Cecil. "My brother was a real piece of work," I said.

"You bet," Cecil said. "Rick Dante was one of a kind. Let's go get another drink."

"Good idea," I said back.

We drank the rest of that day and into the night, Cecil killing me with endless chatter about my brother and his strange obsessions.

In the morning I found myself asleep in my clothes on Rick's living room couch, my brain half crazy. To fight off my hangover it was more of the same—three fingers of bourbon with my coffee. Then a half-pint from my suitcase.

Outside the church I was introduced to Rick's secretary, a pretty rosy-faced forty-year-old who shook her head and filled me in. Rick's doctor told him, she said, that if he kept on drinking and didn't cut back he'd be gone in a year. Then, a couple of weeks after he'd returned to work from his near-death stomach surgery, she began discovering his empties under the daily newspaper in his trash can. Rick Dante lasted another six months.

I had a decent buzz going as I sat with Mom and Liz and Rick's wife, Karin, and their daughter, Mindy, in the front row of Our Lady of the Bleeding Armpits. Mom and I hadn't talked for months but for once she smiled and gave me a hug.

We were inches away from a body that—paint or no paint—had aged fifty years since I'd last seen it.

Then a Mexican priest who'd never set eyes on my brother delivered long measured doses of sweetened snot about Jesus and eternity and a good Christian life to the fifty distracted attendees. Excluded from his homily was any mention of weekends in jail or rehabs or an enraged, penniless wife and teenage kid, or the casual theft of his father's most famous work.

Then, without warning, three feet away, the corpse in the box sat up and glared at me. Rick Dante was dressed in a black SS uniform and helmet. "What's your problem?" the Nazi sneered.

"You, asshole," I heard my voice report. "You're my goddamn problem. You and your double-locked mausoleum where you boozed your life down the shitter."

"Sieg heil!" the Gestapo corpse screeched back.

Liz was grabbing my arm. "Bruno! Stop it for God's sake. You're yelling. What's wrong with you?"

"Him!" I said, gesturing at the body in the box, getting to my feet.

"Sit down," Liz scolded. "Everybody's looking."

I sat down.

"You're drunk," she said.

"I guess you're right. I guess I must be drunk."

Then it was over. My brother's entire life had been neatly dispatched in twenty-five minutes.

We drove the three blocks to the Roseville boneyard and then got out.

The only surprise in the day's festivities came as our group of mourners walked across an acre of manicured graves and up to the top of a small hill to discover the gleaming Golden Hawk standing alone in the openness on the other side. Old Cecil was passed out behind the wheel while two caretakers were trying to wake him up. Tire tracks and skid marks ran in a circle around the tomb. The right front wheel of his Studebaker had gotten stuck in Rick's unfilled grave.

ten

fter returning to Hollywood it took me a week to get my head right. I was still choked by sadness and the memory of sighting of my dead brother's twin only days before his death. The *Jimmy* voice was a nonstop monologue in my head. *You're next, asshole. Keep it up! You're boozing yourself right into the boneyard like your fucking brother.*

But the limo business was picking up and the grind of dealing with the minute-to-minute disruptions and concerns of running a busy dispatch office helped to keep my mind off myself. I'd cut out hard liquor completely after the Roseville funeral. A bottle or two of wine a day and a few vikes seemed to be keeping me mellow and allowed me to get my work done. Portia, on orders from New York, was boss and was watching me like a hawk. I had no interest in another blow up. I needed the job if I was to continue my writing.

Koffman's publicist's newest brainstorm of a formal *wedding-looking* invitation to our California clients had worked like magic. The filigreed announcement featured a color photo of

Pearl, our gaudy white flagship limo. The phones were ringing and the company was really taking off. We had movie people and wannabe celebrities coming out of the woodwork, courtesy of Dav-Ko's publicity and advertising blitz.

Our client roster looked impressive: Famous guys like Mick Jagger, Elton John, Rod Stewart, Ringo Starr, Paul Simon. Lots of the major rock bands too. They all wanted to ride in one of our stretches.

When these guys were in L.A. I drove them all myself on the first run to make sure that the account got off to a good start. But after I'd chauffeured Simon the first time he continued to request me as his driver when his manager phoned in for a car. Paul never talked to me or called me by name when I picked him up and he always raised the glass partition when he was in the car, so my repeated selection as his driver always came as a surprise. It took me a few weeks to realize why: Simon is around five feet tall and I am five foot seven, the shortest driver on the staff.

At the crest of our success wave was my boss. He'd splurged on three more different-colored Town Cars to be "stretched" in Mexico and then shipped north to Hollywood.

Portia and I were barely on speaking terms but her snotty English nitpicky personality and her apparent lust for Frank Tropper were beginning to wear on me. Koffman still *loved* her. He found her "very capable," and her personality "fabulous." And there was no question that she'd covered my mistakes and appeared to be doing a good job. More than once in dealing with an angry corporate client, I'd lost my temper and one of them had threatened to cancel their business relationship with us. Double-bookings and no shows at pickups are among the problems that beset a busy limo company, and Portia had a way of smoothing things over with irate celebrities and bailing us out. Groveling to resurrect an annoyed client was hard for me but schmoozy Portia would do whatever it took to stay on good terms with a customer. They'd find a free bottle of champagne and a rose on the back seat on their next booking. Soon, on orders from Koffman, she began keeping her stuff in an office closet and sleeping over several nights a week on a newly installed pullout couch in the chauffeur's room.

But then the worm turned when slick Frank Tropper was caught with his forked tongue in the cookie jar. He had become our busiest driver and reported to each assignment augmenting his vested blue suit and bow tie with weird accessories that appeared to have caught on with our customers in Hollywood, where appearance is everything. Tropper'd show up wearing dark motorcycle cop shades and black driving gloves and a black, military-looking cap. He called this his hit man uniform. And, to my annoyance, a couple of the other drivers were now dressing the same way.

Over the last few weeks I'd noticed a number of personal phone messages to Frank—excessive phone messages—from our clients, and I'd brought it to Portia's attention. Then, with several customers, he had returned the car to the garage very late after the end of a run. Frank always had a ready excuse and Ms. Portia seemed to go along with whatever account he came up with to cover his ass. But I was beginning to smell a problem—the possibility of a drug dealer on my staff.

On this last run Frank had called in to the office at eight p.m. to report the end of the assignment, but it was two hours later and the limo was still not in the garage.

I decided that enough was enough.

The main client in question was currently our biggest cash account: Marv Afferman, a fifty-five-year-old Cheviot Hills millionaire with a knack for keeping a limo on call as many as eighteen hours a day. Afferman was a player and had a swank house at Trancas Beach and liked to shuttle his women back and forth on summer weekends.

Tropper's hours and the actual in-and-out time for his Afferman gig weren't jibing. I'd called him in the car on his cell phone. His quick excuse was that Afferman had overpaid him in cash and he'd gone back to return the excess deposit.

When Tropper returned to the garage in Big Red, our maroon stretch, I was waiting in the driveway. Portia, still making excuses for his behavior, followed me outside.

There was Frank decked out in his cop shades and black driving gloves. Before he could do anything to cover his tracks I ordered him out of the car. While he stood by I checked through the limo and found a deck of plastic baggies and three empty gram vials under Frank's briefcase on the front seat.

He immediately began shucking and jiving, telling me that he'd found the items on the bar console in the back of the car while cleaning it out. I fired the asshole on the spot.

Portia immediately began yammering at me, trying to come to his defense again, but I refused any explanation.

Standing in the driveway she began hissing at me about integrity and personal trust and compassion and that shit. Then she stormed down the street yelling at me for humiliating her in front of an employee and for overriding her judgment. Now I smelled a cover-up and two slimy brown turds.

Frank whined and squirmed and asked for another chance but I'd been in the limo business long enough to recognize that chauffeurs who sell dope to their clients usually continue the practice. I was sure David Koffman would have done the same thing.

That's when it came out. Tropper chose to take my night dispatcher down with him. It was the jerk's way of getting even with her for not saving his ass this last time.

According to Frank, Portia'd been showing more than favoritism at Dav-Ko. He said that of course she knew what he was doing, that their friendship and her attraction to him permitted the skinny English girl to administer oral sex once or twice a week along with steering a lot of the cash work at Dav-Ko his way. Bottom line: Portia was a pole smoker and a coconspirator. Nice.

I'd never liked Tropper but the story didn't sound like a rope-a-dope. It was too damning not to be true.

I made him turn in his cell phone and his credit card and his sets of limo keys, then wordlessly escorted the jerk down the block to where one of his girlfriends was parked and waiting.

"What are you going to do about Portia?" he asked, getting into the new red Mustang convertible.

"Well," I said, "I don't think she should run for mayor."

"What's that supposed to mean?"

"It means mind your own fucking business. You're lucky I don't have you arrested. Have a nice day, Frank."

But now I had a choice: I could inform Koffman of Portia's foolishness and be rid of her once and for all or I could let the matter slide. I knew my boss. His business principles were unwavering. The sex angle aside, if Koffman found out a driver was dealing drugs and she'd been overlooking the behavior it would mean the axe for her too. All I had to do was say the word and she'd be gone.

When the bony English girl returned around midnight I switched the phones to the answering service and sat her down in the dispatch office. She was still pissy and oozing with self-righteousness.

"What's this stuff about you and Tropper?" I said.

"The truth is you never liked him. That's the obvious issue here."

"He was dealing coke, Portia. You allowed the asshole to endanger our business."

"That's absurd. Totally preposterous and unjustified. Frank is a superb employee. And you questioning my integrity is an insult that I will not tolerate. I suggest we contact David in New York. I believe he'll see my point of view in this matter."

"Frank tells me that you give a decent blowjob; pretty nice tongue technique and all. That's an interesting trade-off."

Miss Britannia looked as if she'd just choked on a thick French fry. "I beg your pardon," she whispered.

"Look, here's how I see it: I've owed you one for my boozing and throat-cutting stuff. Now we're even. I'm willing to let it go at that. But, for chrissake, no more driver favoritism and looking the other way on dope deals, and no more flirting with the staff. And I'd cut back on the cocksucking in the office if I were you."

I held out my hand.

Portia was twitching like crazy and chomping away on her nicotine gum, her eyes on the floor. Finally she looked up and nervously shook my hand. "Thank you for understanding," she whispered.

"No sweat. We've all made our share of dumbshit moves now and then."

I checked my watch. "Hey, it's after midnight. How about a drink to seal the deal?"

The bony blond girl with the actress face mustered her first smile of the day. "Thank you," she said. "Perhaps another time."

It was two a.m. a week or so later. An accident in one of the stretch limos that afternoon, an angry road manager and a screaming chauffeur, and a few drinks after dinner to level things out had turned a bad day into two pints of Schenley and a badass drunk.

Upstairs in my bedroom, with the house phones patched over to the answering service, I had been phoning sex ads from the *L.A. Weekly* for half an hour. Calling out-call hookers. But because I didn't have enough cash I'd been turned down, pissed off, and hung up on a half dozen times.

Finally, pretty drunk, and determined to get laid at any price, wearing only my T-shirt, I made my way downstairs.

In the dark office I opened drawers until I located the petty cash box. My plan was to make a loan to myself before I got my check. One of the girls at one of the 800 numbers—who said her name was DeVon—said she was ten minutes away on Fairfax, and if I had two hundred in cash she'd be right over.

My problem was Ms. Portia. I was buzzed enough to forget that she was asleep in the chauffeur's room on one of her overnighters.

The commotion of me opening and closing the desk drawer then rattling the cash box woke her up. She stood in the dim light from the hall wearing a long, open man's dress shirt—her giant tits half exposed above the two pole lamps she used for walking.

"I heard a noise. Is everything all right?" she whispered.

"Jesus! I forgot you were here! Sure, everything's peachy. I'm just in need of a few bucks from the cash box."

"At two-fifteen in the morning?"

"Exactly. Precisely. At two fifteen a.m. Or twelve seventeen in the afternoon. Or whenever the fuck I want to. I didn't know I needed your permission?"

"Of course you don't. I was simply inquiring. I wasn't asleep anyway. I was reading."

Brushing passed me she opened the desk drawer, then the cash box, then handed me several fifties that she'd paper-clipped together. "I think that's three hundred dollars," she cooed. "I counted it myself this afternoon. Do you need more?"

"Three hundred's fine."

"Let me make sure." She turned on the light.

"Right. Thanks."

And there she was. Under the fluorescent bulbs I could see she was naked beneath the shirt.

I was staring. Leering. But I didn't care.

"Please, let me go slip something on," she whispered, looking away.

"No. I like you the way you are. Just stand there."

I held up my jug. "How about a nightcap? One drink for the good of the company. It won't kill you."

"Actually, I've had a bit of wine already . . . it helps me sleep."

"C'mon."

"Very well. But only one."

I took a hit then passed the bottle to the skinny girl. She downed most of what was left with one gulp.

Screwing Portia on the pull-out bed in the chauffeur's room was like trying to run backward. Clumsy. Elbows and knees everywhere. And nearly without participation.

Ten minutes after we started, when I couldn't cum, she sucked me off.

"Well . . . did you enjoy that?" she asked finally.

I checked my jug. It was empty. "Any liquor in the office?"

"There are two bottles of that inexpensive limo champagne in the fridge. Shall I get one?"

"Get both."

"I feel quite good. Sex relieves stress, you know."

"You're right. So does drinking."

"Well . . . I'll get the champagne."

"Good idea."

For the next half hour we lay wordless, sipping fizzy wine, crunched together on the mattress. Two fools connected by the darkness.

eleven

The next morning I picked up one of our freebie geriatric clients. My dispatch slip read, "J. C. Smart: The Garden of Allah Villas." Portia had mentioned that Mrs. Smart was eighty-seven years old.

I knew the address on Crescent Heights Boulevard because I'm into Hollywood history and used to drink coffee at Schwab's drugstore around the corner on Sunset.

The Villas was an elegant retirement community composed of a dozen thirties-vintage single Spanish-style bungalows at the mouth of Laurel Canyon. It had once been Scott Fitzgerald's old stomping ground.

I was a few minutes early so I parked on Laurel Canyon Boulevard, in front, and read from the new novel by the underground writer Mark SaFranko.

J.C. lived in bungalow #1. The outside of her tiny, white-fenced yard was well manicured, and her small garden was festooned with freshly blooming roses and carnations.

I knocked on the door.

No answer.

I knocked again. Maybe J.C.'d had a heart attack and was floating facedown in her tub, the old girl's aluminum walker tipped over on the bathroom floor.

Then the door swung open and there she was, dressed to the nines and fully made-up and holding a big, expensive-looking red leather handbag. "You're late," she barked.

"Our pickup time is for nine o'clock," I said. "It's nine o'clock."

She was grinning. "I beg to differ. It's nine-oh-two Greenwich meantime. You might possibly consider resetting your watch."

"You're Mrs. Smart, right?"

"You may call me J.C."

"Well, good morning, ma'am."

"My proper name is Joyce Childers Smart. I'm a retired English lit teacher and not a bank president. So the diminutive J.C. will do just fine. And you are?"

"Bruno Dante."

My reply seemed to lighten my client's expression. "Dante," she smiled, "as in *La Divina Comedia*?

"The same," I said.

"Ah, the *Comedia*. How appropriate given your propensity for tardiness and embarrassing justifications. Tell me, Mr. Bruno Dante, have you read your namesake's work?"

"Yeah, I have, but it's been years," I said.

"And . . ."

"Well, it's okay. Not my favorite piece of literature, but interesting, I guess."

"Interesting? And not your favorite tidbit of writing from the Middle Ages? *The Divine Comedy*. Really?"

"The car's in front. Shall we go?"

"Are you, by chance, related to a writer named Jonathan Dante?"

"He was my father."

J.C. was beaming. "Well, well, well. My husband and I knew Johnny. He was a fine writer. As I recall he died and then all of his books were republished a few years later. He got quite famous."

"That's right."

Mrs. Smart extended her hand and I shook it. "How nice to meet you," she said. "Nothing replaces good breeding."

Then my new client leaned past me and glanced at the black stretch limo parked at the curb. "You want to take me—in that?"

"Sure. First-class transportation. You deserve the best, right?"

"Mr. Dante, son of Jonathan Dante, I did not just win second prize in one of those lurid televised game shows. I'm a rich old lady and not a crack dealer. I do not hold with glitz and ostentation. Please tell me, does your firm have other, smaller cars?"

I thought about it for a second. "Only my own car. My Pontiac," I said. "It's twelve years old. But it is a four-door."

"What color is this Pontiac?"

"Color? Light brown. Beige, I guess."

"That'll do for next time. I now intend to open an account with your company. I'll provide my credit card information and whatever else you require."

"Sorry, I thought you knew. You ride free of charge. Our deal is to drive seniors in the neighborhood to and from their doctor's appointments at no charge."

"I pay my own way. I always have."

"Hey, no problem. You're the customer."

"Precisely," she nodded. "Now wait here a moment. I'll have to get Tahuti."

"Tuhootee?"

"T-A-H-U-T-I. My cat. We go everywhere together."

J.C. closed the door in my face then stepped back inside her bungalow.

Half a minute later she was back, beaming, holding in her arms the fattest monster black cat I had ever seen. "Bruno Dante, meet Tahuti."

The beast opened its heavy eyes, glanced at me, then closed them again. "We can go now," J.C. whispered.

On the street I opened the rear limo door for my passenger and her beast. J.C. shuffled toward me up the sidewalk then waved me off. "I'm not an oil sheik nor am I with the State Department, Mr. Dante," she said. "Tahuti and I ride in the front seat."

"Whatever you say," I said back, knowing when I was licked.

After I got in behind the wheel I was about to start the car when J.C., now done situating Tahuti on her lap, leaned toward me. "And Mr. Dante, one more thing," she chimed, eyeing me coldly in my chauffeur's cap.

"What would that be?" I said, fearing the worst.

"Please, no cheap thrills."

It turned out my passenger was also a speed-talker. While I drove I learned that she was an avid reader, that she'd gobbled up every mystery series of novels ever written. Every one. Her unoccupied garage space behind the Villas contained, at her count, thirty-five thousand books. J.C. still read four books a week and had once spent time as a fiction editor at DeMoore Brothers in downtown L.A. Her poetry and short fiction had been published in anthologies and literary journals and she'd been married to a screenwriter named Arthur Smart who had cashed in years before on the ninth fairway at Riviera golf course. Art once worked at MGM Studios as a contract writer with Jonathan Dante. His big hit was the fifties musical film *A Crowd of Stars*, and as a writer/producer-partner he'd made a fortune from his percentage of the gross and willed the whole bundle to J.C.

My customer went on. She once sat between Charlie Chaplin and Greta Garbo while dining at the Brown Derby with her husband and William Saroyan, after Saroyan had been awarded but declined the Pulitzer Prize. She and Basil Rathbone had been intimate pals. The last blast of spontaneous unsolicited information aimed at me was the strangest: I learned that, for the last thirty years, in her spare time, J. C. Smart had become an expert tarot card reader. Ba-boom.

My customer's doctor's appointment was in Santa Monica, half an hour away. Tahuti purred loudly during the whole ride.

The ritzy building had gold-rimmed double-glass doors and a new bright green awning that reached to the street. I parked in front in the handicapped zone.

I got out to help her but before I could hurry around the car J.C. had opened her own door. She and the cat were on the sidewalk.

"I'll be back in half an hour. No more," she said. "Where will you be?"

"Right here," I said. "Waiting."

J.C. handed me her credit card. "Will this do to open an account with your firm?"

"That'll be just fine," I said back.

Twenty minutes later I'd called in J.C.'s information and was waiting, reading the movie reviews in the *L.A. Times*, when my passenger door popped open. She tossed her purse on the seat, then she and Tahuti got in. After situating the cat on her lap she turned to me. "Shall we go?" she said.

"Where to? Back to your bungalow?"

"No, actually. I've got a special errand," she beamed, ten thousand facial wrinkles appearing, then flattening out. "I'm meeting my granddaughter. We're off to Neiman Marcus in Beverly Hills. Do you know where it is?"

"Ten-four," I said.

"Tell me, Mr. Dante, what does the recitation of those numbers signify, if anything?"

"Sorry. That's two-way radio jargon. It means, 'Okay, I heard you loud and clear.'"

"May I suggest that we continue our conversations absent trucker shorthand?"

"Sure."

"Thank you."

I shifted into "D" and began pulling the big stretch out into traffic. "So," I said, breaking a clumsy silence, making small talk, "how did it go at the doctor's? Is everything okay?"

J.C. snickered. "Well, I'm dying, Bruno, if you must know. That's how it went. May I call you Bruno?"

"Sure. But c'mon, you look fine."

"I am fine. But I have a vertebral-basilar aneurysm. Apparently it's inoperable and could rupture at any time."

"You're smiling?"

"It amuses me because I received that diagnosed eleven years ago and I'm still very much here. Doctors are fools: Pompous, overeducated, self-important, boring, pedantic frauds. I've had better luck reading my horoscope in the *Times*."

And then my customer sighed deeply, stroked her fat kitty, and turned toward me. She quoted a guy I knew and admired from my wasted days at college.

> And at the closing of the day
> She loosed the chain, and down she lay;
> The broad stream bore her far away,
> The Lady of Shalott.

"Do you know that one, Mr. Dante?" she asked.

"Believe it or not, I do," I said. "Tennyson, right?"

"You may go to the head of the class, young man. No homework for you tonight. By the way, I want the side entrance to Neiman's, please."

Reaching over, J.C. pulled a magazine out of her purse then held it up. A thick copy of the fashion magazine *Ooh La La*. On the cover was a glossy photograph of a beautiful, tall girl with long black hair in a low-cut white dress. Two huge dogs were sitting at her feet.

"That's her, my granddaughter," J.C. said. "I'm meeting *her*."

"That's your granddaughter?"

"Marcella. Marcella Maria Sorache. I call her by her given name but everyone else, including her mother, my status-obsessed daughter Constance, uses her nickname, Che-Che.

I find it absurd and insulting. The name makes the child sound like a stripper."

"She's a very beautiful woman."

J.C. snorted. "My daughter Constance's second husband is a Milanese ne'er-do-well named Gianluca. He inherited a good deal of money, but thank God, also excellent genes. Against my protests the child was raised in Italy and schooled in New York and Switzerland."

"Sounds like she could have done worse."

"Bruno, kindly do not annoy me. I'm an old lady and I don't want to burst a blood vessel and breathe my last in this ridiculous automobile."

Outside Neiman's side entrance were half a dozen photographers, milling around, waiting for someone—a celebrity or a movie star—to leave. J.C. eyed the group. "Nuts," she whispered, "I might have expected this. They're here for Marcella."

"They are? Are you sure?"

"Clearly you don't read tabloid newspapers or watch enough television, Bruno."

"I guess you're right," I said. "Help me out."

"My granddaughter is a model. That should've become obvious."

I smiled at J.C. "Believe it or not I somehow put that together on my own."

"What you may not yet have *put together* is that Marcella is the spokesperson for a cosmetic line called La Natura. Her face appears on television commercials twenty times a day.

"Oh."

"And the child just divorced her drug addict husband, Todd. Todd Adamson."

"The guy everybody calls Terrible Todd? The rock singer?"

"Now you're current. Apparently, in the last few months, they've become quite the tabloid couple."

"Hey, well now I know. Che-Che and the guitar player everybody calls Terrible Todd. Ooo-eee."

"I'm pleased to have spared you the *thrill* of reading *Snitch* magazine."

"Hey, maybe I'll buy one just for fun."

J.C. glanced down at the two books on the seat next to me. One novel was by Mark SaFranko and the other by Tony O'Neill. "So, you're a reader too?"

"I am, believe it or not."

"Who are these writers? I'm not familiar with either of them."

"I guess you could say that O'Neill and SaFranko are part of a new wave of fiction writers. I like their stuff."

"Are you also following in your father's footsteps? Are you a writer as well?"

"Yes, I am."

"I shouldn't be surprised. If James Patterson can have a bestseller I presume that any day now some homeschooled lackwit with fifth-grade credentials will win a Pulitzer and become the new John Steinbeck."

"I wasn't homeschooled, J.C."

"I wasn't referring to you."

"That's good to know."

"It appears that I will need your help, Bruno. A small favor."

"Sure," I said. "Whatever."

"I'd like you to go inside and tell Marcella that I'm waiting for her here in the car and that there are photographers everywhere as well. Will you do that?"

"Sure. Do you know where she is?"

"I did mention that La Natura is a cosmetic line. Where then would you suppose that the spokesperson for a line of makeup, making a personal appearance, would be in Neiman Marcus?"

Once again I felt my pee-pee being slapped. "At the makeup counter?" I said.

"Bravo, Bruno!"

There was Che-Che surrounded by women and fans and a cable TV camera crew. She was six feet tall and ridiculously beautiful. I made it past the crowd then whispered to her that her grandmother was waiting in the limo at the side entrance and that there were guys with cameras there too. Che-Che smiled and nodded and said she'd be out in a few minutes.

As she left the building I was standing by the rear door of the limo waiting to open it. After signing an autograph or two, when she started to cross the sidewalk, one of the photographers—a guy a foot taller than me wearing an L.A. Lakers cap—jumped in front of her and began clicking. I sidestepped the guy, then body-blocked him in an effort to clear Che-Che's path. He got even by elbowing me in the stomach. Hard. Then the jerk was right in her face again, snapping away.

I wasn't hurt but I was mad. It had been a couple of years since I'd clouted anyone and this guy was twice my size and must have assumed he could bully me. Eddie Bunker, the writer, once told me the secret to brawling: Always get in the first punch. This putz had it coming. Eddie would have been proud. A nice surprise left hook to the cheek, à la Bernard Hopkins.

The guy looked shocked. He grabbed his face then fell against Che-Che as his camera hit the ground and broke.

I opened the back door and hustled J.C.'s granddaughter

into my limo. As we pulled away, "Laker Cap" was still standing on the sidewalk holding his face.

J.C.'s hand was on my arm. "Thank you, Bruno."

"No big deal," I said. "I don't like being strong-armed. The guy was out of line."

"I won't forget today," she whispered. "That was very gallant." Then she turned to her granddaughter. "Are you all right, Marcella?"

"The cocksucker deserved it. What a *cazzo*. Nice hook, Bruno. That's your name, right?"

"Right," I said. "Bruno."

"That motherfucker's been in my shit for three days. Ever since I got to L.A."

"Marcella, do you mind? I'm in the car too. That language is simply uncalled for—I know, how about lunch, dear? Let's put this unpleasantness behind us."

"Sure, Nana. That's a good idea. Anyplace where I can get a drink is fine with me."

Then Che-Che lit a cigarette. She was rattled and pissed off. "You know, that blowjob Morty Shiff isn't paying me enough to go on TV and front his line of goop and powder. I don't need this crap. I should've asked for more money. A lot more money."

"*How sharper than a serpent's tooth it is to have a thankless child*," J.C. whispered. "Please dear, you're upsetting me. That's quite enough." Grandma was now attempting to comfort wide-awake, jumpy, fat Tahuti. "And please, do you mind not smoking in an enclosed car."

"Okay, Nana, you're right. I'm sorry," she said, then tossed her butt out the window. "But between fuckin' La Natura Cosmetics and that coke-slamming guitar player ex of mine, my goddamn life is a zoo. I'm really sick of this shit."

As it turned out our problem wasn't over. A few blocks later I saw two cars following us: a green two-door and an open, yellow sports car. I recognized both the guys riding in the passenger seats from outside the department store.

Che-Che noticed me checking my mirror then looked back and saw them too. "Now what?" she snarled. "These dickheads won't leave me alone. *Menica!*"

"I think we'll be okay," I said. "My company does a lot of concerts. I've been through this before."

With that I punched the gas pedal, crossing the double line on Wilshire and speeding past the three stopped cars ahead of me waiting for the light. Then I swung a quick right on a side street. Reeves Drive.

I pulled over in front of a little residential hotel that was just off the corner—a hangout I knew about that catered to out-of-work studio musicians—called the Saint Paul.

"Look, Che-Che," I said, pointing at the hotel, "I've got an idea. I know this place. There's a lobby inside. If you get out here and give me about half an hour to get rid of these guys, we can swing back to pick you up."

The beautiful girl sighed. "Sure. Whatever. Fuck it. Just be back here in half an hour."

When the two cars finally caught up with my stretch Che-Che was safe in the hotel and J.C. and I were two blocks away.

On Roxbury Drive off Olympic I pulled over at the big park, slid all the limo's tinted windows down, then parked in a blue handicapped space.

Getting out, I opened the door for Grandma and Tahuti. The guys in the two cars slowed down and drove past. They could see that Che-Che was not in the car. After a few minutes of J.C. sunning herself on a bench with black fatso, the paparazzi lost interest and drove off.

When we eventually got back to J.C.'s bungalow on Crescent Heights, it was four o'clock. Grandma and Che-Che had eaten lunch at Jimmy's in Century City while I'd watched Tahuti snore and read two chapters from my book. Then we dropped the beautiful model at the Beverly Hills Hotel.

This time my customer allowed me to open the car door for her and help out by carrying her handbag up the walkway.

At the bungalow entrance the old lady was smiling. "Well, it's been quite a day," she said. "Honestly, I'm exhausted."

"You're home and everything's okay," I said. "I hope you'll call us again—when you need a ride in an *old Pontiac.*"

J.C. wasn't used to giving compliments. She had to look down at Tahuti for inspiration before she could squeeze one out. "You're a decent man, Bruno. A good man. Marcella and I are both grateful," she whispered.

"*Ten-four,* J.C.," I said.

"And I'd work on my excessive misuse of your native tongue if I were you."

"I'll keep it in mind."

Then she unlocked her door and set her cat inside. After turning back she opened her purse and handed me four one hundred dollar bills. "Here. This is for you—for your trouble."

I looked at the money. "That's a big tip."

"*Ten-four,*" she said, grinning. "And as my stunning granddaughter might say, 'You earned it. Big-time.'"

I began to turn away but I wanted to ask a favor—so I faced her again. I wasn't sure how to do it. The words refused form in my mouth. "I . . . I," I said. "Would you mind . . . if . . . very much . . ."

The blue-gray eyes fixed on me. "Speak up, Dante, for the love of God. I'm eighty-seven. I haven't got that much time left on the planet."

"Well, would you mind reading some of my stuff—a few stories?" I blurted. "I know it's a big favor to ask, but . . ."

J.C. was beaming. *"A man was starving in Capri,"* she quoted. *"He moved his eyes and looked at me . . ."*

"I know that one too," I shot back, amazed at myself. *"I felt his gaze, I heard his moan, and knew his hunger as my own."*

"Not bad, Mr. Dante. You've read Millay. You may send me your work, or bring it. I will read what you've written . . . and give you an honest literary assessment."

"I'll drop it by tomorrow. Thanks, J.C."

No reply. The door slammed and she was gone. Inside to the darkness with her mystic Tahuti. This ancient publisher and poet with a great mind and a short fuse.

twelve

I hate banks. And lines. I get uncomfortable and impatient anywhere there's a queue and not enough help behind the counter, especially at the bank.

It had been an okay morning so far and on my drive down Sunset Boulevard I'd been thinking about my new customer, J. C. Smart, and our meeting and also about her beautiful granddaughter, Che-Che. The idea came: Maybe I'd try writing some poetry again. It had always been a welcome distraction. For years in New York I'd carried a notebook and a pen around with me and jotted down lines that might later become a poem. Maybe I'd try doing that again.

For some reason most L.A. banks never have enough tellers and no matter how long the line gets, or who's running the branch, the suits behind the rail, sitting at the desks, apparently never look up or give a rat's ass how long their customers are logjammed.

Wells Fargo Bank is at Sunset and Vine streets in Hollywood. My habit, on instructions from David Koffman, was to deposit all the checks and cash from the previous weekend's work on Monday morning. Sometimes, some days, I'd need to go twice after the mail arrived in the afternoon if we were short on payroll. I'd come to hate the process.

This particular Monday I also needed to cash my check to pay back the advance I'd taken from the cash box.

As I entered the moneyshrine there were eleven people in the line in front of me with only three tellers to service them. Then one of the tellers mysteriously—spontaneously—slapped her "Next Teller Please" sign up and went away. Nine-fifteen on Monday fucking morning and the guy awards himself with a break while a line full of people are kept waiting. My brain went crazy.

Jimmy suggested that I tell these flimflam cocksuckers, in the loudest voice possible, about how arrogant this abortion clinic they called a bank was. His voice was so loud that I had to tell him audibly to shut-the-fuck-up. The guy in front of me turned and shot me a look, then saw my eyes and wisely began to mind his own business.

My deposit and check-cashing took a total of thirty-one minutes. My sanity was gone.

On the way back to the office I got into a yelling beef with a motorcycle needlehead on a Harley who'd cut me off in front of Hollywood High, so to soothe myself a stop at the Liquor Mart on La Brea Avenue was inevitable.

I picked up six cheapo champagne bottles to replenish the office fridge and also purchased three pints of Hiram Walker for my personal relief and comfort.

By the time I reached the office I was four fingers down on pint one and had dropped two vikes to further take the edge off. My sanity was returning.

Three drivers were in the chauffeur's room reading newspapers and watching Dr. Phil while Portia yapped away on the phone with another driver, oozing hyper-anxiety.

I went upstairs, closed the door, and turned on my computer. I was still fuming about the bank. I needed to write something. It didn't matter what. Then the idea came: a love note to Wells Fargo Bank. Here it is:

Wells Fargo Bank
6320 Sunset Boulevard
Hollywood, CA 90028

Attn: Mr. Ignacio Jones
Branch Vice President

Dear Ignacio:

We have never met but I am pleased—no, proud—to announce that I am a longtime Wells Fargo Bank financial patron. Fact is I have been *stuffing* my paychecks into your bank on and off for around five years. Ha-ha. So I guess that makes me an A-1 client. I am also a citizen of the United States of America and though I have never personally spilled blood for my government, let me assure you that I hold the cause of freedom as a sacred trust and a highly elevated big deal. I say God bless America to myself at least five times every day. No kidding.

But here's the reason for my letter: As I said, I use your bank a lot, especially on Mondays, and it was during this morning's visit that something especially stimulating caught my attention. So much so that I wanted to take time out from my daily schedule and write you a letter. Fact is, Ignacio, my helmet's off to

you and the marketing guys at Wells Fargo Bank,
Hollywood Branch, because after waiting in line the
normal thirty-five-plus minutes to transact my banal
business snot, when I actually did get face-to-face with
one of your clerks and handed that human my deposit,
your trained, grinning operative looked me dead in
the eye, then asked, *"Have you heard of Well's Fargo
Bank's <u>new</u> ATM Rewards Program?"*

Wow! Talk about impressive! I mean, even before I
could start to conduct my own banking, your rep had
me right by the short hair delivering a full two minute
sales pitch.

Yes indeed. A walking, talking, real-life banking
commercial! I was rendered speechless. I actually had
the sensation that the teller's boot was right there on
my neck the whole time. It made me wonder; I'd even
be willing to bet that you and the crack marketing
dudes at Wells Fargo often become aroused while you
brainstorm new ways to present financial promotions
to your captive and squirming clientele.

As I sit here at my desk I can close my eyes and
visualize you standing at the conference room table
dramatizing an all-important new sales spiel to your
team of salivating operatives—then bending one of
the younger trainees over a nearby typing table—his
slacks and skivvies down around his ankles—while
you deliver the full measure of your insight to the pink-
cheeked fellow one mighty stroke at a time.

Anyway, I know you're busy. All I can say is: God
bless America and God bless the banking industry.

Sincerely,

Bruno Dante

thirteen

The sex thing with Portia continued and I was becoming more crazy and edgy and angry with myself. The brutal mind attacks and the messages of stupidity and self-judgment were relentless. It was far worse in the morning after a night of booze. *Jimmy's* voice screaming at me: *"Coward! Fool! You screwed that skinny, crippled bitch again! You're using her. You're a pussy. A needy cheesedick. You can't manage this company. Koffman knows it and Portia will know it soon too and even your drivers think you're a nutjob. Just wait. This'll cost you. I promise. You're on your way over the fucking edge!"*

We were having sex three or four nights a week but I had to be buzzed to do it so the drinking and madness had risen back to an unmanageable level. Though the woman grated on me with her high-flung, know-it-all snootiness and nonstop mouth, like an addicted fool I continued the affair, getting drunk and pulling her into the chauffeur's room or up to my bed, or leaning her over an office chair to hammer her from behind, or demanding that she suck me off.

The only thing that made it bearable was that when Portia got drunk too she could be funny, imitating different English accents and telling me crazy tales about the paramedic company in New York and plastic surgery doctors and her philandering cop ex-husband and his friends harassing the transvestite hookers in SoHo.

My daily writing became my only escape from *Jimmy*'s voice in my mind. I was now writing first thing in the morning at six a.m. no matter what—an hour to two hours—and had managed to produce ten decent stories. None of which I showed to Portia. In my experience the best time for a writer to write is when he is completely fresh with no distractions. I'd tried it again and again and there was no possible way I could concentrate later in the day if I'd been drinking. This nonsense about writers who are boozers and conceive their best work while half-jacked is simply crap. No writer can write drunk. It's impossible.

Finally, one night alone in my room, after sex with Portia downstairs, I did something insane. I'd decided that I wanted to clean my gun. The thing had belonged to my father and I kept it in a shoe box in my drawer, an old S&W .38 Police Special he'd had for twenty-five years. Pop had taken it in lieu of a poker debt.

I knew it was loaded because I always kept it loaded. I'm not sure what possessed me but I fired it at my bedroom mirror. Twice. The bullets passed through the wall and one ended up in my bathroom sink and the other lodged in a can of shaving cream on the shelf. The noise of the explosions rendered me immediately sober.

A minute later Portia was up the stairs and banging on my door in a panic. I lied and said that the gun had gone off by mistake. She knew this was crap and it took me over an hour to calm her down until finally I opened her shirt and began rubbing her tits, telling her how smart she was and how much I trusted her. She demanded that I give her the gun to throw away.

"You know you can be a very frightening person when you drink," she whispered. "You're a dangerous man. I see a kind of madness in your eyes."

"That was my father's gun. It's a memento."

"Was he like you when he drank? Was he this way?"

"Not really. But he was no pushover. He was filled with rage and long periods of silence. But when he drank too much he usually got mellow."

"Did you love him?"

"No, I worshipped him. Look, I said I was sorry."

"You should seek help."

"I've tried—nothing works. I'm afraid that I'm crazy. I'm afraid I might just kill myself some night."

"Commit yourself to therapy. You can go to a clinic. Hollywood is rife with free programs and therapeutic facilities. I overcame my issue with bulimia. If I can do it you can too."

"Great. What about the hundred pieces of nicotine gum you chew every day? You're a crackhead for that shit."

"Think progress—not perfection. I'm in deadly earnest. You need help."

"I hate those brain-sucking assholes. They're crazier than their patients. Read the statistics some time. I hate that shit."

"Promise me. Give me your word that you'll at least consider it."

"Okay. I'll give it some thought."

Then we screwed—her on top, moaning, pounding up and down, her ass bones digging into my thighs. After that we fell asleep. By noon the next day the incident was put to rest.

• • •

A couple of days later I made the decision to turn the day-to-day management of Dav-Ko over to Portia, giving her the title of office manager. She liked the business end and her new authority and I knew she'd be good at it. I had arrived at the point that I didn't care about my job and dreaded being stuck alone in the office with her all day.

In the last month we'd added three more cars and two more drivers so I assigned myself the task of training the guys and buying their chauffeur uniforms and showing them the best routes to the airport and downtown. Busy work.

When the one-week training period was over I decided to begin driving more of our clients in the afternoon and evening, forcing sobriety on myself, absenting myself from the office.

In response, because she sensed me pulling away, Portia made the decision to hire a new night dispatcher: tit for tat. The kid was Joshua Wright, a twenty-nine-year-old black guy, a part-time actor and an ex–corporate bookkeeper with a master's degree in theater. Portia interviewed Joshua twice then wanted me to talk to him too. I approved him right away because he was smart and had showed up to both meetings dressed in spiffy sports jackets with a shirt and tie and because he sounded like the Channel 4 guy on the TV news when he talked. Her plan was to have Joshua dispatch and do our company books in his evening downtime. Over the phone to New York David Koffman rubber-stamped the hire because we were saving money, covering two gigs with one employee.

On his first night of work Joshua arrived driven by his fiancée, a pretty, sexy college girl from USC dental school, Katie Sanders. A white girl. He introduced us and then announced that they would be married the next spring. I was hoping that now I'd be off the hook and for once everything might be okay at Dav-Ko.

One of the clients whom I began driving regularly was Ronny Stedman, a film producer and a true Hollywood asshole. Ronny was originally from Australia but had been raised in L.A. from the age of ten. Now, at twenty-eight, he had made three films and had recently formed his own movie production company. His famous gay uncle Robert owned Adelaide Records and Adelaide Films. He'd passed on a few mil to Ronny to give the kid a running start in L.A. Ronny loved our stocked-bar limos and made up excuses to rent our cars two or three nights a week to hang out with his pretty singer-actress girlfriend, Carol.

When I drove them together they'd hit the Polo Lounge at the Beverly Hills Hotel or Sammy's in Century City or Matteo's in Westwood. Carol was a big baseball fan and when the Dodgers were in town the couple never missed a game. She was a former Texas beauty queen and a hot number, ten years older than Ronny. If they'd been partying late and had visited her coke dealer in Westwood on the way home to his Los Feliz condo, the center passenger partition would go up and she'd jump him right in the car. I like that. I liked her. She was funny and pushy and oversexed and refused to take any shit from her asshole boyfriend.

There were some nights when Ronny would go gambling alone at Hollywood Park Casino or one of the clubs in Gardena. I'd sit in the parking lot smoking cigarettes, reading a book, or jotting short story notes in my binder. Portia had instructions from me to only ring my cell phone in an emergency. Stedman didn't know that I was Dav-Ko's main guy in L.A. and I wanted to keep it that way.

He continued to request me to drive him primarily because I kept my mouth shut. I wasn't a wannabe anything,
not an actor and not an aspiring director and I didn't need a
job in film production and I wasn't one of the hundred people
a day trying to get over on him or his uncle.

When, a couple of weeks later, he began a new film, I
became his driver on a twelve-hour-per-day basis, shuttling as-
sistants back and forth from the production office and running local errands. I was determined to stay busy and stay
away from Portia and my boozing. I drank only a pint of Jim
Beam while I worked, stretching the jug out as long as I could,
plus a few wine coolers mixed in with my normal Xanax and
Vicodin regimen to keep the edge off. I put in three days
straight and had logged thirty-two hours behind the wheel.

The first day of actual shooting on *It Creeps* was a location
at Santa Monica Beach beneath the Palisades, a quarter mile
away from where a hundred *Baywatch* episodes had been
filmed. It was a summer night-swimming scene where two
girls are in the water nearly nude and their stalker, a tattooed
serial killer called Kozmo in the script, wades in to slash
them both up with his barber's razor.

I drove Ronny and his secretary Kimberly around L.A. all
that day running errands and then to the location during the
setup at sundown. Ronny was edgy—barking orders—and
constantly on his cell phone. We'd been fighting the home-
ward-bound rush-hour traffic that feeds north on the Pacific
Coast Highway from the 10 freeway.

As we pulled into the parking lot young Ronny became
unglued. Some unsuspecting human shitball that was working on the film had been in a hurry and parked his Toyota
sedan in the spot marked "X-Producer."

Stedman threw his cell phone across the car, smashing it against the wooden console. Then he got out and slammed his two-thousand-dollar briefcase on the roof of the limo. Then he stomped over to where the director and the cast were running lines in preparation for the scene.

Kimberly had been putting up with his crap all day. She sighed deeply then jumped out too, hustling after him carrying the briefcase.

Standing there by Pearl, waiting for the shit to fly, was one of the grips, who came over to check out the stretch. He said his name was Chico but he wasn't Mexican. Chico asked to look inside the limo and ogled the red leather and the woodwork and the TV and stocked bar. "Nice ride, my brother."

"Thanks," I said back. "Holllleeeewood. You know."

"So how long have you been driving Mr. Big?" he asked.

"Not that long, but he's become a damn good customer."

"This is my third film with him. Ever been to his office at 9200 Sunset?"

"No," I said.

"So you've never seen *The Orchid*?"

"*The Orchid*?"

"Yeah, he has an orchid in a big pot behind his desk on the cabinet. Ronny's famous for that orchid."

"Okay," I said. "How come?"

"Well, you know that Mr. Big almost never leaves his office during the day. He never goes out. During business hours when he gets busy on the phone and that stuff, when Mr. Big has to take a squirt, what do you think he does?"

"He pisses in *The Orchid*?"

"Yup."

"Isn't it dead by now?"

"It's a fake orchid. The thing's plastic. He sprays air stuff around the office but it doesn't matter. You can always smell the stink. *The Orchid* and the piss smell are Ronny's claim to fame in this town. His trademarks."

I nodded. "He's a pretty intense guy," I said.

"His receptionists get the pleasure of emptying the planter every couple of days. That's why he never keeps one for very long."

"C'mon. Straight dope?"

Chico was grinning. "Straight dope, my man. Hey, anyway, gotta go. Nice ride."

"Okay, see you."

I looked over at the group standing by the director's chairs. There was young Ronny. He'd found the culprit, an assistant director kid named Matt. Thirty feet away from my limo with two dozen crew members watching, Stedman was yelling and lambasting the guy for his stupidity and unprofessional conduct.

Matt was sorry, he'd been in a hurry delivering extra copies of the last-minute scene notes for the actors. But *sorry* ain't shit. *Sorry* just didn't cut it. Ronny Stedman was boss and he took this five-minute opportunity to make sure everyone present could completely comprehended how a true Hollywood jerkoff actually conducts himself.

fourteen

That night I got back to Dav-Ko after one a.m., exhausted and a little buzzed, and as I was rolling over the drive and pulling into the raised carport, I misjudged the distance and bumped the rear of our brown stretch with the tip of Pearl's right fender.

Hearing the thud I got out to take a look. I'd dislodged a piece of front chrome molding. Surely a five-hundred-dollar repair at the Lincoln dealer's body shop and the loss of a day's rental for the car, another twelve hundred bucks.

I was pissed. When I got inside Joshua was just leaving for the night, shutting the office down and forwarding our phones to the answering service.

After he'd gone I remembered what Jackie, our New York mechanic, used to do when a chrome strip or a piece of molding came loose on one of the older Caddys. I located a tube of Krazy Glue in our tool cabinet and went back outside to see if I could reattach the molding.

The glue worked. Five minutes later Pearl's fender strip

was in place and as good as new except for a tiny, almost un-noticeable ding.

Back in the office I entered my "Time-In" in the computer after tossing the glue on the desk. I could hear an Etta James CD playing in Portia's chauffeur's room/bedroom. I knew that I'd better go in and say hello.

"Bruno!" she called from across the room. "Hi, darling."

She wasn't alone. She was close-dancing with a partner, a young guy. Portia pulled her head from his shoulder to intro-duce us. "This is Sidney," she whispered. "He's my friend. A personal trainer and massage therapist."

The kid was tanned and overmuscled and looked as if he'd stepped out of a gay men's magazine.

Both of them were giggling and nicely gassed on drinks and whatever else they'd been drugging that night. Portia was wearing her favorite oversized man's dress shirt and her thonged panties. Sidney, a tight tee and sweat pants. L.A. fit-ness casual.

I knew that the kid being here with her was payback, Por-tia's way of showing me what a jerk I was for pulling back and avoiding contact with her.

She asked me if I wanted a Cuba libre. I said yes because I needed a pick-me-up after the annoyance of Pearl's fender ding.

Crossing the room I sat down on one of the puffy velour chairs Portia had brought in weeks ago to dress the place up.

The shit was starting. "Sidney and I first met in a yoga class at my gym. He's from Chicago," she purred. "My young friend has a spectacular body, don't you think?"

"Sidney looks like he lifts weights day and night," I said. "He's an impressive physical specimen."

Portia was leering. "Sidney darling, slip your shirt off,

beautiful boy. Bruno ought to see what's possible when a fellow devotes himself to improving his body."

Apparently Sid was shy but equally as drunk as his skinny, grinning host. He also stuttered a bit. "Ca-ca-c'mon Porsh, you're ma-makin' me nervous. You know I don't la-like to show off."

"Bruno, Sidney's bisexual."

"That's just swell," I said. "He's in the right town for it too. The very rectum of deep thinkers and financial opportunity. How about that drink?"

"Of course" she said. "Help yourself?"

"Don't mind if I do."

Across the room I spotted a one-third-empty half gallon of rum, ice, some limes, a tall glass, and a quart of Coca-Cola on the magazine table. But, as I started toward the bar, Dav-Ko's office manager changed her mind, breaking her hold on her personal Ken doll. Her shirt was open, exposing her tits as she slinked her way across the floor to mix me a drink. "No, no, no," she purred, "I'll get it for you. My treat. Service with a smile."

"Mind going easy on the mix," I asked.

It was then that the bell went off in my head and I fully got the message. Earlier that night, when I knew my assignment with Stedman was ending, I'd phoned in to tell Joshua my ETA to the garage and to let him know my out-of-pocket expenses for the run. Portia was in the office, in the background. I could hear her lecturing a driver. She knew I was on my way in. But the extra glass on the magazine table was the real giveaway. She'd been expecting me.

I decided that I didn't care. Let the woman have her even-steven for the way I'd treated her. Let it play out. Screw it. I deserved it. I had it coming. Maybe after tonight we'd be able to get back to where we were before the whole mess began.

She handed me my drink and I took a hit. A good one. The glass was mostly rum and ice. Now I was okay. I could relax. I was fine. I took another long hit.

Ms. Portia was smiling, a drunken leer, her teeth stained by red lipstick, her boy's white hair and pretty face glowing in the soft light. She rejoined Sidney and pressed her tits against his chest and began dancing again. Etta on the CD player wailing out "At Last."

"Don't mind us," she said.

"Hey," I said back. "Just pretend I'm a tired chauffeur having a well-needed nightcap."

"That's nice," she whispered.

"Mind if I help myself to another?" I said, pointing at the liquor table.

"Pleeezzze," she slurred. "Sidney's been promising me a mah-sage. You don't mind if we just go ahead? It won't embarrass you, will it?"

I nodded no. In for a peso, in for a pound.

With that she picked up her glass, took a last hit, draining it, then crossed the room to pull open the sleeper couch.

She slipped off her panties and long-sleeve shirt to lie on the bed, her ass in the air.

Sidney, as if choreographed, finished his drink too, then stood above the bed peeling off his clothes, down to his red bikini underpants, attempting to appear nonchalant. Near naked, the guy was a living cartoon: the perfect tanned steroid vision of what his West Hollywood clientele expected and paid for.

He produced a bottle of massage oil from his fanny pack on the table then got on the bed with Portia, on top of her, sitting upright, fitting his ass just behind hers. After squirting her with the oil he began rubbing her shoulders.

Portia let out a sigh, then surprised me by doing something

she'd never done with me; for once, she removed the nicotine gum from her mouth, tossing the wad on the nightstand.

At the magazine table I made myself another blast. A big one. I had a secret that neither of my hosts knew about: One more drink and I wouldn't care. I wouldn't give a damn what happened.

When I sat back down Sid was in the same position above Portia, except now he was working his hands down into the crack of her ass.

I lit a cigarette and took a long hit at the rum.

"More?" he whispered. Portia's eyes were closed and she was humming. "Oh yes. Please. Please."

Now her legs were wide apart and his bikini shorts were off and lying on the floor.

Sid was behind her rubbing his cock against her wet cunt and asshole. Portia opened her eyes then looked over at me as if asking permission.

I lifted my glass to toast the event.

He removed a rubber from his fanny pack on the night-stand and slipped it on. Then he fitted himself deep inside my skinny girlfriend.

A minute into it he leaned forward and breathed in her ear. "How 'bout the ass too? I know you like it up the ass."

"Oh yes, the ass too," she purred. "Do me in the ass, Sidney. Please. Fuck my ass."

My drink was done and I got to my feet. "Okay," I said, "I'm leaving. Thanks for the demonstration. I'm working to-morrow."

"Wait, Bruno," she breathed, stopping, looking up at me, her fat tits dangling beneath her against a pillow. "Don't leave." She pushed Sid away.

"You've made your point," I said. "My dick's in the dirt. I've seen enough."

"Please. There's some excellent *Peruvian* in my purse," she breathed. "Have some. Have as much as you like. I don't want you to go. "

The drug invitation made me change my mind. I was now drunk enough. "Okay, you win," I said. "Don't mind if I do."

I located her handbag and found a two-gram bottle of blow in a velour pouch along with a gold straw and a mirror.

With the two of them lying on the bed I cut out three fat rails on the magazine table then snorted them. Coke has never been my drug of choice and I hadn't done any in months so the effect was immediate and euphoric. I was whacked—drunk and wired.

"How about sharing," she purred. "Bring it here, darling. Join us."

Sitting on the corner of the bed I handed the bottle and straw and mirror to Portia. She cut out several lines, snorted two fatties, then passed the works to Sid, who did up the rest.

Her hand was on my arm. "Can I do you?" she whispered. "Can I suck on you?"

"Why?" I said. "This isn't my party. I'm not needed here."

"I want to. I want you to cum in my mouth. You know I love sucking your penis. I love tasting you."

Unzipping my blue chauffeur's slacks, I pulled them down to my knees. My cock was iron.

Lying back against the pillow I watched as her tongue began circling the head of my dick. Then I closed my eyes. She wasn't a deep-throat artist. If she took too much in she began to gag. She was more of pole licker and helmet sucker.

When I opened my eyes again it was because Sidney was banging her from behind, long jarring strokes, interrupting her rhythm and my fun.

"Wait," I said. "Let her finish with me. Then you can go next."

Sid smiled but kept at it.

Then Portia stopped and pulled his cock out. She turned around and began sucking him off too. Then back to me.

Finally, sliding his cock from her mouth, she purred. "Sidney, let's give Bruno something special. You and me. Okay, beautiful boy?"

Sid was ready for anything. Beaming. "I love it."

So they both went to work on me, tongue kissing each other and passing my cock between them.

Sidney was a master at giving head. Cocks were his expertise. He'd take my entire joint in his mouth in one gulp then let it out slowly, holding it in his lips before allowing the head to pop from his mouth.

Then, while she was sucking on me, Sidney dropped down and started tonguing my asshole. Deeply. Then around the rim and back inside again.

A minute or two later, when I came, it was like a planet exploding against the sun. Boom boom boom.

Portia held my jizz in her mouth until she could lean across to Sidney and pass my cum through her lips to his. They tongue-kissed while swallowing my load.

When I opened my eyes the two of them were cutting out lines with the last of the coke. I reached for the rum bottle and sipped from it instead.

When Portia offered me more I refused.

She was smiling. "Did you enjoy that, dear Bruno? Am I back to meeting your needs?"

The words that came from me were a mistake. I was drunk and stoned and stupid and not conscious of the damage I was doing—or if I was I didn't care. But saying what I said made me realize I had just pronounced my own death sentence.

"Your guy Sidney is a master at sucking cock." I said. "He's better than you. Blowjobs should be Sidney's life's work."

Portia was off the bed and slipping into her panties and shirt. "I'm tired now, Bruno," she hissed. "I'd like to go to bed. Leave, please."

I struggled up the stairs leaving the two of them in the chauffeur's room. I knew she was pissed off, but in my mind she had it coming. Anyway, I didn't care. I'd figure out what to do in the morning.

When I awoke it was because daylight was blasting through my curtains and I badly needed to pee. It was just after dawn and my head was pounding and *Jimmy* began yammering away: *Good morning, asshole! Have fun last night? So it turns out that now you're a faggot too. Just swell. You don't care what you stick your dick in, do you? By this time next year you'll be wearing lipstick and working downstairs on Selma with the rest of your swish pals.*

I began to hear noise downstairs too. Real voices. The front door slamming shut.

As I tried to get up, swinging my legs toward the floor, there was a sudden sharpness of pain in my groin, a pulling at my thigh and testicles.

Slipping back down on the bed to a sitting position I tried my best to clear my head. That's when I realized the problem: My penis and balls were stuck to my leg and some substance—something hard and dry—was covering my crotch area. My pubic hair was a thickened mesh of cemented steel wool. I tried pulling my dick away from the gathered skin of my testicles. It was impossible.

A foot away on the nightstand I saw a folded piece of yellow legal paper. On top of the paper was an empty squeezed tube of glue. Krazy Glue.

Unfolding the note I read the message:

> Good-bye Bruno. You're insane and I despise you. You are a monster and a prick and a son of a bitch!
>
> P.

The emergency surgery to remove my superglued penis and testicles from my thigh lasted two and a half hours. After first trying an array of solvents and stinging chemicals it was determined that nothing short of cutting away the skin would do any good. I had a choice, the doctor said. I could lose the flesh from my cock or they could cut away the tissue from the leg.

Because I had alcohol in my blood the guy refused to put me under. I was numbed but fully conscious as I watched him sweating, cutting away at my thigh, removing a seven-inch-long patch of tissue. Part of the urethra opening at the tip of my cock had been glued shut too. An incision was made there to reopen the hole so I could pee properly again. In all, sixty-one stitches were needed.

In my room after the surgery and when the meds wore off and the pain began, I started to shake. I was jonesing in alcohol withdrawal, a tonic-clonic reaction. My body was out of control and the tremors were getting worse all the time.

I rang for the nurse. When she came in and saw me shaking and sweating the on-call doctor was summoned and they hooked me up with a diazepam IV. Half an hour later I was okay.

fifteen

The towering white-haired figure that stood in the hospital doorway blocking out most of the light was part man, part water buffalo. David Koffman had flown to L.A. from New York to help Joshua run the company while I would spend several days at Hollywood Presbyterian.

In bed, in my ward room while he stood there wearing his newest Panama hat, which made him nearly seven feet tall, I gave David my account of the accident—about being in my underpants trying to attach the section of chrome molding back on to the front bumper of Pearl when the tube of Krazy Glue burst open against my shorts.

The lie sounded only semi-convincing and it didn't account for Portia's abrupt departure, but the look of pain in my face and my apparent discomfort were real and Koffman was genuinely sympathetic and upset for me. His sombrero came off and he set it down. It covered the lower half of my bed.

When the opening was right I reminded him of something that I'd only realized myself the week before: Our company had just passed its six-month mark in business. I was now a full 25 percent partner.

"Were you drinking when the accident happened?" he asked quietly.

I blew up: "No, for chrissake, it was six a.m. in the morning! I was getting the car ready for an airport run. Remember, we had a deal about my drinking. I really resent that kind of question."

David apologized. He could see what I was going through. And Portia's quitting, I added, was an unfortunate coincidence—icing on the cake to a really fucked day. Nothing more.

The meds I was on were starting to make me feel a little giddy and I went on to tell him about my run-in with Frank Tropper a few weeks before, and his dealing drugs, and explained that Portia had been put on probation as a result. This, of course, was a lie, but her resignation the morning of the incident was now beginning to fit in nicely with the stream of bullshit I was concocting. "Bottom line, we're better off without her," I said. My new partner had no choice but to nod his head in agreement.

Then two of our drivers, Marty Humphrey and Cal Berwick arrived to pay their respects, both of them dressed in cop shades and black driving gloves. It surprised me when Koffman approved of the new thug look and he even suggested that we might consider advertising our driving staff as chauffeur-bodyguards.

I was on a roll so I blurted out that the idea was absurd, that advertising that nonsense would open the door to legal licenses and hiring restrictions that could make the task of hiring decent drivers even more difficult. The white-haired giant in the plantation owner outfit seated near me nodded his head in agreement.

• • •

The next day Dr. Rilke, the guy who did my surgery, came into the room to give me his evaluation. He was freshly tanned from a long weekend. It came to me that this was the first time in three years I'd gone this long without a drink—or a hard-on.

Rilke, who had body odor and seemed perpetually distracted, checked my chart then put it down. He peeled away my bandages, poked me and pressed and squeezed, then offered his assessment of my red and oozing crotch. "You're progressing well." The guy needed deodorant—a class he must've ditched in med school.

"What else?" I asked, turning my head away to cop a gulp of fresh air.

"Well, you'll experience epidermal numbness on your penis and testicles. But that's to be expected as well."

"Permanent numbness?" I asked.

Rilke was folding my bandages back down and taping them closed. "Doubtful," he said. "Just give it all time to heal."

"Hey, good news."

Now done with taping my body, Dr. B.O. pulled up a chair and sat down. He made some notes on my chart. "There is another factor that comes into play: the psychological component."

"Which means what? Don't tell me that I may never get a hard-on again?"

"That's not my area but anxiety after this type of injury can become a factor. If you'd like I can refer you to someone. We have people on staff here."

"Not interested. Thanks."

"Then, if I were you, I'd give myself as much time as necessary. Don't rush things." He looked at my chart again. "You're unmarried, correct?"

"Correct."

"Avoid sexual contact for a few weeks."

Portia's face suddenly popped into my brain and I felt myself wince. "That won't be a problem," I said.

The twitchy doctor adjusted his glasses. "There another issue we need to discuss," he said. "Something I'd think long and hard about if I were you."

"Okay. What? Tell me."

"Your blood test showed significant liver deterioration and we had to administer anticonvulsives. You're a heavy drinker, correct?"

"That's genetic," I said. "It runs in my family—my father and brother."

Rilke was whispering. "I'm not talking about genetics, Mr. Dante. Your problem is substance abuse. When you were admitted you had a blood alcohol level of .16 and there was evidence of cocaine and traces of the chemical compounds found in Xanax and Vicodin."

"Like I said that stuff runs in the family. From time to time I deal with anger and depression. The pills help."

"There's a newer compound out called Lexapro that's been quite successful in treating those symptoms. Patients in recovery have reported excellent results. You should look into it."

"Thanks anyway. I'll pass," I said.

The next day was release day. A new Filipino nurse came in to check my meds and change the dressing. She was tiny and in her early twenties with a pretty dark face and eye makeup. Her long black hair wrapped in a bun. Her badge name tag read "Esperanza."

Esperanza removed my sheet and blanket from the bed,

then pulled off my blue hospital shirt. Then she peeled away my bandages and began a sponge bath starting with my back and chest. When she got to my crotch area and began softly dabbing my cock and scrotum with the warm cloth I knew I'd be okay. Bingo!

sixteen

Dav-Ko's senior partner apparently wanted to keep tabs on the day-to-day operation of the company so he decided to stay on in Hollywood for another week or two and help run things. He'd unlocked his private suite upstairs and taken up residence. A steady stream of his gay pals invaded the duplex. The smell of hors d'oeuvres and gourmet dinners began flooding the building.

Resting in my room I spent the next two days writing a story about a paralyzed guy in the hospital who has an affair with his cute night-shift nurse but has no sensation whatever in his lower body, and watching old episodes of *The Twilight Zone* on DVD.

Even before I was up and around Koffman put an ad in the *Los Angeles Times* for a new day dispatcher. We got lucky and hired sixty-year-old Rosie Camacho the Monday after the ad ran. Rosie was a retired L.A. city bus route manager with twenty-five years on the job. Both of us liked her and it was an easy decision after the first interview. Her experience and her congenial phone manner made it a done deal.

Then it became a twofer package deal because Rosie had a grown son named Benito who had just recently started up his own lube and oil storefront business, close by on Western Avenue.

The day after she began work Rosie came back from a lunch with him and mentioned the nice coincidence of her son's little company being only ten minutes away. David Koffman met with Benny that afternoon and put him on the payroll as our moonlight mechanic.

These days Dav-Ko was almost constantly busy. I was better now and in the afternoon and evening when Koffman was out making business calls or on the rounds of the West Hollywood clubs, I came downstairs to help dispatch. We never turned down a limo order and frequently our stretches were double-booked and Rosie needed help to call our list of affiliate companies to farm out our overflow.

Then, suddenly, my chickens came home to roost. I was helping Rosie learn how to do future cash bookings in the computer when Koffman returned from a lunch appointment and stomped into the office. He opened the top desk drawer and pulled out our company checkbook, then asked me to step into the chauffeur's room with him. His face was stone; expressionless. I could tell something was up. Something ungood.

Marty Humphrey was watching a baseball game on the wall TV and waiting to do an airport run—the Dodgers were playing at San Diego. Koffman switched off the game and asked him to leave. The he barked the order: "Bruno, step in here with me. We have business to discuss."

Once I was inside David closed the door then flipped the

lock down for privacy. He dropped his big body heavily into a chair then folded open the check ledger. The shit was about to hit the fan. I could feel it.

"Sit," he snarled.

I stayed standing. "Sure, what's this about" I said.

"I had lunch with Portia today."

My attempt to appear blasé failed badly. In the back of my mind I was aware of the possibility that Koffman might try to contact the vengeful bitch but I was hoping I might get lucky and also hoping that if he did talk to her that she wouldn't spill her guts on every sordid detail. But now, standing in front of David Koffman, I was pretty sure the jig was up—my ass was in flames. "Oh," I said. "So, how's she doing?"

Taking a pen from his breast pocket I watched as Koffman printed my name on the top two checks in the ledger. "I'm writing this first one out to you for five thousand dollars," he sneered. "I feel that's a more than reasonable value of your 25 percent share in Dav-Ko."

"Wait a minute. What's up? Let's talk this through," I said.

"No discussion. No more deception. I've been an unthinking fool. But no more. I'm dissolving our agreement and our partnership as of today."

He ripped the first check from the book then kept on writing. "This next one," he said, "is a week's severance pay. One thousand dollars."

"C'mon, what the hell's going on?"

"Do not screw with me, Bruno. You know precisely what this is about."

"Do I get a chance to talk? This is still a partnership, right?"

"You're unstable—an alcoholic and probably a drug addict too. Christ, bullet holes in the walls of your room!

That's plain insanity. On top of that you've abused your fiduciary responsibility to this company. There's no adequate excuse for what you've done and no explanation for it is required."

I sat down. "Look, what did Portia tell you? You owe me that much."

The tall man folded the checkbook closed then used his ballpoint pen as a scepter, pointing its silver Gucci tip toward my head. "I was told things that, in confidence, I will not repeat here. But essentially, in substance, you're a train wreck. And I agree with Portia's view that you should be in therapy or some sort of recovery program. But, after today, that's your problem. Your choice. I'm washing my hands of the entire matter."

"The gun thing was an accident, David. I'm not crazy. I made a mistake."

He handed me the check for a thousand dollars then folded the big one, the one for five grand, into his shirt pocket, then patted it. "You'll get this one when you sign the release my attorney is drafting. Another ten days at the most."

"Look," I said, "my brother died. I had a hard time dealing with it. I fucked up. I started drinking again. That's the truth. But I'm okay now. I'm back on my feet."

Big David frowned. "No sale, sir."

"So I'm out on my ass. What about hearing the flip side?"

"Frankly, for me, there isn't one."

"That's just swell, David. I sober up and try to pull my shit together and then I get blindsided—and you get my quarter share in the company. That's a lousy deal and I don't deserve it."

The tall man glared at me in silence, then snarled, "You have until tomorrow afternoon to pack your things and vacate your room," he hissed.

"So that's it?"

"That's it. I have nothing else to say. The matter's settled."

That night I only slept an hour. Being off booze and pills was brutal and *Jimmy* was at me nonstop.

I was up early the next morning driving the alleys of Hollywood searching for boxes to help me pack up and move. After filling my Pontiac with collapsed cardboard I stopped at Ace Hardware on Sunset and bought a roll of clear tape that had a built-in cutter.

Back in my room I packed my clothes and began to unhook my computer and printer. There on my writing table was a stack of stories, now fifteen in total. Over a hundred and seventy printed pages of work. Good writing. Good stories. No matter what came next down the pike after Dav-Ko, I had these. My life wasn't a total shit sandwich. These stories were the upside. I was also now an experienced L.A. chauffeur with a major company. I'd be able to get work. The hell with Dav-Ko. I'd start over. I knew the drill.

Then I began doing the hard part—boxing up my books. There were several hundred.

An hour later I had four full boxes on the floor. Novels, poetry, and plays, all sorted and ready to go on a shelf wherever I landed next.

I heard a knock at my door. Figuring it was my ex-boss coming to check on my packing progress, I yelled, "I'm busy. Come back later."

The door opened and he stood there framed in the doorway, a granite statue outside a public library. "Can we talk?" he asked.

"My stuff will be out of your company by this afternoon," I said. "I reserved a U-Haul. I'm picking it up in an hour or so. And frankly, David, I've had my life shoved up my ass by a boss for the last time. So let's just save anymore replay for down the road, some other time. Okay?"

He stepped closer. "You should know that I had a conversation with Frank Tropper this morning. I've been waiting for his return call since I had my meeting with you."

"Swell."

"After we spoke I decided to dig deeper just to satisfy myself. I hope you realize that I didn't take this matter lightly."

"But you fired me anyway."

"I did what I thought was best under the circumstances. Getting drunk and shooting off a pistol in this building was simply the act of a madman."

"Have a nice fucking day, Mr. Koffman."

"There's more to discuss."

"I've just been evicted. I'm busy here."

"Do you want to know what happened on my call with Tropper?"

I'd begun stuffing books in a new box. "Sure, David. Sure," I said.

"First, a question: Why is it that you never mentioned he was having an affair with Portia?"

"You said you didn't want to hear anything from me."

"I mean at the time you fired Frank. Weeks ago. Tell me what happened there."

"I don't know. The guy's a snake. Dealing drugs out of a limousine. I squashed a snake. Case closed."

"That incident was important. Portia never mentioned her relationship with Frank. She omitted any discussion of that can of worms."

I sat down on a box of books. "Portia's an angry, poisonous whackjob. Take my word for it," I said.

"Go on. What happened?"

"Now it's important," I said, slinging the words at him. "*Now* you want to know. Forget it."

"You have my full attention. What happened?"

"Okay, sure. Fuck it," I said. "Why not?"

"Precisely."

"After I found out she was his part-time backup pole smoker I made her tell me what they'd been up to. I'd suspected for weeks that she'd been playing favorites and pushing all the company's cash work his way but I couldn't be a hundred percent sure, so I had let that part slide. After I fired the jerk and he could do no more damage, I thought it over and decided that Portia deserved another shot. My reasoning was what-the-hell, people are human. Shit happens. She made a mistake."

Big Koffman sat down on the box of books next to me. "I thought as much," he sighed.

"So that's it. Anything else?" I asked.

"Well, I may live to regret this, but I've decided to reverse myself and give you the same chance you gave Portia. With strict conditions."

"Jesus Christ!"

"Setting aside the insanity of your shooting spree, you've done a good job, basically. I don't want to overlook that."

"Okay, so what conditions, David?"

Buffalo Bill flipped a chunk of his gray hair back over his shoulder then folded his arms across his chest. "You are no longer a partner. You are now an employee and you will immediately return the one thousand dollar check I gave you."

"No problem. I can do that."

"And you are now on strict probation. If you can stay sober—completely sober—then we'll take it from there. You will attend three AA meetings per week and get the signature of the secretary at each meeting. Then, in ninety days, after I'm satisfied that you really want to make this work, we'll discuss reinstating our partnership."

The worm had just turned. But, instead of me having to do more groveling and slithering and backpedaling, I now felt myself getting pissed off. "No deal," I said. "Not that way."

"I beg your pardon?"

"I worked my ass off for this company and for that twenty-five percent. Screw that. Our partnership stays as it is or I move on."

Big David scratched his head. "Okay, I agree," he said. "I'll meet you halfway. But the ninety days probation stays in effect and your attendance at AA meetings is mandatory."

"Deal," I said. "Fair enough."

We both stood up. David Koffman put his arms around me and gave me his best lovey-dovey partner hug.

seventeen

Later that afternoon I got the number of AA and called the main office in L.A. and was given the address of a night meeting in Culver City.

The guy's name was Harvey. He was all business and got right to the point and let me choose one from the long list of cities he'd read out. I didn't want to go to any more in Hollywood. Hollywood is a snotpile. But I was willing to try. I would do whatever I could not to lose the limo job.

I'd driven by the Marina Club a hundred times when I lived in Venice and I'd seen people standing outside on the sidewalk smoking and holding Styrofoam cups but I had never been curious enough to stop and find out what was going on inside.

I parked my Pontiac up the block on Washington Boulevard just in case I needed a quick getaway, then walked back.

The meeting time posted outside on the door on a stick-on blackboard was eight o'clock. A guy with long sideburns in a Harley jacket, smoking a cigarette—blocking my way—

stopped me going in and shook my hand. "Hi. I'm Vince," he said grinning. "Welcome to the Marina Club."

"Thanks," I said.

"First time here?"

"Yeah. Does it show?"

"Like neon," he said smiling. "So what's your name, brother?"

"Bruno."

"Well, welcome, Bruno. How many days you got clean and sober?"

"I've stopped counting," I said. "A week or so."

Vince sneered, then pointed. "Coffee's all the way in the back. The meeting starts in five minutes. P.S.: You came on the right night. It's Phil S.'s twentieth birthday. He sponsors me and five or six of the regular guys here. Big doings. He'll be the main speaker."

"Lucky me," I said.

"No joke, Phil's a miracle. Twenty-five years in the slam—pronounced dead twice—he gives a great message."

"I'll bet."

"Hey Bruno . . . keep coming back."

"Ten-four. You too . . . *brother.*"

The fluorescent lighting in the Marina Club reminded me of the intake corridor at old County Jail, downtown. The meeting hall contained over a hundred chairs and was filling up fast.

After waiting in line and getting my free cup of coffee there were only a few seats left, so I decided not to sit down and subject myself to small talk. I stood at the back of the room near the bathrooms.

As it turned out Harley Vince in the leather jacket was also the guy leading the meeting. He called the room to order. As before, at the last meeting I went to in Hollywood, someone got up to read part of the Big Book: Chapter 5.

I was starting to feel trapped and closed-in. Beginning to sweat. This was a bad idea. There were way too many bodies—people pressing against me—a crowded hall populated by smiling, miracle-oozing, AA robots. The smells of bad breath, sweat, and the unventilated men's room behind me was beginning to make me want to bolt.

Then a pimpled teenage girl standing next to me, with ratty pink hair and torn jeans, held out her hand. "I'm Jeannie," she whispered.

"Bruno," I said back.

"First time here?"

"Yeah. You?"

"No. But I'm back again," Jeannie sighed. "I had ninety days then I had a bad slip. My boyfriend's back in County on a probation beef. I decided to try the program again."

"I hear that," I said.

"It's really because Phil S. is speaking that I'm here. His wife sponsors me—well, she used to sponsor me. Anyway, everybody loves Phil. Have you heard him talk?"

"No. But I met Vince at the door—the biker guy leading the meeting. He filled me in that old Phil has pretty much been canonized around here."

Jeannie was smiling. "Canonized?"

"Forget it."

"*Just keep coming back*, Bruno. *It takes what it takes*. If I can do it anybody can."

A couple of minutes later, when the reading was over, Vince was back at the podium. "Any newcomers?" he yelled.

Five or six people stood up and gave their names and how

many days they were off booze and drugs. Ten dozen of the faithful cheered and hooted and clapped.

Then pimples next to me raised her hand. Vince motioned for her to talk.

"I'm Jeannie," she yelled. "I'm back. I'm an alcoholic. I have two days sober."

"That's great, Jeannie!" Vince boomed over the mic. The crowd clapped.

Now Captain Harley was pointing right at me. "And the guy next to you . . . Bruno? Right? Your first meeting, right?"

Jeannie nodded yes on my behalf.

More clapping and a few cheers.

"C'mon up here, Bruno. First timers get a seat right up front. Right here next to our speaker."

Trapped. All eyes on me. I had no choice.

The great Phil S. went on for over forty minutes. He was sixty-six years old and skinny and gray. He'd robbed twenty-six supermarkets and been stabbed in prison and shot in the knee and crashed his bike into a police barricade at a hundred miles an hour and been pronounced dead and lots of other stuff. All until he found God and AA and the Twelve Steps. Right.

Eventually, when old Phil was done, the cheering went on for a full half a minute.

Then Vince and a couple of his Harley henchmen presented Phil with a twenty-year cake.

More adoration. More applause.

Finally, when Vince announced it was time for sharing, hands went up around the room.

One by one people they came to the podium to deliver the Good News and congratulate Phil S. Saved marriages and walking on water and commuted sentences and transplanted livers, and not one juicer among 'em. Whackos and drunks and doper pillheads all cured of a hopeless malady of mind and body.

Finally, the meeting was winding down. Almost over. I'd had more than enough. I felt like I hadn't had a drink in a hundred years and my brain was tuned to internal scream. *Jimmy* wouldn't let me alone—hissing in my head—mocking me.

My shirt was wet and I felt my brain becoming unglued.

Vince was back at the podium. There were plenty of hands still raised in the room but he pointed down at the front row. At me.

Standing there facing a horde of the anointed, on the podium, sucking in air, I had come to hate Vince and the great Phil S. and Jeannie with her stringy fucking pink hair. It occurred to me that I had arrived at a place in my life where I was willing to commit murder—to do anything—but be where I stood.

"How long are you sober?" someone near me yelled.

I was unable to make my lips move. I could not speak.

Then Vince was beside me at the podium. "Take your time," he whispered. "You're doing fine. Just say whatever comes to your mind."

Near me on the podium was a half-full plastic bottle of Sparkletts. Phil's leftover speaker's water. I didn't care. I took a sip anyway.

"My name is Bruno Dante," I said, shaking a little, clearing my throat. "And to tell you the truth I have never heard so much bullshit in all my life."

On my way out, after I got the meeting secretary's signature on the attendance sheet given to me by David Koffman, Vince spotted me as he stood by the door shaking hands.

"How ya doin'?" he whispered.

"I'm here. I made it through the worst part," I said.

He handed me a printed card with his phone number printed on it in bold Century italic. "Take this," he insisted.

I slipped the card in my pocket.

"Hey, look, Bruno, don't worry what people think."

"I don't," I said, now annoyed. "I don't give a fuck what people think."

"Use the number. It's my cell. Use it twenty-four seven. Anytime you need to talk."

Outside, up the street in my Pontiac, I lit a smoke and took a deep hit. *Jimmy* began sneering. *You really are a limp-dicked mental gimp. You belong in that room, bigshot—you and the rest of those tit-sucking Jesus whiners. Nice going.*

But when I began to calm down I realized that old Phil S. had said a few things in his *drunkalog* that had stuck. Number one: He said that "AA is for the people who *want* it, not for the people who *need* it." I concluded that the statement was accurate. Judging from the assembly of zealous outpatient whackjobs gathered in the room that night, the *want-it* tag made a lot of sense.

Number two: "Wear the AA program like a loose garment." His meaning there, I decided, was to not to be too hard on yourself. To just do the best you can. A reasonable bit of advice.

And Number three: "Fake it 'til you make it."

Number three fit me to a tee. Faking it would be no problem. Faking it would be a breeze for me.

eighteen

A week later David Koffman was gone and I was back as a full-time chauffeur and part-time manager, still going to an AA meeting four times a week and waiting in line afterward like a weak suck to get my paper signed.

Cal Berwick, one of the regular drivers, had been filling in for me on the all-day, *It Creeps* movie job. I finally took over for him at Stedman's request. When I knocked on Ronny's door at five thirty a.m. on my first day back, the guy's grin was ear to ear. "Bruno! My lad! And just where the fuck have you been?"

"Long story, Mr. Stedman. But I'll tell you this and drop it: It involved a crazy woman."

"Say no more. Been there—done that," he sneered. "Hey, I like your guy Cal. He's a decent lad. Don't get me wrong, though. He ain't you. You're my driver. My man! From now on, right?"

"Ten-four."

The best news for me was that I had printed up my short

story collection, *Belly Up*, and was ready to send it out to publishers. One hundred and seventy-five pages. In *Writer's Market* I found five new publishing houses that specialized in short fiction. I had copies made at Kinko's on Cahuenga Boulevard and then stopped off at the post office to pick up a stack of Priority Mail envelopes. The stack was sitting on Pearl's front seat waiting to be mailed.

It Creeps had moved its location to Malibu and was using the former home of Michael Landon, the TV cowboy star who died of cancer a few years before. Young Ronny liked the high-end ambiance because it was near the *fucking fabulous* homes of Bob Dylan, Barbra and Cher and Anthony and Nick and Lewis and Martin and Mel and Goldie. Ronny apparently had a sycophantic desire to be noticed by his peers while he worked.

Cal had told me that the days with Stedman were twelve to fifteen hours and there would be lots of down time. I planned to spend it reading and writing stories in longhand in my notebook, sitting in the Malibu sun. I still didn't like Stedman much but he was a good cash tipper, and as a driver I was hoping to knock down some decent daily money on top of my Dav-Ko partner salary.

David Koffman had grudgingly agreed with me that it would be tough getting to AA meetings while I was on-call with Stedman and decided to cut me some long-distance slack. I said I would find a local Malibu group and go as often as I could on my meal break. But I was free now, unhampered by the ball and chain of a Twelve Step program. My new plan was to take a pass on the local meetings and have a couple of different guys on the crew sign my attendance paper in the column marked "Secretary's Signature." I was friendly with the assistant director and one of the lighting guys. Both of them were juicers I had met at the slashing-surf-scene beach location. We'd drunk beers together and watched the filming, so signed meeting papers would be no problem. *"Fake it 'till you make it."*

It Creeps had been adapted from a book by a true crime writer named Lawrence Scuccimarri, an *In Cold Blood* kind of story. It took Larry three years of traveling the country taking photographs and doing interviews and getting legal releases to finish the thing. I'd read the first twenty pages of the hardback the night they shot the slashing scene on the beach, for fun, then left it to gather dust in Pearl's trunk. It was pop slop, sensational and disposable.

Scuccimarri, I'd heard, had been paid peanuts for his book and the screenplay by Ronny's company. When Larry arrived on the set to do scene rewrites Stedman had condescendingly introduced him to the cast and crew as "Scooch." This was because Ronny Stedman couldn't pronounce the name Scuccimarri correctly twice in a row. Larry's day job was as a professional translator. He was an immigrant from Calabria, Italy, and what my father, Jonathan Dante, used to refer to ungently as a *Mustache Pete*—a greenhorn and a patsy for the sharks in the American movie business.

That afternoon I was working on a story in my notebook with my stack of ready-to-mail envelopes next to me on the front seat, trying to find a sitting position that didn't bother my red and still-healing crotch. Stedman stormed out of the house and down the driveway and got into Pearl before I could get out of the car and open the rear door for him. His director, Mel Kleinman, had been filming a garage suicide scene where a fat mother of one of the victims decides to hang herself but fails when the rope breaks.

"Just drive, Bruno," Stedman snarled. "Head up the Coast Highway toward Trancas. I've gotta get away from that fucking guy. That goddman imbecile is ruining my movie . . . Hey, is there booze in the car?"

"Sure," I said. "In the console. Ice too. You know where it is."

As we drove Ronny poured himself a tall Scotch and ice, lit a cigarette, horned two toots from his coke vial, then tossed his Prada sunglasses on the seat next to him. Five minutes later he was more sociable. He leaned through the partition opening to talk to me about something but instead saw my stack of envelopes.

"Hey, Bruno, what are those?" he asked.

I hesitated. "Nothing special," I said.

"So, you're in the direct mail business or some goddamn thing?"

"No," I said, "just stuff I'm sending out."

"Like what?"

"A manuscript. A collection of short stories."

"You're a writer?"

"Yeah," I said, "but not like Larry Scuccimarri. Not that kind of writer."

"You never mentioned that."

"You're not a publisher. It never came up."

"What do you write?"

"Fiction," I said. "Short stories. Some poetry too."

"Anything published?"

"Look, Ronny, I don't like talking about my work, if that's okay."

"Hey, man, just tell me. I ain't the book police, for chris-sakes. You know me. I'm always looking for new material."

"I have a book pending with a publisher, but nothing in print right now. This is my newest collection."

Ronny Stedman was smiling. "Can I have one? I'd like to read it."

I handed him one of the sealed packages. "Sure Mr. Stedman," I said. "Whatever. No problem."

When we reached Broad Beach I pulled into the parking lot and Ronny got out. After he threw his sports jacket onto the backseat next to my envelope he climbed down the path to the sand and took a walk by the ocean.

nineteen

That night I got back to Dav-Ko after dropping Stedman off in east Hollywood at one thirty a.m. I was
beat. It had been an eighteen hour day. Rounding
the corner off Highland Avenue on to Selma I saw
flashing patrol car lights in front of our office—three sets
of pinball machines stinging the darkness. A crowd of two
dozen of the local hustler talent, unable to conduct business
because of the confusion, stood by smoking cigarettes and
nancy-baiting the cops.

Joshua, our night dispatcher, was on the front steps talking to two of the uniforms who held notebooks, and my driver,
huge Robert Roller, his suit and shirt torn and his nose caked
with dried blood, was splayed out across the hood of one of
the prowl cars that looked to have crossed the curb in a hurry,
coming to rest on our front walkway. Robert was in handcuffs.

The limo he had been driving, Big Red, was a few feet
away, parked in our driveway with a smashed-in hood and
two broken headlights. One of the front wheels had scraped
itself bald on a dented fender.

Roller had been chauffeuring Nick Tallman and his manager to a concert that night at the Staples Center. Tallman was the co-headliner and had just completed a two-year bit for spousal abuse and drug possession. This was to be the first of his comeback gigs.

I interrupted the cops telling them I was one of the owners of the company, then pulled Joshua aside to get the full story. According to my night dispatcher, Tallman apparently was still a full-on juice mooch and had chosen to anger his audience by being too drunk to finish his set.

Joshua retold what happened. Half an hour after Tallman left the stage, as his limo pulled out of the underground limo entrance, two dudes in motorcycle boots who had not gotten their seventy-five-bucks worth stopped the car and did what is known in *limo-eze* as a *raindance* on the hood, causing the damage.

Apparently Robert Roller was the right guy for the job at the wrong time for the two bikers. A former bouncer and mixed martial arts fighter, Robert got out of Big Red to offer a short dissertation in pain management. After the beating he drove Nicky and his manager back to their hotel. The upshot was that someone in the parking lot had taken down the limo's plate number, and as Robert pulled into our driveway he was swarmed by the three squad cars and six uniforms. My driver was busted for assault with a deadly weapon—his fists.

I had David Koffman on the phone at five a.m., New York time. He'd just gotten in from an after-hours club and was half gassed, but he woke up our L.A. attorney and by ten o'clock that morning, after interviews and witness confirmation, the charges against Robert Roller were dismissed. I drove down to County Jail to pick Robert up as Big Red was being limped to the local Lincoln dealer where we had our limo warranty work done. The damage estimate was $7,560.

Then, a crazy twenty-four hours got even crazier: the strangest day I'd ever spent in the limo business.

While I was on my way downtown to pick up big Robert, Rosie Camacho received a frantic call from Don Simpson's mansion in Beverly Hills. Simpson was a new client for Dav-Ko, our richest client along with his producer partner, Jerry Bruckheimer. The two guys had ten of the biggest-grossing Hollywood films in the last few years.

According to Rosie the emergency call came from Simpson himself. He'd been standing in his bathrobe outside his pool house. He demanded that we immediately dispatch three limos. The EMTs and the fire department, he screeched, were already on their way.

Two of the cars were to go to shops in Beverly Hills to transport their owners, fish experts, and the third was to pick up a guy named Dr. Atwalt at Universal Studios.

After getting Robert at County Jail we drove directly to the store on Little Santa Monica Boulevard and found a frantic lady, Nora Hiramoto, waiting outside at the curb.

Simpson's gated mansion was on Calle Tu Juevos, back in the mountains above the Beverly Hills Hotel. When we got there the carport looked like an aerial scene from a *S.W.A.T.* TV episode. Twenty vehicles, among them several limos, but mostly cop cars and emergency trucks with flashing lights, made it impossible for us to get near the home's entrance. I parked outside on the street, then me and Robert and Nora Hiramoto made our way down the one-acre lawn toward where everyone was gathered at the ninety-foot, Marilyn Monroe–shaped, swimming pool.

I recognized one of the other drivers in a black suit from a competing limo company, Music Excess. We had worked together at concert gigs. His name was Zeke. "Hey, Zeke," I said. "What's up? What's all the commotion?"

"Hey," he said back. "It's just goddamn Mr. Winkie. He's at it again."

"At what?" I asked. "Who's Mr. Winkie?"

"Don Simpson. Mr. Nutcase himself. Your customer and our *former* customer. You've got three or four cars here. Right?"

"Right," I said.

"Mr. Winkie. Jesus, you can have him. I can't stand the jerkoff."

"He's been good for us so far," I said.

"Just wait," Zeke said. "You'll find out. He rides around to studio meetings with the partition up and his pants down smoking meth and talking to his cock, asking it for advice. They have meetings together in the back of the car."

"C'mon. You're joking. Right?"

"Straight dope. The dude's a total squirrel cage. A rich, crazy, meth-sucking asshole. You should hear the stuff he says to his dick."

"Like what?" I asked.

"Forget it. Just trust me. He won't be your customer for long. You'll want nothing to do with the guy in a month or so, millions or no millions."

And there was Simpson in his open bathrobe, a cigarette in one hand and a telephone in the other, his back to the huge koi pond that rimmed the decking of the swimming pool, frantic, screaming into the telephone while simultaneously barking orders to the police and firemen.

According to Zeke the madness had started innocently enough. An hour before, while one of his groundskeepers had been cleaning the koi pond, one of Simpson's fish had jumped from the guy's net and fallen into the swimming pool. The little guy had been frolicking in the water with the chlorine and chemicals for over half an hour and death, the panicked Simpson insisted, would be certain and inevitable unless he was rescued.

Dr. Atwalt, the Universal Studios animal curator, had arrived with two rolls of fishnetting. Here was a man of action. Atwalt understood command in an emergency situation. He began barking orders and selected four volunteers from the three dozen bystanders gathered around the pool. The men stepped forward. All firemen. They removed their clothing down to their underwear then descended into the evil, chlorine-filled waters at the deep end of the pool.

The nets were unfurled by Doctor Atwalt and the foursome, now wearing varying colored fins and goggles from Simpson's pool house, slowly began swimming from the deep end toward the shallow end in an attempt to entrap the eight-inch koi, who still appeared to be having the time of his life.

Ten minutes later the rescue had been a success and Simpson, who'd since managed to tie his bathrobe closed, was shaking hands, passing out cigars and hundred dollar bills, congratulating all concerned.

twenty

Back at the office in the chauffeur's room, through the window, I could see our driver Marty Humphrey, chain-smoking and guzzling a Big Blast energy drink, waiting to talk to me. He'd had an incident the night before with one of our clients and Rosie let me know that he was very upset and I needed to meet with him immediately.

I entered the chauffeur's room and closed the door behind me, then turned off the Dodgers game.

"Look," Marty said, getting to his feet, "I just want to know: Am I fired or not? I need this job. Just tell me if I'm bumped. Yes or no."

"What happened?" I asked. "I know nothing about this. I just got here. I've been chasing fish in a swimming pool all morning."

"Okay, right. Look, you know that we started driving Jennifer Lopiss, right?"

"Right," I said. "We got the account from her management company. Damn decent new clients according to Koffman. We drive them in New York."

"Well, last night after a party in Hollywood, like around two a.m., I was taking Lopiss back to her place above Sunset and she's in the back of the car talking on her cell most of the ride. Just this and that kinda stuff, but you could tell she was pissed-off at someone. Her manager or an agent or somebody."

"Okay."

"So, I didn't realize that she ended the call. I was doing something else. You know, checking her street address on the GPS. Something. But then she starts yelling at me. 'Hey, jerkoff! Whaz your problem? I'm talkin' to you! Hey, moron, don't fuckin' ignore me!'"

"So I look in my rearview mirror and now she's right behind me on the jump seat. She's kicking the console with the heels of her pointy boots. Screaming. Going nuts, you know. I mean I'm thinking maybe she's on dust or speed or something, but I can see she's doing some real damage to the car."

"Okay. So what happened?"

"We were on La Cienega. I put the flashers on and pulled over and got out. I walked around to the passenger side and opened the back door. 'Look,' I say. 'I'm sorry I didn't hear you. I thought you were talking on your cell. I'm very sorry. But you've got to stop kicking the car.'"

"I'd have done the same thing," I said. "You can't put up with that stuff. It doesn't matter who she is."

"But now she's completely out of control, calling me bitch and cocksucker and faggot and screaming and all."

"So . . . ?"

"So I pulled her by the arm out of the car. Then I handed her her purse. I couldn't think of anything else to do. I left her on the sidewalk and drove off. Right there."

Marty's account sounded true and I knew him as a decent

guy. Reliable, presentable, and always on time. I was sure that the story had already gotten back to David Koffman and that there would be major problems. "Well," I said, "as far as I'm concerned you're clean. You were looking out for company property."

"But when I come in this morning for my airport run Rosie's frantic 'n' all. She got calls from Lopiss's manager and two different attorneys. Rosie says they're going to press charges for assault and sue the company for this and that."

"Spoiled-brat central, pal," I said. "Welcome to the exciting and glamorous limo business."

"Look, man, I didn't hurt the woman. I was trying to do the right thing is all. I just want to know: Will I get fired for what happened? Is my job at risk here?"

"No," I said, "you're not fired from this company. Of course I'll go over the details but if everything you just said is on the money, you and I have no problem. That's a promise."

"What about David Koffman? He gets upset. I've seen it. He's pretty picky."

"I'll handle David."

"You mean we're cool?"

"Just keep doing your job and I'll straighten this out with Koffman and our attorney and whoever else is hunting your scalp."

"Thanks, Bruno. I mean *really*, thank you."

"You're a good chauffeur, Marty. Go in and tell Rosie to put you back on the schedule. Tell her I said it's okay."

twenty-one

y Friday that week the Malibu shoot with Stedman was over. The director of *It Creeps*, Mel Kleinman, had been sacked and I was hoping for a week layoff between locations. That, apparently, was not to be. My Monday morning dispatch instructions were to pick up Ronny at his production office at 9200 Sunset.

I was parked at a meter outside the building when my cell phone rang. It was Ronny's new secretary Brandi telling me that Mr. Stedman wanted me to come up to the eleventh floor.

When I got off the elevator and walked into the lobby of Hollywood Star Productions, sexy no-bra Brandi asked me to have a seat, then went into Ronny's office to report my arrival.

I was sure that I'd screwed up but I couldn't figure out what I'd done. I hated to lose Stedman as a client for Dav-Ko at twelve to fifteen hundred bucks a day. I hadn't had so much as a beer in over a week and aside from a few vikes and Xanax here and there I was totally clean, so I searched my head for an insult or some off-color wisecrack I'd made but could only think of one incident where I'd told an actress after a bedroom scene that I liked how her thong fit. But that was lightweight snot. Nothing. They hear that stuff all the time. Then I realized Stedman might somehow have heard about the crazy incident with Don Simpson. They were both movie producers. Maybe my remarks by the pool with Zeke about his tweaked-out weirdness in calling the cops and the fire department over a fucking koi fish had been overheard by Snipson himself and had gotten back to Ronny Stedman. This meeting might be retribution for my big mouth.

Brandi appeared again and directed me to step into Stedman's inner office.

Once inside I took off my chauffeur's cap and Ronny got up from behind his desk. I prepared myself for a shitstorm.

But Stedman was smiling. Instead of a face-off confrontation I was introduced to the new director of *It Creeps*, a twenty-five-year-old film school grad named Billy Cohen—a kid with a short Afro sitting across the room on the plum-colored velour couch.

The knot in my stomach went away. Long-legged Brandi wanted to know if we'd all like some coffee.

Then Ronny picked up a stack of manuscripts from his desk and, in a gesture of mock exasperation, tossed three of them in the wastebasket. I saw the title page of the one he was still holding. It was *Belly Up*, my story collection.

"This fucker is gold," he barked. "Remember, in the car, I told you that I'd read your stuff. And I did. I kept my word."

I nodded.

Ronnie went on. "And 'Santa Monica Pier' is perfect for a film. Billy read it yesterday and thinks so too. Right, Billy?"

Young Billy nodded approvingly.

"Edgy shit, Bruno," Stedman went on. "Raw and gut level

and *in-your-face* writing. This is the kind of stuff—L.A. street stuff—that, as a film, just might get hot the way *Pulp Fiction* got hot. Both Billy and I think *raw* just might be the new wave in the film business. Know what I'm sayin'?"

"Yeah," I said, attempting to get my head into the conversation, "I think I know what you're saying."

"Billy thinks we can combine three of the stories into a single plotline and pitch it to HBO as a movie or a series. With a little editing, 'Santa Monica Pier' and 'Two Beers' and 'Granite Man' are ONE idea. Ya follow?"

"Okay, I hear you," I said, now sure that Dav-Ko and a bite out of my ass was not going to be the topic of conversation.

Ronny went on. "The cab driver theme is spot-on. The jaded eye of your main character Ricky is exactly right for someone like Colin Farrell or maybe an older guy like John Travolta."

Then Billy spoke up. "Or Robert Downey, Jr.," he chirped. "He'd be great for it too. I know Robert's agent. We went to Pali High together."

Stedman pointed at a matching plum chair. "Sit down, Bruno. Let's talk this idea through."

I sat down and lit a cigarette.

Then Brandi appeared again, dancing back in with a tray of coffee and pastries.

Stedman's arms were across his chest. "Hey, do you mind, my man? My office is a smoke-free office."

I put the smoke out on a brass dish that Brandi provided, then reminded myself that Ronny snorted more blow than almost any of my customers. *Absolutely*, I thought. *Secondhand smoke is poison. The shit kills millions every day.*

Now Stedman was grinning again. "So how would you like to be in the film business, my man?"

The question put a knot in my stomach. Brandi passed me

my coffee mug and I dumped in two teaspoons of sugar and milk. "I've never written anything like a screenplay," I said finally, tasting the concoction. "It's not something I've even thought about."

"Not a problem, Brun-issimo! The point is you pick up a copy of Final Draft software and the goddamn program writes the thing for you. It's a no-brainer, I promise."

Brandi, in the miniskirt, was leaving the room with her empty coffee tray in hand. Me and Stedman and Billy couldn't help but watch her exit. After she closed the door behind her Ronny was leering. "I'm a lucky guy to have talent like that in the next room. *Fabulous* broad, right? Am I right or am I right?"

No one disagreed.

Ronny's next leer was directed at Billy. "Hey, even the kid here can write a fucking screenplay. He's written three already. Right, Billy? Or is it four?"

Billy faked a smile. "The point Ronny's making is that with the right tools it's not that difficult, especially since you've written the stories already."

"So what about it!" Stedman leered. "Welcome to Hollywood. Join the team. It's who ya know and who ya blow. We take your three stories then connect the themes and come up with one kick-ass, edgy, mothafucka of a movie?"

"Sure, I guess," I said, trying to act like I was going along. "But at the moment I write in the morning. Two hours a day. I'd have to stop what I'm working on to concentrate on the screenplay."

"You bet, my man! The faster I get your pages the sooner we go into production. Ninety days later I can guarantee you one ballbuster of a movie. We can start pre-casting next week."

My look went from one guy to the other. "So I guess my

question is, what do I get paid for my stories and the screen-play?"

Ronny paced across the floor, across the big, black, red-and-gold rug in the middle of the room; a bizarre woven, mock-Persian piece that depicted two swans dismembering a fish—possibly a koi. He flopped down next to Billy on the *fabulous* velour couch where the kid was seated. I asked myself: Was I that goddamn fish?

Stedman slurped has coffee then wrapped his arm around Billy, mussing his hair. "What a team! We've got everything we need right in this room. Okay, look, Billy and I talked this out before you came. Naturally production costs are the major factor, I won't bullshit ya, Bruno. But the good thing with a cab driver story like yours is that it has real advantages cine-matically—a lot of the film will be exteriors. Street stuff. L.A. grit. That really helps keep the friggin' costs manageable."

Now Billy chimed in: "We see L.A. itself as a major char-acter here. That's the vision so far."

"Right," I said. "So what do I get paid?"

Stedman's expression became somber. He shot a look at Billy, then turned back to me. "Well, the way it's structured is that there's really no front end for any of us. I, as producer, am taking all the risk. I front all the production expenses myself. Right, Billy?"

"Right, Ronny."

The head of Hollywood Star Productions continued weav-ing his flimflam. "Billy and I have a similar arrangement to the one I'll make with you. A percentage of the net from the movie. Right, Billy?"

"Right, Ronny."

Stedman began closing the deal. He was on his feet. "In other words we're all eating out of the same pot here. True communism—ha! just kidding, Bruno. One guy wins—we all win. Fair is fair. Are you with us?" He extended his hand.

I looked from one guy to the other to try to read their expressions. This cocksucker was in the film business. Didn't he know that this kind of scam was legendary in Hollywood? The net! There never was any NET in a movie! I grew up in Hollywood. Didn't he know that? Hadn't he done his homework? I'd spent summers sitting around writers and directors and actors guzzling gin and tonics on my old man's back patio in Malibu listening to just this kind of step-'n'-fetch-it, the-check'll-be-good-on-Wednesday yarn, summer after summer. Jonathan Dante had once even punched a producer in the nose after the fool offered Pop a net profit film contract. NET was a bad joke.

For once I kept my mouth shut. Ronny Stedman was a Dav-Ko account. A client. His business was important to David Koffman and I was skating on thin ice with my partner as it was. If I told these guys to go fuck themselves that would be the end of their business with my company. No more Hollywood Star Productions work.

I set my coffee cup down and got to my feet. Then I pointed behind Stedman's desk. "By the way," I said. "Nice plant. Is that an orchid?"

Ronny looked distracted. "Yeah," he said, "it's an orchid."

I started for the back of his desk. "I like how plants smell. Do you mind?" I asked.

My question caused Stedman's eyes to open wide. "Hey, do you mind, Bruno? We're talking business here."

But now I was at the orchid. My nose close to the stinky fucker. "Funny smell," I said.

"It's plastic, for chrissake."

"Oh," I said, touching one of the fake white blooms. "And

it actually looks real. But, you know, it smells funny. A bit like piss."

Without saying good-bye or shaking Stedman's hand I began moving toward the door. "Look," I said. "Let me think all this over. There's a lot to consider. How about that?"

Stedman appeared puzzled but immediately recovered himself. "Abso-fuckin'-lutely, my man! Give yourself a day or two. The point is, after we have the screenplay—the pages— we get the ball rolling. You write it—we shoot it. No screwing around. *Belly Up* is now our next project."

"I hear you," I said, still backing across the flesh-eating swans toward the door.

"Billy," Ronny bellowed, "I'm really excited that the three of us will be working together. Aren't you?"

Billy nodded. Billy now looked excited. Maybe Billy would perform oral sex on Ronny too after I left the room or empty his piss pot for him.

Stedman grinned again. His best million lira, *I gotcha*, film-producer leer. "It was—like—an amazingly cool surprise when I read those stories. Like finding a diamond in a Dumpster."

"Really," I said, "A diamond in a Dumpster? No kidding? That's an interesting choice of words."

"Hold up," Ronny barked. "You're driving us to see the new location, right? We've got a full day ahead of us."

"Yeah," I said, putting my cap on, "I meant to tell you. I guess I've got the flu or something. I'm sick to my stomach. I'll call in and get you one of the other guys to drive you for the day."

Ronny Stedman gave me a long look. "Well—okay—I mean, if you're sick. Sure."

"Yeah, I'm sick. I'm sick to my stomach."

In the elevator on the way down to the street I felt my

crotch scars itching like crazy. I began shaking. I needed to smash something, anything. Then in my mind *Jimmy* gave me a direct order: *Listen to me, asshole: drive yourself to the nearest gun store—buy a used .38—the same kind that you got from your old man—the kind that Portia took from you and threw away—and come back here and shoot these two cocksuckers deader than the deadest lowlife snakes that they are.*

Then I noticed the glued-on, maroon-colored nameplate next to elevator button #11 that read HOLLYWOOD STAR PRODUCTIONS. I took out my pen knife and pried the plastic fucker away from the fake formica paneling, then snapped it in half, tossing the pieces onto the floor. From now on, no matter what, I promised myself I would not set eyes on Ron Stedman again. Let Rosie and Joshua at the office deal with the slithering feral fuck. I'd develop a slipped disk in my back or contract hep C or whatever excuse I needed to come up with to avoid being in the same car ever again with these pricks.

Down on the street behind the wheel of Pearl I phoned Rosie with instructions to replace me with another limo and chauffeur, telling her a sudden and important business appointment had come up.

On the way back to the office I stopped at Wells Fargo Bank, waited in the usual line of eleven people, then cashed my check: $1,357.00. I told the smile-trained imbecile behind the counter to give me my money all in twenties. I wanted to feel the weight and the roll in my slacks. The kid sighed and ha-humphed and mimed his best Jay Leno, roll-your-eyes to the camera expression, then reached under the counter for more bills.

Back at Dav-Ko I parked Pearl in the driveway, walked into the office past Rosie, then wordlessly grabbed the keys to my

Pontiac and took off. For the last hour my mind had been a screaming monkey. I had to escape, to go anywhere and to be anywhere else. I despised Hollywood and the bizarre greedy deranged mutant jerkoffs it had spawned. I hated myself for not facing Stedman and telling him how I felt about him and his obvious and ungenuine conniving manipulations and stupidity. I hated the limousine business. I hated it all.

twenty-two

I t happened to me rarely these days. Working and making money and writing and managing Dav-Ko was all that I'd been doing for months. But I now clearly had a serious case of the *fuckits*.

I can't say it was Ronny Steadman and I can't say it wasn't but within me there is this leveling device thing that, when my mind exceeds a certain point, just goes on *tilt*. Snaps. I know that normal people can take a pill or go to bed or call their friend Bob and watch TV or have sex with their wife or jerk off, or some goddamn thing. But that stuff doesn't work for me.

I know what I was thinking. I was thinking: *What's the big deal. Life is too short for this shit and I need to take the edge off. Fuckit. I deserve it. Fuck it!*

A door slammed. I woke up.

It was a strange room. It looked to be a nearly unfurnished one-room apartment with only a small window and dark yellow walls. No pictures.

Clearing my head, I rolled toward the floor and looked down—a woman's dirty underwear and a pack of cigarettes and a strange half jar filled with blue liquid tucked just beneath the head of the bed.

Lifting the jar up I studied it: a set of false teeth, bridges, uppers and lowers. The sight of these in the strange colored water unnerved me and the glass slipped from my hand and fell to the floor. A pool of blue liquid now flooded the linoleum and nearby underpants.

Reaching back down I picked up the teeth again and held them in my hands, examining them.

How the hell did I get here on this bed with these goddamn things? The top bridge had six fronts with one missing space. No back teeth. The bottoms had no molars but like the uppers, all the front teeth were there. In other words whoever owned these had no real teeth on the top and bottom. My brain collated this information and gave me an image of the toothless bitch who owned them. Whoever had slammed the door must have left in hurry and neglected to put her teeth in.

Near the underpants on the floor, but away from the blue pool, were my pants and socks. Both my shoes and my jacket appeared to be missing.

Reaching for the pants I found that the pockets had been turned inside out. The wallet was gone. My money was gone. The cell phone too.

Pulling back the sheets around me I discovered several hairpins and a sex stain. I was naked except for my torn and soiled shirt. Two buttons were missing.

Finding the bathroom I vomited again and again until my head hurt so much that I had to fall to the coolness of the tile floor and curl myself around the porcelain toilet, in a ball. Then the shakes started.

Fifteen minutes later I'd pulled myself together enough to leave the crapper. But lighting a cigarette forced me back into the bathroom to puke again.

Back in the main room I checked for more signs of where I was and what had happened. I saw more dirty women's clothes and underwear strewn in the corner. Under some socks was a stack of supermarket coupons held together by a rubber band. Nothing else except a large, gold plastic crucifix looked down from above the apartment's main door.

The window was partially covered by a sheet. The only furniture other than the bed was a dresser. I opened the drawers. They contained a child's clothes. Old and worn.

Outside, looking down from the second floor, the neighborhood appeared to be Ghost Town, in Venice—a row of old, rundown houses with sad, unwatered lawns. But maybe not. Maybe I was in Compton or Old Torrance or even Long Beach. I couldn't be sure.

On the window sill were two green plants. They still had their price tags stuck to the black plastic pots.

Then something shiny got my attention: my car keys. Across the room in the corner.

But that was it. Nothing else belonged to me. All of my shit was gone—gone with whoever slammed the door and departed in a rush.

Back in the bathroom I washed myself. There was no soap. No towel. No toothpaste. Nothing.

I gulped as much water as possible from the faucet until I felt myself wretch convulsively, but somehow I kept the liquid down.

So far so good.

Drying my face with the end of my shirt I then ran water

through my hair with my rattling hands in an attempt to smooth it into place. Then I used the last of a toilet paper roll that sat on the toilet tank to clean my teeth.

I now had a sudden and immediate need for a drink. Without a drink I would start puking again or pass out. Or die.

Picking up the set of teeth I stuffed them in my pocket, one in each, along with my car keys. Then I pulled on my socks.

On the street in the heat I intended to circle the block until I found my car. But a few minutes later, with no luck, I reached a main drag with a sign: North Van Nuys Boulevard. Fucking Van Nuys Boulevard. The ghetto. Had I spent the night with a Mexican hooker? That figured. My *thing* had always been Latin women.

My feet were starting to burn badly and swell as they scraped the asphalt. A mother with her two young daughters averted her glance as she passed me crossing the street.

I kept moving, my brain aching and slamming itself inside my skull. I couldn't stop. I had to locate my car and I had to have alcohol. A drink. Immediately. The voice of *Jimmy*, my hangman, scorched my brain. *Well done, fucko! Lost in the goddamn Valley! No shoes. No money. Just swell. You've outdone yourself once again. You're a gutless juicer and a loser just like your fucking brother. You deserve this. Hey cheesedick, with a little luck you just might get yourself arrested for vagrancy—or drunk in public.*

There was only one way I'd ever been able to shut *Jimmy* up: drown him in bourbon.

Finally, my fists sweating and still clenched around the teeth in each pocket, I reached a section of shop fronts: A ninety-nine-cent store. A 7-Eleven. Instant payday loans. A porno arcade. A pawnbroker. In the window above a display of beat-up used watches, the pawnshop clock read ten twenty a.m.

I stopped. I felt myself starting to pass out.

Leaning against a wall I sucked in air. It took thirty seconds for the dizziness to pass, then I was okay. I could walk.

Maybe the 7-Eleven? I decided to turn back. I had no money but maybe I could steal two talls or a forty-ouncer while the guy's back was turned. For once *Jimmy* screamed some good advice: *Hey nutcase, are you completely crazy? You've got a torn shirt and no shoes! . . . Keep moving, for chrissakes.*

So I kept going.

Then, on the corner, I saw it. A bar! It was open—a square neon sign in the window flashing.

I pushed the door open and went in.

Two working guys sat at the rail drinking bottled beer. The jukebox played mariachi music.

Then it happened. I was inches away from the stools. The bartender had seen me and was moving toward me when I felt the spasmodic rush of hot liquid hit the inside of my pants. I'd crapped myself! Without underwear I felt the heat of the mess running down my leg.

As I reached the stools I tossed my car keys up on the bar, trying to appear self-confident.

The bartender's expression changed. He knew. The stench had been immediate and overwhelming.

"What's up?" he snarled.

"Look," I said, "I've got an idea. Hear me out, okay? Do you want to make some money?"

"I ka smel jour idea from ober here! Take a walk, *cabrón*! Now. No chit. I mean it. You wann troubl in disa plaze, you got troubl!"

I raised my hands in the air like a guy under arrest. "No kidding!" I blurted. "Do you want to make a hundred bucks? For real."

"For wha, chitman?"

"For a pop. One drink! A hundred dollars for one drink. Straight business."

"Lemme guez, okae. Jour problem is jou ain't got the hundred on you. Am I rie?"

I nodded.

"*Mira, stupido,* jou got ten seconds to get jour stinky *culo* outa here and go bak on da stree. Ten seconds, *comprende?* Nine . . . eight . . ."

"Two hundred! No joke!" I was panting now. Gulping air. "I'll pay you two hundred bucks for one drink . . . and a phone call! I run a business. I'll have someone bring the money. It'll be here half an hour after I make the call. C'mon, cut me a break."

"Thaz it, chitpants! Timz up!"

The guy scooped my car keys off the bar and held them toward me. "I tole jou, take a fukking walk!" he hissed. "I ain no kiddin'!"

Then something happened. With my key ring in his outstretched arm, the bartender's expression changed. He was looking at what he held in his hand. "Whaz about thez?" he said.

"What?" I said.

"Deez one, my man!" he snarled, pinching the coin on the ring between his fingers.

It was a fifty-cent piece. A silver half dollar. The coin and chain had been a gift from my ex-girlfriend Cynthia years before, when I bought the Pontiac.

I felt my body breathe again. "What about it?" I asked. "You want it?"

"I collek. I collek koinz."

"So?"

"Dis one iz a 1916. Firss jear minn. Walkin' Leebertee. Goo *condicion* too."

"I know what it is," I lied. "How about a trade?"

The guy folded his arms across his chest. "Hokay, chit-majn, herez dee deal: Jou get jour stinky, shakin ass to the bahroom 'n' clean up an when jou come back I giff jou one drink—an one phon call. For dis."

"Two drinks" I blurted. "Two drinks and you have a deal. Double shots. Deal?"

"Deal," he snarled. "Now go wass jour ass."

It took Robert Roller almost an hour to travel the twelve miles from Dav-Ko to the Tanampa Bar and Grill in our brown stretch, Cocoa.

When he walked in he stuffed the hundred dollar bills in cash in my hand, wordlessly eyeing me up and down, shaking his head.

We found my Pontiac where I assumed I'd left it, in the alley behind the rundown apartment house where I'd come too. There were no new dents and it was unlocked. And I was okay now. Feeling much better. Two more sets of doubles at the bar and a quick stop at a liquor store for a pint of Jim Beam had restored the calmness to my brain.

While big Robert sat in the limo I looked inside my car for signs of trouble. There were none. But in the backseat, in a box, I discovered some old clothes and two pairs of shoes I hadn't yet returned to my closet after the firing episode with David Koffman.

No one was around, so I took off my shirt and shitstained chauffeur's slacks and replaced them with a pair of jeans, an old warm-up jacket, and tennis shoes.

Telling Robert to wait for me I went back inside the

building and walked upstairs to the one-room apartment. I knocked. When no one answered I tried the door. It was still unlocked. Inside I could tell that whoever she was, she had not returned.

I put the set of dentures down next to the plants on the window sill where they could be found, then checked again for anything in the room that might be mine. There wasn't anything. I'd been picked clean.

I took a long pull from the bottle in my pocket, then went to the door. Above me was the big gold plastic crucifix. A new thought caught my attention and stuck: A choice. An option.

Returning to the window I removed the plants from the sill, then put them down on the floor in the blue puddled water.

Then I unzipped my pants, took out my cock, and pissed in each one.

That done, I picked up the two custom-made bridges and set them down in the mess on the floor next to the whore's dirty panties. Then I crushed each one with the heel of my shoe.

Back at the door, ready to go, I looked up at the crucifix on the wall. Big Jesus was smiling.

But, as it turned out, I wasn't done. I wasn't done at all.

After Robert followed me back to the Dav-Ko office I took seven hundred bucks from the petty-cash drawer, left an IOU, and informed Rosie that I was taking a payroll advance. Then I told her that I was taking a day or two more off, telling her that if David Koffman or anyone else asked, I was using up sick-leave days to attend a weekend AA seminar. Rosie's expression was blank. "It's Wednesday," she said.

"Yeah, well, I'm getting an early start. Is that okay with you?"

"You're the boss, Bruno."

"Correct-a-mundo, Ms. Rosie. That I am," I said smiling.

My favorite porn is anal action. Number two is deep-throat blowjobs with oral cum shots.

At the liquor store I picked up large bottles of Mad Dog 20/20. Mogen David. It had been years since I'd hit "the dog," but this was a special occasion. I needed to get *downtown* in my brain and Mad Dog is the best and fastest train there is. After picking up the wine I made a stop at the best X video store in Hollywood, on Santa Monica Boulevard. I rented half a dozen titles that looked promising then drove back to Highland Avenue to an upscale tourist motel against the Hollywood Hills called the DeMille, off Franklin Avenue. I knew the day manager, Russ. He'd been my new pill connection since I moved to Hollywood.

To me Mad Dog and porn in a clean motel is the best vacation a person can take. A spiritual retreat.

twenty-three

'd never had two blackouts in a row before. Until now. I came out of this one in Venice, parked at a beach parking lot against the sand behind the wheel of my Pontiac. My pants were around my knees leading me to believe I must've been jerking off before I fell out. I was wet from my chest down and on the seat next to me were my soaked shoes . . . and my arm was stinging like crazy. The bright lights from the car behind me were blasting through my windows. I looked at my watch. It was 4:05 a.m.

Now there was a guy banging on my driver's window with his flashlight, dressed in blue. I saw the badge too.

"Last time, pal! I said *open the door! Out of the car!!*"

"Sure sure sure. Hang on," I said. "I'm doing it. No problem."

I pulled up the jeans and tucked my cock into my pants, fastening the snap.

. . .

"Open the goddamn door!" Blue repeated.

I unlocked the button and was then yanked from the seat. I did the drill: hands on the roof. Blue yanked my pockets out, then took my money.

"No driver's license? NO ID!"

"I misplaced them . . . I guess."

"Turn around," Blue snarled.

I turned around.

"Now close your eyes, asshole."

I closed them.

"Now put your arms out, and touch your nose with the tip of your left index finger!"

"I'm right-handed," I said.

"Shut the fuck up, jerkoff. Do it now!"

I did what he asked but the result was apparently unsuccessful or unsatisfactory.

"You're under arrest for driving while intoxicated and not having a valid license. Any questions?"

"Can I smoke?"

"You can shut the fuck up! Where's your car registration?"

"Can I talk?"

"Shut the fuck up!"

"It's in the glove compartment."

"Get it."

I found my paperwork and my cigarettes and lighter, then handed the envelope to Blue. I was about to ask him if I could smoke again when he said, "I told you to shut the fuck up."

I decided not to ask—not to smoke.

Backup arrived suddenly, screeching into the deserted parking lot. The pinball machine flashing. The works.

"Whatcha got, Tessman?" A much larger Blue snorted.

"DUI, sergeant. And no ID."

"Didja call for the tow?"

"Not yet."

"Can I smoke now?" I asked, looking from one blue to the other.

"Shut the fuck up."

The big sergeant reminded me of someone dead. A guy I'd known in New York when I was a street peddler. Tooty LaPardo. Tooty sold watches outside the Time-Life Building. One Wednesday he said he had a stomach ache. The next Monday he was dead. Forty-eight years old.

After handcuffing me, Blue stuffed me in his police cruiser.

"Can I have my money back?" I asked.

"Shut the fuck up."

At the Pacific Station I was ordered to take a breath test. I refused. Then I was placed in a holding cell and allowed my one call. Joshua, our night manager, answered on the first ring at Dav-Ko. I told him to call Perry Busnazian, the attorney who had represented Robert Roller, and to tell Busnazian it was a personal matter and not a Dav-Ko business situation. I made sure that Joshua would keep the conversation to himself until we could talk personally.

Sitting in the cell alone it was the first chance I'd had to examine my sore, stinging arm. I rolled up the right sleeve and there it was. A red, swollen tattoo, made worse by the sand and salt water. Three lines of black letters, in all caps, raised above the rest of the skin. Line 1: RICK DANTE. Line 2: DEAD FROM BOOZE, NAZIS. Line 3: STUDEBAKERS & STUPIDITY.

I stared at the thing. Why had I done it? My brother never liked me and I never liked him. But there it was. Shit.

• • •

*Well well well, you've really done it now. So long limo career—
hello orange, County Jail jumpsuit. How 'bout this, needledick:
Go find that fucking .38, stick it in your mouth, and do world
ecology a small favor.*

When I was released the next morning after court, Busnazian
drove me to the impound in Marina del Rey to pick up my car
and pay the $150 towing and parking fee.

Busnazian knew his job. After stopping at the DMV for
me to get a temporary license we went on to the impound. As
we drove my attorney wanted to know the details of what happened and began a series of questions. Where was I exactly
when I was arrested? Was there an open bottle in the car?
What did I say to the cops? That stuff.

Back at Dav-Ko I wrote him a $2,000 check. A down pay-
ment. There would be more, he said.

After I walked him to his black Benz in the driveway he
eyed me up and down. "DUI is serious business," he said. "The
new laws have sharper teeth. I'll have to see what I can do."

"Will you keep this confidential? I don't want my partner
to know my business."

"You're my client in this matter. No one will hear anything
from me."

"Will they pull my license?"

"You refused the breath test, right?"

"Yes, I did."

"Not good, Bruno. Not smart. I tell everyone the same
thing. Always cooperate fully. If you're convicted, refusing
the breath test is an automatic one-year license suspension in
this state."

"Swell. I didn't know."

"You seem to be a guy with a chip on your shoulder. Did you resist the police at any time?"

"No. Just the breath test thing."

"Then what's bothering you?"

"I'm upset, for chrissake. I just got out of jail."

"Have you been to AA?"

"Goddamn right. I go to AA."

"How often?"

"Periodically. Once in a while."

"I can pretty much guarantee that will change if we manage to retain your driving privilege," he said.

"What are my chances here? I just want to know?"

"California is a rough state."

"Will I lose the license?"

"You're a chauffeur. With first offenders there are generally imposed driving restrictions. But the breath test issue is a significant hurdle. And in California DUI convictions stay on your record for ten years."

"Fuck."

"Look, I have a couple of ideas. Just don't piss on our shoes again, if you get my meaning."

"I'm a chauffeur. You're telling me I might not have a goddamn job?"

"Let me look into it. I'll just say this: It pays to have friends in tall glass buildings."

"No shit," I said. "And it pays pretty goddamn well too. Two thousand bucks worth."

"You just shot your horse, sir. You've been charged with drunk driving. Now let's see what I can do to remove the bullet. For the time being just calm down and get some rest. I'll be in touch."

"Thanks for the pep talk."

"Take it easy," Busnazian said, patting me on the back.

"This is what I do. One of my partners specializes in DUI and drug cases. I'll earn my fee. You have my word on that."

Then my attorney glanced down at the fresh, swollen tattoo on my forearm. "What's that?" he asked.

"A mistake. Another fuckup."

"Don't be too hard on yourself."

"Thanks for the advice. And thanks for cheering me up. Have a swell day, Mr. Buznasian."

Then I walked into the office to find out from Rosie just how deep the shit around me was piled. But I was pretty sure I would be okay. Unlike crazy Portia, Rosie and Joshua regarded me as their boss. They knew that as far as I was concerned they were replicable and they were aware of my reputation for having a short fuse.

twenty-four

The following week, Wednesday, mostly sober for four days except for a few pills and some wine coolers here and there, I got a long-distance call on my cell from Che-Che Sorache in Manhattan. Against her protests La Natura cosmetics was dispatching her to do a statewide personal appearance tour of New York department stores. The whole deal would be filmed and turned into part of a national TV campaign. But Che-Che hated flying and she hated trains. Her idea was for me to catch a plane back east and drive her from store to store throughout the tour. She said the gig would take no more than a week.

The idea appealed to me. I liked the tall model and getting out of L.A. for a few days to be back on the East Coast sounded more like a vacation than a job.

I telephoned Koffman and he approved the assignment. I'd drive one of his limos while I was there. A new light-blue Benz that had just been stretched forty-eight inches in Mexico and shipped north. My partner had visions of some kind of advertising coup for the company if our limo made it into a TV ad.

Dapper Joshua, night manager/bookkeeper, who'd lately appeared twice a week in a new sports coat and a made-to-measure dress shirts, would move in and run Dav-Ko Hollywood until I got back. I'd stay at David Koffman's condo on Riverside Drive when I wasn't chauffeuring Che-Che around to do her gigs.

I left the next morning.

In the baggage claim area at American Airlines at JFK I was greeted by Dennis, Che-Che's blond, six-foot-two-inch boy toy. The guy looked like he'd just left a modeling shoot for Calvin Klein sportswear. My client had sent him to greet me and escort me back into town.

In the limo on the Van Wyck Expressway Dennis let me know that he and Che-Che had met three weeks before in the lobby at Quick, the ad agency where they were both under contract. They were *totally hot* for each other and he'd been crashing at her place in the Village ever since. Apparently Dennis was a moron. Nineteen years old. A kid from Paramus with a football scholarship who'd passed it up for a modeling career. A real lightbulb of a kid.

On the on-ramp to the Triborough Bridge Dennis raised the car's tinted partition window then pulled a two-gram bottle out of his shirt pocket. "How 'bout a pick-me-up," he sang.

"Pass," I said. "Maybe some other time. My tastes run more toward bottled in bond."

"Huh?"

"My drug of choice is bourbon," I said. "It comes in bottles with a government stamp covering the cap." Then I pulled a pint bottle of Early Times from my inside jacket pocket and showed Einstein the cap and seal.

"No shit?" says Dennis. "I never noticed. Hey, I just learned something new."

While he began horning two big scoops from the vial with the end of a penknife, I turned to him, actually taking the kid in for the first time. "Well, there ya go," I said. "Always happy to help."

"Uh-huh," Dennis said.

The first series of gigs that week began on a Friday. The department stores on Fifth Avenue. While I drove beautiful black-haired blue-eyed Che-Che, she had her face touched up in the backseat by a sweet girl name Ida.

My client was a kick. By the second stop her wardrobe was all over the car, slung on top of the limo's jump seats and stacked in my front passenger area. When she'd do a dress change she'd pull the last outfit off and be near naked in her thonged panties. Che-Che never wore a bra. She knew I couldn't help but watch but she didn't care. It was just business.

"You getting your kicks up there, *pisano?*" she snickered as she slipped into a pair of fitted slacks, her pelvis in midair.

"You bet, blue eyes," I said back. "I'm having the time of my life."

And everyone was a cocksucker. The store managers, the leering, fat pimple-faced security guy at Saks, the rep from the Quick Agency. All of 'em.

Outside Lord & Taylor there were photographers and no one except a lazy security guy to escort her into the store.

"Hey Bruno, tell that dipshit door-shaker cocksucker I'm not getting out of the car until he gets rid of the fucking mob in front. Tell the *cazzo* I'm twenty minutes late and I'll rat him the fuck out unless he wakes up and does his fucking job!"

"Okay, Che-Che, I'll tell him," I said.

Then the amazing smile. "Hey Brunissimo, you havin' a good time? Need anything? A soda or something?"

"Your twin sister. Do you have one?"

Later that night Che-Che and her Rhodes Scholar boyfriend attended a private screening at Clearsky movie theater on Eighty-sixth Street. On the way from her place in the Village to the Upper East Side she and Dennis kissed a little and groped each other, then started drinking from the bar and snorting lines.

"Hey, Bruno," Che-Che giggled up from the backseat a few minutes from the theater, "how are you getting along with long-haired Rip Van Winkle? Your partner, Kong Koffman?"

"Okay, I guess. Mostly okay."

"Did you know I quit using Dav-Ko as my New York limo service? Like, a year or so ago. I switched over to DEMURE. But, now I'm changing back because of you, Bruno baby. Because you're the only blue Benz stretch guy for me."

"Thanks, Che-Che. I appreciate the business. You know that."

"Know why I quit using Kong Koffman's Camel Caravan?"

"No, I don't," I said. "But I bet you're gonna tell me."

"It's because Kong was padding my goddamn bill all the fucking time. Twenty minutes here, half an hour there. Once the asshole charged me for a full day because I left the car at one in the afternoon. I mean, it's not like I didn't spend a grand a week with the big dufus queen."

I decided to change the subject. "How come you call David, Kong?" I asked.

"C'mon Bruno, you're shittin' me. You know why, don't you? I mean, that's his nickname. Everyone at the clubs calls him that. Kong."

"Honest to Christ, I really don't know. David and I don't exactly move in the same circles, other than business."

Che-Che was laughing. "Well, sweetcakes, it's because your dear partner is rumored to have a twelve-inch *schwanz*. Kong is famous. He even has his club groupies. They wear chauffeur's caps and follow him around."

"Okay. I mean I *actually* know what you're saying."

"Ah ha! So you've seen the caged beast for yourself? El Grande. The big gorilla. Please do tell us. From personal experience, I assume."

"His robe was open."

"Uhhhh. So it's true! You've seen the beast."

"I guess it is. The man does have one giant cock."

Che-Che giggled all the way to Eighty-sixth Street.

When we got to the movie my client demanded that I go in and watch the film with her and Dennis. I paid one of the outside ushers fifty bucks to watch the big Benz limo and make sure it was out front at the curb when the show let out.

Che-Che bought me popcorn and Gummi Bears and a box of Milk Duds. The large size. We sat in the middle seats in the back row with Dennis on her left and me on her right.

Before the film started, the young director, who was dressed in a too-tight black turtleneck, ratty blue jeans, and Dominick Donne–shaped black horn-rimmed glasses, stood by the screen holding a mic, introducing the cast and acknowledging his film-school mentors and each of the seven or eight executive producers and everybody else he could think of.

I figured that I might be in for a long ride so I decided to take a squirt and get a refill on the popcorn.

In the men's room after my piss I had a quick smoke and finished the last of the pint in my pocket, then dropped one of my remaining stash of Xanax from my stay in the hospital.

I felt smooth and under control. After that I went to the candy counter and got a refill on the ten-dollar box of buttered popcorn.

In the movie Che-Che was playing the slutty girlfriend of the lead man's business partner. A five-minute scene. She was standing at a Vegas crap table heckling the guy throwing the dice. The performance was okay. Believable.

When the theater lights went up everyone clapped for the director and the lead actors and then, in turn, the supporting cast. When beautiful, tall Che-Che stood up and took her bow every man in the theater's eyes were on her.

As people began to leave, I was setting my popcorn box down from my lap when I noticed a foot-wide dark stain on the crotch of my blue chauffeur's pants. The "butter flavoring" goop had drained through the bottom of the box and darkened my slacks.

On the way out, now wearing my chauffeur's cap and feeling pissed off and feisty, I stopped at the candy counter and showed the teenage kid in the striped jacket the bottom of the box and my stained suit pants while Che-Che and Dennis stood by watching.

The candy guy couldn't have cared less. "Hey, that's too bad," he grunted, faking a look of detached bullshit concern. "It happens."

"It happens!" I said.

"Yeah, tough break," says candy stripes. "My advice: Use more napkins next time, is all." Then he went back to stacking paper cups.

I wasn't done. I wasn't done by a long shot. "Look, kid, this is crap!" I snarled. "I'm from out of town. I work in this suit. I've got one pair of pants with me. Now they're screwed!"

Candy boy refused any eye contact and continued replenishing the fucking cup supply from a big cardboard box.

When he finally looked back and realized I wasn't going away he stood upright and faced me. "On behalf of the staff and management of Clearsky Theaters, I want to extend our heartfelt apologies, sir," the wiseguy punk parroted from some jiveass "How to Handle Complaints" pamphlet.

"Fuck you!" I yelled.

"Calm down, Bruno," Che-Che whispered. "This is no big deal. I'll buy you six goddamn blue suits tomorrow."

I ignored her. "Where's the manager?" I demanded.

The little shit behind the counter was apparently a master at treating people with blasé nonchalance. To him I was another stack of paper cups.

"Look buddy," he whispered, "just cool it. I hear what you're sayin'. Okay?"

"I'm not your buddy, asshole!" I said. "I'm YOUR CUS-TOMER."

His new expression said it all. The kid rolled his eyes in an *aw, fuck me, I got a real piece-a-work here* look. He walked away down the counter, then threw the words back toward me over his shoulder. "Mr. Aftar went home," he said. "He leaves at ten o'clock just before the start of the last show. Sorreee. He'll be in tomorrow at eleven."

Now Dennis was shushing me. "Bruno, man, knock it off. You're attracting attention. Just chill."

I got the movie house manager's name and the kid's name and wrote them on the back of my ticket stub.

The evening ended early. Che-Che and the professor went to eat at Umberto's down in Little Italy, then she said she was tired, so I dropped her and Dennis in the Village, at her place, right after one.

Since I was already downtown and still pissed off about my

pants, I decided to stop in at St. Adrian's bar on West Broadway for a few drinks. Five or six years before the place had been a favorite night haunt of mine. They had twice-weekly poetry readings and a couple of local newspaper guys who write columns had frequented the place from time to time.

When I got to the bar the building was the same but the name was different. It was now called Euphoria.

As I was parking the car, a pretty girl in her late thirties or early forties, wearing a short skirt, stepped out the entrance door for a smoke. When she saw the light-blue Benz stretch her eyes lit up. "Is that yours?" she called as I was clicking my driver's door locked.

"Yeah, it is," I said. "Not exactly a low-profile ride, is it?"

"Damn," she cooed, "what a beautiful limo. The car. It's a Mercedes, right?"

"Yeah, it is."

She was smiling and, for sure, a little drunk too. A very sexy smile on the face of a very sexy girl. "Hey, would it be okay if I looked inside?" she asked.

"Sure," I said, "let me open it up for you." I pressed the remote in my hand and after the locks popped, I walked over and chauffeur-style opened the back door for her.

When she stepped in and sat down I checked out her legs. They were beautiful—all the way up to her pink panties.

After sliding across the seat to make room for me, I got in too. "THIS IS ME," she giggled. "This is WHO I AM. The bar, the moonroof, the DVD TV! I'm in heaven."

"What's your name?" I asked, trying to take my time.

"Oh cripes. I'm sorry," she giggled. "I'm Heidi. And who are you? I know! Don't tell me. You're Prince friggin' Charming."

"I'm Bruno. Bruno, from L.A."

Heidi shook my hand.

"How about a ride in my Benz, Heidi? Would you like that?"

"Geez, Bruno from L.A.," Heidi giggled. "I'd like nothing better but I'm, you know, with somebody. How about a rain check?"

"Too bad. I'm out of town in the next day or two. Some other time, maybe."

Pretty Heidi was still smiling. "You going in?"

"I'm planning to."

"Can I buy you a drink?"

"You sure can, Heidi."

Inside, the bar was the same as I remembered, minus the short stage and the sound system. A few more tables.

Heidi was at the bar with a straight-looking guy in a sports jacket and tie. She introduced us. He was Biff or Bill or Benny or Buck or Barney, or some goddamn thing. He sneered and shook my hand, reaching across Heidi. I could tell that the asshole was cordial because he had to be and not because he was a friendly person. He was with the hottest girl in the bar and he had to put up with guys like me saying hello to captive fox. Then he went back to his scotch-rocks and me and Heidi chatted on about the limo business and rock stars and what it was like for me to do my job driving *all those cool celebrities*. Somehow her smile and confident manner reminded me of a much younger J. C. Smart.

Eventually, three drinks later—doubles for me—her guy stepped outside for a smoke with one of his bar pals and Heidi, still flashing the amazing, sexy smile, leans close to me and says, "Excuse me, Bruno honey, I've got to make a pit stop. Be right back."

From time to time, in my years in bars, boldness and being pushy with women has worked for me. So, a few seconds after she'd gone, I decided to make my move.

I followed Heidi to the ladies' room, then waited outside

the door until I was sure she had entered a stall. Then I walked in quietly. There were only two booths. I opened the door to the one next to the one she was in, then stood up on the seat and looked over the top.

There was Heidi taking a squirt. I watched and waited. When she leaned back to unroll the paper from the fixture against the wall I got a shot at the sweet little cookie between her legs. It was shaved. Heidi's hips and thighs were as pretty as her legs.

"Need any help with that?" I whispered.

She looked up. But her reaction wasn't the one I'd hoped for. "Hey, Jesus Christ, man! That's just plain rude. Get the hell out of here!"

Back on my stool at the bar, I waited. Five minutes later, Heidi finally appeared. Not smiling. I leaned close, "Hey, look," I said. "Can't blame a guy for trying."

She wouldn't look at me. Then, before she could answer or say anything, necktie returned and took his place on the seat next to hers.

There was some whispering back and forth, then he stood up.

He was behind my stool. "So you're a peeper," he snarled. "A fuckin' asshole perv."

The punch came quickly and was unexpected because usually, in bar fights, I get a chance to stand up first. But not this time. The blow caught me at an angle, on the side of the head. I fell against the empty stool next to me and whacked my ear on the bar rail.

Outside by my limo Biff or Benny or whatever his name was, and one of his friends, each took another turn. His pal was a bigger guy with some kind of apparent martial arts background. When he clouted me it was with an open hand—

the butt of his palm—right in my mouth. The blow split my lip and blood gushed down my face onto my white shirt and suit jacket.

All in all I hadn't had a good night.

It was after three a.m. when I got back at David Koffman's condo on Riverside Drive. I cleaned myself up and even used some remover stuff from a kitchen cabinet to try to get the popcorn blotch off my pants. No sale.

twenty-five

hat Sunday morning at three a.m. a day later my cell
phone started ringing on the nightstand by my head
until it woke me up. It was Che-Che. I could hear
in her voice that she was buzzed on something. "Yo
pisano, how ya doin'," she sang.

"I was asleep," I said. "What do you need, Che-Che?"

"Pick us up at my place in half an hour. I feel like having
some fun."

An hour later I was standing in front of Che-Che's condo
in the Village buzzing apartment number 16B.

No answer.

On the third try my pissed-off sounding client finally
pressed her "talk" button. "Yeah!"

"It's me. Bruno," I said. "I'm downstairs." In the background I can hear someone yelling and something crashing.

"Hang loose, okay," Che-Che snarled. "I'm dealing with
. . . a situation here."

"I'll be downstairs when you need me."

• • •

An hour later the building's oak doors swing open and out struts my beautiful customer, alone, wearing a formfitting exercise outfit, with a Nikon strapped around her neck. In her hand is a brown shopping bag turned on its side.

After she got into the blue Benz stretch I turned around to face her. "Is everything okay?" I asked.

"What happened to your face?"

"A long boring story with no happy ending."

"But," she forced a smile, "you're okay?"

I tried to act nonchalant about the bruises and my cut lip. "Sure. At your service," I said. "But the real question is, how are you? I heard yelling. You look upset."

Che-Che slid a long dinner platter out from inside her shopping bag, then rested it on the console opposite the backseat. On the plate was at least half an O-Z of cocaine and a glass straw. "Everything will be just peachy-fuckin'-dandy in about thirty seconds," she said.

"Whatever you say. Ma'am."

I watched my client snort three long fat lines, then she looked up at me. "Get on the West Side Highway, Bruno. We're headed upstate."

"Soo, no Dennis?" I asked. "We're riding alone?"

"I'm done with that putz," Che-Che hissed. "That punk struts around like a frikkin' Greek god but the asshole slams steroids twice a day and, pardon the expression, he can't get it up for love or Jesus."

"That can't be good."

"The boy's hung like a fucking miniature Chihuahua. He goes to the gym twice a day but it sure don't help my love life. I mean he gives decent *head* and all, but, so does my neighbor's pug. Then the *stronzo* tells me this caca crap about, 'Geez, baby, I'm sorry. I'm feeling tired.' I mean, what am I, Bruno, fucking brain-dead? Do I look neutered to you?"

"You emphatically look anything but neutered to me, Che-Che."

"What a waste. He acts like Hulk Hogan but fucks me like an eight-year-old choir boy!"

"I'm here for you, Ms. Sorache. My services come free of charge. With a willing smile."

"Shut up, Bruno. I'm into pretty young guys is all. If I wasn't I'd take you up on it. Look at me. I'm twenty-nine, for chrissake, and all I do is strike out."

"Keep swingin', Che-Che, you'll hit one. But you might try not eating the picture off the front of the menu. I mean, before you order, make sure that you're getting the real deal."

"No shit!" my client whispered.

We arrived at West Point at seven a.m. My customer was completely stoned, sipping straight from a glass decanter of vodka in the car's minibar. Her eyes were two huge black holes.

After we entered the compound, Che-Che pointed toward an elegant stone cottage at the far end of the parade grounds. "Pull over at the front door of that house," she said. "That's the commandant's residence."

"I don't feel good about this," I said. "You're pretty whacked. You could get us both in a huge jackpot."

"I was on a shoot here last year for *Elite*. A cover. I know what I'm doing. Trust me, okay? You're about to see just how far a smile and a tiny pair of tits can take a girl."

"What the hell are we doing here, Che-Che?"

"We're having fun, dummy. Calm down."

"Okay, but let's put the drugs in the trunk. This is military, for chrissake. I don't feel like going to jail on Sunday morning."

Che-Che was grinning. "Damn, Bruno. You come on like some kind of removed, edgy hardass, but down deep you're a pussy."

"But not a stupid pussy.

After I stowed my client's cocaine plate in the boot I pulled the limo around to the front of the commandant's cottage.

Tall, beautiful Che-Che, her Nikon around her neck, her tits half out of her warm-up jacket, weaved her way up to the residence door, then knocked loudly.

A short time later a tall, gray-haired guy, wearing a bathrobe, opens up. From twenty-five feet away, behind the wheel, I watch as Che-Che smiles and charms the colonel.

Back in the limo a few minutes later my client is beaming. "Pull the Benz out on to the middle of the parade grounds on the grass," she commands. "And go get my fucking *toot* out of the trunk."

"No! Have a drink. Settle down, for chrissakes."

"Fucking pussy!"

Not long later, perhaps a quarter of an hour, there are nine hundred cadets in full dress uniforms, in formation, on the grass, ready to march.

Che-Che Sorache, filmless Nikon camera is hand, half her body protruding through the car's moonroof, begins snapping away, unable to stop herself from laughing.

On the way back to Manhattan my customer is now very drunk and very sleepy and slurring her words.

"Hey, Bruno?"

"Yeah, Che-Che."

"That was a kick, right? I mean all those boys marching

around on the grass, looking so pretty, on Sunday morning. Fun, huh?"

"Right." I said. "Just great. Now go to sleep. We'll be back in town in an hour."

"When you see Nana, don't tell her about this, okay? She'd be so annoyed with me."

"I won't tell anybody, Che-Che."

"Hey, Bruno, you're not really a pussy. You're a good friend. I mean it."

"Thanks," I said. "Ditto. It's all in a day's work."

My first-class airplane ride the next day, featuring half a dozen double Jack Daniels, was paid for by Che-Che.

Back in L.A. at Dav-Ko, up in my room, after unpacking, I sat on my bed and sipped at a beer, opening my mail. I had returned to the madness of Los Angeles. I was home.

Among the bills and junk mail were two thick manuscript envelopes I had addressed to myself and put return postage on. I knew what they were. They were publisher rejections. My short story manuscript had been returned. Both the boilerplate letters said essentially the same thing. They weren't looking for more short fiction. They were cutting back.

Flipping the pages of each manuscript I concluded that neither one had even been read.

I could feel my stomach tighten. Once again I had failed. Nobody even looked at my work. Across my room was a wall of books. All I had ever wanted was to have my words rest among theirs. My Kafka and Shakespeare and Miller and Steinbeck and Selby and O'Neill and Tennessee Williams and Wallant and Hemingway. I was a forty-two-year-old loser. A man who'd fallen between the cracks of an empty life. A freak. Not a writer but something else—another dime-a-

dozen lost Los Angeles mutant. One of the thousands of drifting if-come asshole wannabes who had attached his heart and
mind to a fraud and squandered his life for the rancid, empty
wet crotch of hope.

Jimmy's voice had been right all along. I amounted to shit.
I was shit. I was simply a washout. A juicehead. A drunk. A
talentless, empty fool. The son of a drunk, the grandson of a
drunk, and the brother of a dead drunk.

But I'd become sure about one thing. The events of the last
few weeks had made me certain: I had to get out of the limo
business. It was madness. It was making me drink. I'd be
better off in a phone room, flogging pens or copier supplies,
than caretaking and servicing a clientele of self-indulged celebrity brats. I no longer had the stomach for it.

twenty-six

t was one-forty-five in the afternoon several days later. Attorney Busnazian was waiting alone outside the West L.A. Courthouse, dressed in his double-breasted black suit and pink tie, a coordinating hankie stuffed in his breast pocket, carrying his Gucci briefcase. He chuckled when he saw me walking toward him. "Right on time, Bruno. Good. Excellent."

It felt like a drug deal, except not. I handed him a white, sealed envelope. It contained the additional thousand dollars (twenty fifty dollar bills) we had agreed upon over the phone. "There you go," I said. "As promised."

Without counting the money he stuffed the envelope into his inside coat pocket. "Cheer up," he said, grinning. "I've got news. Good news, actually."

"A total of three grand's worth of good news, I hope."

"Your hearing is scheduled for two o'clock. They moved us up in the calendar. The drunk driving charge against you will be dismissed."

"Wait! No kidding? Dismissed?"

Still the leer. "You were motionless in the car when the officer arrested you, correct?"

"That's right. At the beach. I was asleep."

"The vehicle's motor was not running. Correct?"

"Correct," I said.

"Well, it's generally a useless technicality, but sometimes, depending on the presiding hearing officer, it works. To be guilty of a DUI the law states that you must be operating the vehicle."

"C'mon!" I said. "That's it?"

"You weren't driving. Ipso facto the DUI will be quashed."

"That's amazing. I don't know what to say."

"You'll recall that I mentioned to you that it pays to have friends in tall glass buildings. This was strictly a quid pro quo situation. A favor. Any other time you'd be convicted. Your appearance today in court is perfunctory."

Busnazian extended his hand and I shook it. "Thanks," I said. "Good job. You earned your money. So—let's go in and get this deal over with."

"In a minute. First, there's the Dav-Ko matter of your driver, Martin Humphrey."

"Right," I said. "The lawsuit. Jennifer Lopiss. The assault thing. That stuff. Marty's still on the payroll. He's a good employee. Marty's not going anywhere. I gave him my word."

"I'm gratified to report to you that the entire situation has also been resolved. Just this morning, actually."

"What about the pending charges?"

Busnazian was smirking. "Let me say it this way: Sometimes unreasonable people become reasonable. When their unreasonableness is documented and presented in a persuasive manner by their own attorney, they return to a more rational mode of thought. But candidly, I wouldn't expect any more business from that particular celebrity management firm.

"Hey, no problem. I don't need that kind of business. As a matter of fact, fuck those guys. I mean, who needs the headaches?"

"That's very cavalier. But, as we both know, it is your livelihood."

"Yeah, it is. Unfortunately."

"Anyway, a good day, all in all," Busnazian smiled. "Now, shall we go in?"

"Hey, you're three for three, counselor," I said, "including the Robert Roller arrest. My partner was scared to death about that lawsuit."

"I pride myself in my ability to earn my fee. You fellows are getting what you paid for. My job is to smooth out the bumps in the road for those glitzy cars of yours. So far we've been extremely fortunate."

"How about this; your next limo ride is on us. Our treat."

"I'm going to Boston on Monday. I'll take you up on it."

"Done. Call the office and book the car."

Attorney Busnazian now modulated his voice for maximum dramatic effect. "One last caution: In your case you may not be so lucky next time. I'd be mindful of that."

"I hear you."

"No more drinking and driving."

"I know. Look, there's something else. Can you and I talk confidentially? I need your advice."

Now my lawyer put on his best, most serious barrister expression. "I'm your legal representative. As I've said before, whatever we discuss remains in confidence."

"I want to get out of the limo business."

"I see."

"Can you help me with it? I'd need your help in writing up an offer to my partner."

"In a word, no. Unfortunately, I represent your firm. You

and Mr. Koffman jointly. My personal association with you in the matter would represent a conflict of interest. But I can refer you to a very competent man."

"Okay, good. Have him call me."

"I have to say that I'm a bit nonplussed. Dav-Ko is doing quite well. You fellows have a successful, thriving operation."

"I'm tired, okay? I live where I work. That company is up my ass twenty-four-seven. And I hate Hollywood. I hate my job and I hate my clients."

"Just a suggestion: Move. Get your own place. You can easily afford it."

"It's beyond that. Way beyond that."

"You strike me as an impulsive person, Bruno. I would restrain that emotion for the time being. Perhaps talk it through with your partner. But certainly, don't piss away all that you have worked to achieve."

"I'm tired of being a garbage man. Koffman can have it. But first I'd like to know my options."

"Very well, I'll have my associate contact you. He's with a good firm. Now, shall we go in?"

"Sure. Let's do it," I said. "Today I'm a happy camper."

twenty-seven

The next afternoon, following up on my plan to cut loose and get free from Dav-Ko, while Rosie was dispatching, I began to go through Joshua's computer files trying to come up with a precise monthly gross income for Dav-Ko. The current figure that Koffman and I and Joshua had come up with was roughly 30K per month. But some months were a lot more and Koffman, for his own reasons, liked to downplay how well the company was doing. He and Joshua would talk on the phone twice a week for an hour discussing money stuff and expansion strategies and that shit. Then Joshua would meet with me in the chauffeur's room and give me the short version if I asked for it.

It took me an hour, but after totaling the last six months of business sales on the computer, I came to an actual average gross figure of nearly 41K per month. I printed out the pages and stuffed them in a legal envelope to take upstairs to my room.

Then I went to the file cabinet and pulled all the open accounts payable folders. Then the paid ones too. I wanted to get an accurate number, then make my own copies of everything. The first file I came to was American Express. Each tab inside represented one card, one employee. There were twelve in all.

That's when I got the shock! It was almost unbelievable. Joshua Wright's personal credit card charges were over $4,500 a month. Sometimes higher. Twenty-three thousand dollars in total. Restaurant charges! Charges for online gifts to his friends! Roundtrip first-class airline tickets for someone named Todd Kraft from Seattle, $1,500. A hotel charge for $800 for that weekend was beneath it. Joshua's clothing transactions alone came to over $1,100 a month. What a fucker! Then I came to another page. On it were charges for porn sites. Subscriptions to all-male links. Then the kicker: a balance transfer of 23K to a new separate Visa card in the company name in an attempt to hide the whole snot-filled caper.

Still in disbelief, to backup the porn site charges, I clicked on the "downloads" tab on Joshua's PC. There they were. Full photographs of cocks and men and young boys having sex. Cum shots and anal action. Pages and pages, file after file of the stuff. In his "sent" e-mail file there was more. Cell phone and webcam photos of Joshua himself. Jerking off. Ejaculating. His bared asshole.

On and on. E-mails to guys around L.A. that he'd met on gay websites. Meetings in park bathrooms and their back and forth notes on what they planned to do to each other.

Joshua Wright was two people. One of them was a well-dressed, well-spoken young man engaged to a pretty coed from USC, a clean-cut kid on his way up with a growing company. But Mr. Hyde was a total whackadoo. An embezzler and a homo sex freak.

I had no choice. I had to call my partner and report the insanity.

Koffman was at first in shock too. Then livid. His instructions were for me to do nothing. To say nothing. Business as usual. He would be on the next plane west.

Confronting the kid with his misdeeds was a sad and brutal occasion for me. Rosie had gone home and all the cars had been dispatched and our farm-out business to our affiliate companies was covered for the night. Dav-Ko's senior partner had registered in a local hotel and hadn't let Joshua know he was in town. He and attorney Busnazian entered the office together at eight o'clock. I came down from my room at the same time. We converged in the dispatch office.

When Joshua said "hi" to us no one replied. Wordlessly, Busnazian laid out copies of all the embezzling charges, and the porn photos of the kid's sex stuff, on the desk. "Your employers and I especially would like an explanation of what you see here in front of you," he said quietly.

Joshua stood there looking from one of us to the other. Then, slowly, he leafed through the pages on the desk, saw that he was screwed, then eased himself into his chair. "I don't know what to say," he whispered finally. "I'm sorry, I suppose, is the best way to sum it up."

David Koffman's ire was directed more toward the kid's sexual madness than the crazy credit card shit and the theft of money. "You meet your tricks at public bathrooms," he hissed. "When you have sex with these men do you at least use a condom?"

"Sometimes," Joshua said. "Why?"

"Why! You're asking my WHY, for God's sake!"

"Yeah, if I remember to bring a condom I use one. What's the big deal?"

"Then you go home and have sex with your fiancée. Is that correct?"

"Yes, I guess it is. I mean, we live together and we have sex."

"Unprotected sex! I'm talking about unprotected sex."

"I suppose that's right. Sometimes we do and sometimes we don't. But, I mean, that's my business, David. That's my personal life. It has nothing to do with Dav-Ko or what happened. What I did."

"Spreading HIV is murder, young man. Like holding a fucking gun to someone's head and then deliberately, knowingly pulling the trigger."

It was the first time I'd ever heard my partner, David Koffman, use the word "fuck."

Now Joshua was whispering. "Like I said, my personal life is my own business. But look, you guys do what you have to do. I did it. I mean, I did the things you said. My life and stuff, it all just got out of control."

David Koffman sat there, looking at the clean-cut soft-spoken kid wearing the sports jacket and tie, in dazed amazement. "You need help, Joshua," he said quietly. "You are a person without conscience. You're insane."

In the end, after the showdown and Joshua's bizarre lack of conscience, the matter was settled between Dav-Ko and our night manager.

Of course he was fired. But then attorney Busnazian made an astute suggestion. Joshua held the title to a six-year-old BMW sedan—a gift from his parents as a college graduation present. Online, the car booked out at nineteen thousand dollars. Busnazian proposed that no criminal charges would be brought against him in exchange for the car's signed ownership papers and California registration.

The matter was settled.

twenty-eight

The following day I was back driving Che-Che's nana, J. C. Smart, and my partner was on his way back to New York.

When she needed a car, every week or so, J.C. had always requested me and my old Pontiac and, if I was available, I would drive her and do the job. It had been more than a month since we had last seen each other, and as I was on my way to pick her up I realized that I was now more determined than ever to get free of Dav-Ko. The episode with Joshua had been the final straw.

Mrs. Smart had become my favorite client. I loved her old-time Hollywood stories and nonstop gossip about movie stars and transplanted screenwriters like Ben Hecht and Faulkner and Scott Fitzgerald. She and her husband Art had once spent weekends at Tracy and Hepburn's home in Malibu, on Trancas Beach. J.C. was part of the Los Angeles that was long dead. Expired from totally unnatural causes.

Our routine had been well established. I'd drive her and Tahuti to her doctor in Santa Monica or to lunch in Beverly

Hills or to tea with her favorite elderly girlfriend, Dawn, out at the Motion Picture and Television Fund retirement home in Woodland Hills. Then she and I would return to Hollywood and do her supermarket shopping, then go to the post office to pick up whatever new books she had ordered, then home to the bungalow.

I arrived on time. J.C., as usual, was dressed handsomely and ready to go. I walked her to the car carrying her bag. After she got in my Pontiac and had nestled her fat cat on her lap, I went around to the driver's door and got in too, then placed her bag on the seat between us. "I always appreciate your help with my bag," she said.

"No big deal," I said.

"I beg your pardon," Mrs. Smart hissed.

"I said, no big deal."

"Just say 'you're welcome,' for God's sake. Why on earth would anyone above the age of ten use a phrase like *no big deal*?" The English teacher/critic in my customer was still a tyrant. She could not stop herself. She was like a kleptomaniac in a button store. She couldn't get enough. The shit was relentless.

"In fact, I have a term for your type of grammatical carelessness," she sneered. "I call it TV speak. You, apparently, have mastered it. In lieu of an actual education, the majority of the American population—I don't necessarily mean you— has acquired its English usage by viewing Oprah or that simpering fraud Dr. Phil. Or possibly from the staggering array of situation comedy and police drama implanted nightly in their brains via that absurd and hideous box."

"I'll try to clean up my act," I said, smiling.

"Merciful Jesus."

"Where would you like to go first, J.C.?"

"The usual," she said. "Dr. Prescription-Pad, in Santa Monica. But first, may I change the subject? I have some positive news for you. Would you like to hear it?"

"Yes, I would. I've had nothing but bad news machine-gunned at me for a while, especially from inside my head, so some good news would be nice."

"I've read the manuscript you gave me. Your stories are good, the characters well developed, and your sentences clear and succinct. In fact, absent the vitriol, profanity, and blatant pornographic content, your writing is often excellent. In some ways, in fact, your style reminds me of the writer H. H. Munro. Saki. Are you familiar with him?"

"Yes. It's been a while, but, sure, I've read his stuff."

"May I make a suggestion?" she said.

"Sure. Please do."

"I still have a friend or two in the publishing business. Small press publishers. With your permission I will send each of them your manuscript."

"Thank you," I said. "Thank you very very much. You absolutely have my permission. You've made my day."

J.C. was smiling. "Not at all. You deserve to have your work in print. You're a good writer, Bruno Dante."

In Santa Monica my client was her usual twenty minutes at the doctor's office. For once she left Tahuti behind in the car. Her devoted cat was getting on in years too, but when I petted the monster a little he managed an approving purr.

From Santa Monica we drove over Topanga Canyon to Woodland Hills and the Motion Picture home. J.C. liked that route best because of the green and the natural beauty of the canyon.

She and her pal Dawn had tea for an hour at an upscale English joint in Calabasas. After that we drove back to the Motion Picture home to drop her friend off.

But, as we were getting on to the Ventura Freeway on our way back to Hollywood, I noticed that my client had slumped against the passenger door. Her eyes were closed. I leaned across and touched her arm. "J.C., are you all right?"

She opened her eyes slowly. "I'm not sure," she said. "Please don't be alarmed, Bruno, but I think perhaps you should take me to a hospital. Just now I'm not feeling well at all."

"Sure. Of course," I said. "What's wrong? Do you know?"

"It's probably nothing. But please hurry."

I got off the freeway at Warner Center, where I knew there were at least two hospitals. Five minutes later we were in the emergency room.

They wheeled J.C. in right away while I waited nervously in the lobby.

Forty minutes passed. I went to the admitting window a few times to ask about her condition but no one would give me a straight answer. Finally, a nurse came out to talk to me. "Are you Bruno?" she asked. "You're here with Mrs. Smart?"

"Yeah. I am. How's J.C.?" I asked. "Is she okay?"

"Mrs. Smart appears to have had a fainting episode. We believe she took too much of her blood pressure medication. But she seems much better now. She's asking for you. Would you like to go in?"

"Absolutely. I want to see her."

"Are you a relative?"

"Right," I said, "I'm her nephew." The lie came easily. I knew from repeated trips to the ER with friends over the years that only family members are allowed inside emergency rooms.

I was guided through the set of double doors to one of a

dozen curtained cubicles. J.C. was sitting up on her hospital bed, putting on her coat, looking weak. "You look a lot better," I said, telling another lie. "How do you feel?"

"Alive," J.C. snickered, "as opposed to the obvious other option. Please tell me that you did not call my granddaughter. You didn't call Marcella, did you?"

"No," I said. "I didn't want to worry her. She's three thousand miles from here. She'd just get upset. There's no point in scaring someone who can't do anything anyway."

"Thank you, Bruno. Excellent reasoning."

"I'm glad you approve," I said.

J.C. was smiling. "*Sic biscuitus disintegrat.*"

"What does that mean?" I asked.

The old lady snickered. "It's Latin," she said. "The loose translation is: *That's the way the cookie crumbles.*"

We both laughed.

"Look," I said finally, "are you getting enough rest? You seem very tired. Do you still lay down in the afternoon?"

"What's that?" J.C. snarled. "What did you just say?"

"I said, do you lay down in the afternoon?"

"Bruno, have you no shame? You're well read and apparently semi-educated, but obviously beyond any capacity for intelligent application. Have you so little comprehension of the mother tongue you speak? I do not LAY down, sir. I LIE down."

But then she softened up a little and smiled, eyeing me closely. "Actually, apparently, it is you who should LAY down. You look tired too. I'm certain that you don't get enough rest."

I settled the score by quoting her favorite poet: "*My candle burns at both ends; it will not last the night . . .*" I recited.

"*But ah, my foes and oh, my friends—it gives a lovely light!*" J.C. chimed in. "Well done, Bruno. Edna Millay again."

"Thanks," I said. "Shall I take you home to Hollywood? No post office today, okay?"

"Yes. That would be best," she said. "I suppose I'll remain at the mercy of that buffoon in Santa Monica, at least until I meet my maker. I find it incredible that I was just examined at that man's office this morning. A few hours later I'm plopped down in an emergency room. Perhaps I'll go home and read his cards. There's no question that he's incompetent but perhaps he is actually mad as well."

Back outside in the parking lot, after helping my client into the passenger seat, I shifted my Pontiac into "D," then pulled out on to De Soto Avenue heading toward the freeway. Tahuti, for some reason, suddenly left his master's lap then jumped into the backseat.

"Hey," I said chuckling, pulling the car back toward the curb, "what's wrong with your friend?"

But J.C. was unable to answer me. She was dead.

The following day I picked up a weeping Che-Che and her *in shock* mother, Constance, at the airport, then drove them to the Beverly Hills Hotel.

Two days later, J. C. Smart was buried next to her husband at Hollywood Memorial Park cemetery, at sundown, in their double plot near the lake. Joyce Smart had outlived almost every one of her contemporaries, so the service was only attended by a handful of people.

After the minister read J.C.'s favorite, the Twenty-third Psalm, her daughter Constance got up. With Che-Che standing next to her at the grave, she read two of J.C.'s last poems as a benediction.

I felt myself beginning to come apart.

MY BUNGALOW

The chirp of sparrows waking up
Counterpoints to my clinking coffee cup:
I hear the asthmatic morning cough
Of my neighbor's old Cadillac driving off:
And here and there a garbage can
Vomits at the touch of man:
The substance of my life runs out
Through a rusted, percolating spout
Meanwhile I place upon the shelf
Well-dusted pieces of myself
And cube into my casserole
The severed fragments of my soul.

One continues to decay
Day by day, day by day.
Strange forms of agony are made
By those who have their last years betrayed.
The wolves of nameless doom await
My little house concealed from fate;
And those who lock their door and hide
Will soon be ravished by the beast inside.

And then there was this one too. After Constance read it I
cried my ass off.

ANNIVERSARY

I have lingered too long outside in the late light
Amidst the twitterings of sparrows;
Already the eucalyptus cast their purple shadow
And the owl in the deodar has opened his yellow eyes

Unfolded his wings and flown away.
Tahuti, Lord of Magic, my black cat,
Prowls the lawn, dancing on delicate feet.
Beyond him a full moon begins to rise,
Twice reflected in his eyes.

I have lingered too long outside in the late light,
And now I find myself remembering,

Sixty years ago, this week, you gave me
Violets in San Francisco
Purchased from the last street vendor's cart
Near Union Square
And amid a faint drifting evening mist
I turned my face up to be kissed

I know that tonight
Your ghost will come to me again
And for better or for worse
You will haunt my dreams
And chant my name
But by morning I will wake the same

And another day will pass
Until under different skies
The same ancient and crushing moon
will begin its nightly rise.

On our way back from the cemetery to the hotel, stopped
at a traffic light, Che-Che leaned forward from the backseat
and stroked my head. "You okay?" she whispered.

There were tears streaming down my face. "No," I said.

"No, I'm not okay. That was a great lady. I'll miss her. I'll miss her a lot."

That night Che-Che got drunk while her Mom stayed locked in the bungalow next door with the blinds closed. I was waiting in the limo outside.

Finally, about ten o'clock, she decided to go dancing, so I drove her to the gay clubs in Hollywood: Brown Eye and Chinchilla and Bay City Bistro. But our first stop was at the Chateau Marmont off Sunset so my client could purchase a quarter O-Z.

Because Che-Che Sorache was Che-Che Sorache, wherever the tall girl went she drew a crowd. When she left Chinchilla she loaded two leather boys in the car with her. They were good dancers she said and I knew that she wanted the company and they wanted her drugs. But both seemed to be okay guys. They kissed and cuddled and snorted her dope while Che-Che sipped her black Russian.

It was after one when I got her back to her bungalow. She was blasted and said that she didn't want to be alone and demanded that I come in with her.

We drank for another hour or so, me on the couch and her on the bed. She loved the Eagles so I got to hear their goddamn CD three or four times in a row.

When she got up to go to the bathroom I put my coat and limo cap back on and prepared to leave.

The door swung open and there was my beautiful client, naked and amazing, a big grin on her face. "You're it, *pisano*," she whispered. "Take your jacket off. You ain't goin' no place."

A sport fuck was just fine with me. Che-Che knew just what she wanted and the way she wanted it.

When we were done and smoking and listening to the
Eagles *again*, she began rubbing my belly then plucking at my
pubic hair. "Did you like that, little Italian boy?" she cooed.

"You're kidding, right? It was great. You have a great body.
You're a bona fide fuck monster."

"Yeah, but no tits. I have no tits."

"C'mon, your tits are fine."

"No they're not. But I still get plenty of work, so screw it.
In a few years I'll get Botox. Mid-thirties is when the face
starts to go. Then, maybe then, I'll do the tits too."

"Thatz crazy."

"Hey, in my business it's the price of admission." Now
Che-Che's expression was serious. "Sooo, is it okay if I ask
you something? Something personal?"

"Sure. I guess."

"That thing on your leg and the side of your cock? While
I was down there gulping and choking I could feel it. A big
ouch, right?"

"Gulf War. Special Forces," I said. "Machine gun fire."

"That's crap, Bruno. C'mon."

"Give it a pass, okay?"

"Whatever. You don't have to be a smart ass."

"Okay," I said. "It was stupid. A misunderstanding. But it
is a battle scar. A Hollywood battle scar. Okay?"

"Okay."

"Okay?"

"Sure. But hey, look baby, I gotta say this: you know this—
you and me—was a one-time-only deal, right?" she whispered. "I mean, it was great and all but . . . you understand,
right?"

"C'mon, you're kidding me," I chuckled. "And here I was
getting ready to slip a Corona cigar wrapper on your wedding
finger."

"So it's okay?

"Will you make me another drink?"

"Sure," she smiled. "I'll make you a doozie."

"Then consider us even. How's that?"

Then her expression changed again. "You know," she said, "I've read your stories."

"No. I didn't know."

"Nana copied the manuscript and sent it to me. She told me you were a damn decent writer. She wanted me to see what you'd written. The one I liked best was about the cabbie and a jerk doorman."

"Your grandmother was a fine lady. Full of surprises."

Now Che-Che was fighting tears. "I'm sorry," she said. "It's Nana. I loved her so much."

"Sure. I understand."

She tried to collect herself. "So, you want to write full time? Is that your ambition?"

"I don't know," I said. "But I've also just begun to realize that I don't know anything. I'm pretty much a loose cannon these days. But I do know I'll miss your nana."

"Look," she went on, "if you owned that company you could write full-time. Yes or no?"

"I don't own the company. I have a partner."

"Right," she said, looking okay again. Smiling. "Kong Koffman."

"You got it. The great Dong himself. Where's that drink?"

"What if I bought Kong out and gave you the company? We'd be sort of partners except it would be yours."

"C'mon. Get serious."

"Bruno, I made eleven million bucks last year. I need write-offs. I have investments in a dozen companies. I could buy it and lose all the money from the investment and it'd still be okay."

"Thanks but no thanks. I hate the limo business," I said.

"Think about it. It would make Nana very happy."

"Okay. I'll think about it. Now, who do I have to screw next to get my drink?"

Che-Che was smiling. "No one, baby. I'll get it for you."

"And put the fucking Eagles back on again. I've had all the fun and good news I can handle for one night."

twenty-nine

n my way back to Dav-Ko on Sunset Boulevard, after leaving Che-Che, I was feeling good. It was four a.m. and the streets were deserted. These days, out of self-protection, I made sure to throw away any bottles in the glove box or in my suit pocket while I was doing a limo run. So when I finished my pint of Seagram's before leaving the side street outside the Beverly Hills Hotel bungalows, I slid the empty under the car where it came to rest against the curb. Then plugged in a Bob Seger CD. *Still the Same.* I'd just been in the sack with the most beautiful woman I'd ever seen. And she'd asked me! Jesus.

At the stoplight on La Cienega Boulevard an old Toyota pulled up next to me. Two young Latino guys. They did what so many people in L.A. do at stoplights; they ogled the shiny stretch limo.

When the light changed they took off down Sunset. Then, a few blocks further, when I was opposite the Continental Riot House, the Toyota reappeared out of nowhere, then swerved in front of me. The driver slammed on his breaks.

The wreck was intentional and unavoidable. One of L.A.'s oldest gimme-gimme street scams to collect on an insurance company. I was going twenty-five miles an hour at the time but it didn't matter. If I'd been doing fifty it would have been the same. I couldn't stop. Ba-boom!

Asshole Number Two, the passenger, immediately flung himself out the door of the ratty, stopped Toyota. He lay on the asphalt, moaning and rolling around and holding his neck. Asshole Number One opened his driver's door a few seconds later, then staggered around to the front of his car, feigning incoherence. Then Number One collapsed too. I watched from my driver's seat while he pulled out his trusty cell phone to punch in 9-1-1.

My first instinct was to run. To shift Pearl into "R," back up, then take off. There was very almost no damage to my car and this was an obvious setup. Why make it easy for the two scheming pricks? But that'd be a mistake. For sure one of them had taken down my plate number.

Instead, I was furious. The accident was technically my fault. I'd hit two scamming assholes who would claim injuries.

I got out of Pearl and walked over to Number One, who had just stuffed his phone back in the pocket of his khakis.

"Nice work, you sonofabitch," I snarled. "I hope you're bleeding. I hope your fucking neck is broken."

"Hey man, jou slamm tha big, bling-out chitbox into the back of my car. I'm injored."

I was standing over the guy. "How about if I stomp on your fucking leg and break it?" I yelled. "Then you can sue my insurance company for that too, motherfucker!"

Now Number Two, who'd heard the arguing, was on his feet, suddenly fully healthy. The prick pulled a blade and

stood there mad-doggin' me. "Back off, prick," he snarled
in perfect English. "I'll fucking cut you! *Afuera*! I said back
off!"

(In New York, as a cabbie, for a long time I'd been called
by the nickname Batman, because it was my habit to carry a
cutoff Louisville Slugger in the trunk of my taxi or under the
front seat—the result of being involved in two uptown holdups.
The habit had continued when I went to work for Dav-Ko.)

Wordlessly, I turned and hurried to the passenger door of
my car a few feet away. I opened it, then the glove box. Then
I pressed the trunk release. The two assholes assumed they'd
just scared me off.

With my bat in my hand I walked back to deal with
Number Two. I was pretty drunk and I knew it. But I felt no
fear. Only rage. These shitbags deserved what they got.

When they saw me coming back at them with my Slugger in my hand, they separated. Now Number One pulled a
shank too—a letter opener kind of blade with a taped handle.

"Who's first," I yelled. "Which one of you cocksuckers
wants a piece of this?"

"I'll stick you, *puta*!" Number two screamed. "Get back. I'll
cut your fucking throat out!"

My first swing at Number Two didn't miss by much. Then
I saw Number One circling behind me so I took a cut at him
too, missing his head but sending him falling back on his ass
to the pavement where my next blow caught the side of his
leg.

He scurried to his feet and backed away. They both did.
Number One was screaming. "Jou krazee, *maricón*! The cops
comin'! Dey gonna fuk u up!"

I was. I was crazy. And I wanted to hurt them both.

Now they stood ten feet away and every time I made a

move toward them one or both of the pricks would bolt in a separate direction.

A couple of minutes passed with me yelling and threatening and lunging at the punks with my bat on the empty street. Then, in the distance, I heard the siren and saw the lights of the black and white.

Seeing the squad car speeding toward us, knowing they were now safe from me, the two cockroaches reverted to their original M.O. They knew the drill: They first tossed their knives down a street drain, then flung themselves back down to the asphalt again, continuing their jiveass scam. I had just enough time to fling my bat into a bush.

I was escorted by a cop to the curb, where I blew a trusty .17 on the blue man's Breathalyzer and was cuffed right away. My ranting explanation about the faked injuries of the two guys and the bogus accident was ignored. I was now a drunk driver. I was the criminal. The cops had their man. Case closed. I wisely left out the part about the knives and the bat. I wanted no part of risking an assault charge on top of the DUI.

Justice is swift in L.A. for intoxicated motorists. A few minutes later a hauling truck arrived to transport my limo. I watched, squatting on the curb next to the patrol car with my hands cuffed behind my back, as the two rats were put on stretchers by the EMT guys. Number Two, as he was being loaded into the ambulance, made eye contact with me and grinned, then gave me the middle-finger salute. Then they were gone, sirens blaring.

The next morning without sleep, with *Jimmy*'s voice filibustering in my head and reminding me of every detail of my stupidity, I met with attorney Busnazian. He was accompanied, I was told, by Che-Che. I'd phoned her from booking and given her Busnazian's number to call for me. But I was in L.A. County max lockdown, so only my attorney was allowed in.

Busnazian and I spoke through the thick plastic partition. But first I had to watch as he removed the jacket of his expensive-looking double-breasted brown suit jacket, then adjusted the diamond cufflinks on his pink shirt sleeves to make certain they were the requisite one inch above the end of his hands.

"This is a difficult situation," he said finally while opening his briefcase and dumping my paperwork on the counter. "I did my best to explain the implications of your arrest to your friend, Ms. Sorache, as we drove down here this morning. Might I say that she's a most attractive advocate for your cause."

"Just tell me when I can get out?"

"Your field sobriety test indicated that your blood alcohol was at least twice the legal limit."

"Okay, what does that mean? How long do I have to stay here?"

My representative paused to examine the positioning in the knot of his light-blue tie in the reflection from the Plexiglas. "The charge is felony DUI," he whispered for dramatic effect. "You were involved in an injury accident. In a word, you're in deep shit, sir."

"That's two words. Deep and shit. Look, it was a street scam, for chrissakes. A setup. The punks did it purposely. They caused the collision on purpose."

Now I was getting a whiff of his cologne over the top of the glass wall. Busnazian shook his bald head and glanced down at the papers in front of him. "Not according to the arrest report. You apparently rear-ended vehicle number two in the number-one lane heading east on Sunset Boulevard. We need to be particularly mindful of the facts in evidence. A: You were intoxicated. They were not. B: You collided with their vehicle from the rear."

"I don't care. I want to plead not guilty."

"Unfortunately, you cannot dispute your guilt at this point."

"Fuck."

Busnazian flashed a twisted grin. "*Fucked* describes your situation with accuracy. Felony DUI carries an automatic and immediate driver's license revocation. A jail term is also automatic. Your actual sentence will be determined at your hearing. That's the only area where I can be of help. I've discussed a strategy with Ms. Sorache and she has endorsed the scenario that I have in mind."

"So now you're buddies with Che-Che? Got yourself a new client, do you, Busnazian?"

"That's really not relevant to your situation."

"What else?" I said.

"Well, there can be no release from custody from now until your hearing. No bail is possible."

"Jesus," I said.

"It smacks of irony, doesn't it?"

"And why is that?" I snapped back, really beginning to hate this pompous jerk.

"You recently mentioned to me that you wanted to disassociate yourself form the limo industry. Apparently, unwittingly, you appear to have achieved that end."

"I don't think it's ironic, Busnazian. I think it sucks a big dick."

Busnazian's face was expressionless. "As it happens, unfortunately, I am the bearer of additional unpleasant news."

"Swell. Let's hear that too."

"Your employment at Dav-Ko is officially terminated. Your conviction has ipso facto violated the terms of your partnership agreement with Mr. Koffman. In a telephone conversation with him this morning I was clearly charged to convey that message."

"Thanks, Busnazian. Anything else?"

"We've known each other quite a while now. Our attorney-client relationship has expanded over time. You may now call me by my first name. Dalton. I've asked Ms. Sorache to do so as well."

"Jesus! I've really gotta get out of Hollywood."

I had $4,100 in my checking account. That day I signed a power of attorney that Busnazian already had in his silky leather briefcase, so he could withdraw my money against his fee.

thirty

I n the end I served fourteen days in jail. The original sentence was six months and then a six month rehab, and I was in County awaiting transfer to Wayside jail when I was released.

It pays to have a good lawyer. But better said, it pays to *know* someone who can pay for a good lawyer. At my hearing Dalton Busnazian presented additional facts that one of his law clerks had discovered in the public record: The two greedy assholes whom I rear-ended had been involved in three of the same type accidents over the past two years. They were career victims and stupid enough not to change IDs between insurance claims.

On the basis of that information the judge dismissed the felony DUI charge and reduced my crime to simple DUI. I was resentenced to time served and a six-month inpatient rehab to begin within thirty days.

Busnazian picked me up and drove me to Dav-Ko, where I would be permitted, according to David Koffman's note and Rosie Camacho's instructions, to stay for "a day or two" until

I packed my books and belongings and found another place to live. It was then that *Dalton* let me know Che-Che had paid my fine and the rest of the legal bills above the money I'd already given him. I'd tried to call her many times from jail without success.

Up in my room at Dav-Ko while going through my mail and bills I found a padded brown shipping envelope with her name and New York City return address on the upper left corner. After tearing the package open by the tab I found a get well card inside in a white envelope. The message was handwritten: "Hang in, Bruno. Good luck. Don't call me again. Che-Che."

In another sealed envelope there were thirty hundred-dollar bills. The golden kiss-off.

It took a few dozen phone calls and a little time but I managed to find a temporary roommate deal through an apartment rental agency in Santa Monica: five hundred a month, first and last month's rent payable immediately.

The building was on Lamanda Street in West L.A., about three miles from the beach. I had the back bedroom facing an apartment building across the courtyard, and I had my own bathroom and use of the kitchen. My only furnishings were a bed and a dresser and a table. But Che-Che's money was coming in handy.

Robby LeCash was my roommate. The guy was a sixty-two-year-old jock and fitness trainer at a health club in Marina del Rey, on his way to Europe for four weeks to teach kung fu and endurance training to one of his actor clients who was preparing to film an action flick about a global-warming-mutated, man-eating strain of fish. Buffed-out Robby was *totally* excited about the trip. Our deal hinged on a quickie proposition. He was leaving in two days and needed someone to move in immediately. The clincher turned out to be that I had to agree to watch and walk and feed his bulldog, Tub, while he was away. *No sweat.* While sitting in his living room I reached down to pet the farting old beast and we made friends easily. Tub's main preoccupations appeared to be sleeping and breaking wind.

I put my books in storage and then moved my clothes and computer in before noon the next day. Later in the afternoon, walking the neighborhood, with my driver's license now indefinitely revoked, I found a bicycle shop on Washington Boulevard and made an impulse purchase: a used, beat-up, beach-cruiser bike with a chain lock. Sixty-five bucks cash. It wasn't much but I was riding again.

But then, after Robby was gone a day or two, I could feel myself beginning to sink. A wall of wet muck swallowed me and saturated my brain. I found myself no longer able to do the only thing that had ever saved me from myself: I could not write.

I'd turn on the computer and stare at the keys and blank screen for an hour at a time. There was nothing to write. I had nothing to say.

Unlike jail—where after the first few days of shaking it out and detoxing from tobacco, I'd spent my time reading books in enforced confinement, resigned to my situation, chatting occasionally with my cellmate, a kid calling himself Swank who filibustered me with stories of convenience-store stick-ups and pimping his girlfriend, then grunted loudly as he

jerked off every evening—I was now alone. My only compan-
ion at LeCash's apartment was my mind.

Each night, through my room's thin curtains, the exterior
patio lights of the apartment across the courtyard flooded my
bare walls, making sleep an impossibility. Without sleep my
head's malignant conjuration persisted.

During daylight hours I began to take long walks in the
neighborhood or ride my bike to the boardwalk at Venice
Beach to exhaust myself enough to pass out on LeCash's living
room couch, next to Tub. It didn't work very well. Nothing was
working. I had been weeks without a drink and the messages
from my brain were getting louder and louder until the self-
hate and the endless replay of my squandering stupidities and
the futility of my life—even breathing in and out—demanded
that I stop it. Kill it. Standing at my balcony rail I began trying
to amass the courage to throw myself to the concrete twenty
or thirty feet below. The spell lasted four days.

Tub the bulldog was my only salvation. When he'd get
lonely on the living room couch he'd gimp his way into my
bedroom, see me on the balcony, or at the computer viewing
porno sites and book reviews, then limp over and force me
to pet him by grabbing my arm, saturating my leg or shirt-
sleeves with his slobber.

My cell phone, which I hated and rarely answered and
seldom turned on, had been collecting messages from
Dav-Ko. Three in total over the last few days. "Bruno, call the
office." I ignored the shit.

At Safeway supermarket on Centinela Avenue, a few blocks
away, my madness culminated unexpectedly.

Tub and I were there partly because LeCash's refrigerator contents consisted of four types of organic juices and vegetables and brown paper bags of grains and gluten-free shit that was inedible, and partly because a dog needs beef to sustain himself. Real food, not organic snot compressed into little brown pellets from the Whole Foods pet department.

So, with Tub dragging behind, I rolled my cart down the Safeway aisles in search of bread and hard salami and mayonnaise for me and something decent for the bulldog to eat.

Then I made a bad decision. I came face to face with a bottle of Mad Dog 20/20 in the liquor area. I made a quick, stupid decision and paid for the bottle at the small counter. Then I pulled Tub out of sight behind a stack of boxed Miller Lite Beer, cracked my jug, and slammed its contents. This is *therapy* I told myself. With this at least I'll be able to function and shut down the noise.

After getting nearly immediate relief I rolled around to the deli area and procured a Genoa salami, a loaf of French bread, mayonnaise and mustard, and a plastic-wrapped brick of Parmesan cheese.

In the pet department I stocked up on six cans of 100 percent beef for Tub, then I made my way into a checkout line run by a blond, chubby, college-looking kid whose name tag spelled PAMMI.

Holding Tub by his leash next to me, after my purchases arrived in front of PAMMI on the conveyor belt and she'd greeted me with the requisite smile and "Hi, and how are you today?" and I had nodded back toward her, she gave me my total: "That'll be nineteen-forty-six."

I dropped a twenty on the counter.

PAMMI was dispensing my change. "Would you like to give a donation to support prostate cancer research today?"

she chimed, then flashed me another checker-mandated shit-eating grin.

"Would I what?" I said.

"Would you like to donate to support prostate cancer research?"

"Why do you ask?" I said. "I'm buying groceries here, Pammi. What in Jesus's name does me buying food have to do with the prostate cancer research business?"

Pammi appeared a bit unsettled. "It's a donation, sir. It's for a good cause."

"I'm not here to *donate*, Pammi. If I wanted to *donate* I'd be where they take donations."

"Oh, okay, I see," she whispered, looking away.

"Tell me, what makes you think I give a rat's turd about prostate cancer? And who in hell told you to ask me for money? I mean, along with your instructions to grin and be cordial and that unnecessary nonsense, that *how are you today?* snot, what imbecilic store policy dictates that you harpoon your clients in the checkout line to solicit contributions?"

"Look, it's manager's orders. We all do it. C'mon, mister. It's no big deal."

I could feel myself at the edge. But I couldn't stop. "Where's this manager?" I snarled. "Let's get him over here, Pammi. I'd like to meet your manager personally and discuss Safeway's *donation* policies."

Behind me there were three customers. One of them—a guy—tapped me on the shoulder. "Look, my man, give it up, okay?" he hissed. "The kid's just following orders."

"I know what the kid's doing," I yelled. "How about just backing the fuck off!"

The guy could tell from my expression that I was getting upset. He wisely turned away.

Then Bill arrived. Bill was in his mid-thirties, wearing a

tie, with different colored pens in his starched, white manager's smock pocket, and wire-rimmed glassed. "Yessir," Bill grinned, "how may we help you today?" Then he leaned down to pet Tub, who reacted with a genuine snarl. Bill wisely pulled his hand away.

"I'm a customer here, Bill," I said, now not giving a shit and not caring that a crowd was gathering and was watching us. "I buy my groceries here. So help me out here, will ya? Please tell me, what Safeway policy permits your employees to entrap their customers in the checkout line to solicit charitable contributions? What gives you guys the balls to ask me for money when I'm here to buy groceries?"

Bill's smile faded quickly. "We're just trying to help out. Could you please keep your voice down?"

"And it doesn't tweak you in the slightest that you're embarrassing people—putting them on the spot—forcing them into giving donations?"

"No sir, I guess it doesn't. Our customers seem to like to donate to a worthy cause. I'll ask you again: Could you please keep your voice down?"

"How about this idea, Bill? My personal opinion is that prostate cancer is a good thing. In my view prostate cancer is Jesus's answer to population growth. How would you and your clerks like to join me and solicit contributions to spread my message? *Hey, it's a good cause.*"

"Okay, that's it! I think you'd better pick up your groceries and your dog and move along. If not I'll call security."

Clearly Bill had the sympathy of the customers who stood around checkout aisle #4. Tub sensed trouble and was beginning to get edgy too. But I didn't give a fuck. I scooped up my change and my plastic bag filled with dog food and salami.

I heard myself yelling again. "Lemme ask you another question, Bill. While I have you in front of me the same way

Pammi had trapped me in the checkout line: How would you like to *contribute* to anal herpes? My guess is that you take it up the ass, Bill. You look like a pole smoker too. Are you, Bill? Are you a bum pirate? Hey, I'll bet Pammi would love to watch you go down on one of the young box boys on your staff. I'll just bet she'd want to make a 'contribution' to watching that shit. Cock-sucking is a *good cause* too! Don't you think?"

Out of the corner of my eye I could see the store's security guard moving toward us from the canned soup aisle. I decided I'd had my say.

Bill whispered something to his nightstick door-shaker and then Security Man turned toward me ready for action. But Tub had been eyeing the scene, and the sudden movements of the two guys made the fat bulldog give the security guy a nice growl that backed him off a step. "Time to go, mister," the guard, whose name tag spelled RAMON, barked. "Let's move it out. We don't want no trouble today, okay?"

I gave Tub a good yank on his chain choker leash, which created another immediate and appropriate snarl.

"Hey," Ramon said, "watch your dog!"

I glared back. "You're the one who should watch him, Ramon. You make another move toward me and *Slasher* here just might decide to take a chunk out of your fat ass. He's a fully trained attack animal. So why don't you just chill out and back the fuck off? Then maybe I'll decide to be on my way."

Down the line of stores in the Centinela Shopping Center was a Walgreens drugstore, the kind that carries everything from hair spray to lawn seed to frozen pizza to digital photo enlargement machines. They also sported a large and well-equipped liquor department. The solution to my week of self-imposed insanity was in front of me and suddenly quite simple.

The image of my former partner's elegant living room bar in New York City came into my mind. The thing was an oak replica of P.J. Clarke's on Third Avenue in midtown, complete with several dozen quarts of the best bottled-in-bond shit on the market and a six-foot-high engraved mirror behind it.

I'd always wanted a home bar for myself so I made the decision to give my bedroom back at LeCash's a little room decoration.

I headed toward the liquor area pushing my shopping cart with Tub tied to the handle.

They had it all: bourbons and brandies and vodkas and gins and flavored this and that. I loaded a quart of each into the cart, then headed for the checkout stand.

My total came to $646.00. Twenty-two bottles. I paid the tab with my pocket cash from Che-Che Sorache's don't-call-us-we'll-call-you, hasta-la-vista-baby, kiss-off fund.

Then I asked the counter guy to remove the cardboard packing boxes from around the bottles that came boxed to make the stuff easier to carry. He didn't ask for a donation and appeared happy to oblige me. He triple-bagged everything in plastic. Six sacks—three on each arm. Then me and Tub headed up the street toward home.

Lamanda Street was five blocks away but by the time we'd covered half the distance, the plastic bag handles were cutting into my the hands, and yanking Tub along the sidewalk was no help either.

I negotiated with two street guys at the bus stop and offered to pay them ten bucks each to carry four of the bags. Their names were Clemence and Don. "You must be having some kinda partee, my man," said Clemence. "I mean, you're doin' it up right. Am I right?"

"I'm decorating my room," I said. "I just moved in."

"Good idea, bro. Excellent. And while you're at it, gettin' your own self ready for the holidays."

"Never hurts to have an early start."

"Right as Ripple, my man," said Don.

thirty-one

That night, after I set up all the bottles on my fake-oak dresser, Tub and I got drunk in the living room watching TV cable reruns of a sadistic crime show where normal-looking guys make dates with young decoy girls online in chat rooms then go for a visit and get humiliated on camera by a self-righteous prick *investigative reporter*, then busted as they leave the house by the local Gestapo. Me and Tub watched five episodes in a row. Real quality TV snot.

But my brain's peace had been restored. LeCash's bulldog seemed to favor black Russians topping his all-beef canned burger meat, while I stuck with straight-blended whiskey after a couple of salami-and-cheese sandwiches.

Around midnight we took our evening walk. It was later than usual and I had to rouse Tub from a deep sleep. While getting my jacket from my room I noticed that a party appeared to be in progress across the courtyard. My neighbor's two bright exterior wall lights were on and a couple was drinking and talking against the rail on the deck.

Half an hour later when Tub and I got back, the people were gone but the lights were still blazing. I took off my clothes and poured four fingers of Schenley and was ready to get some sleep, but as always, my room's thin curtains were useless against the searing beams from beyond the court-yard. Just for once I wanted to sleep in my own bed. I didn't feel like crashing on the couch again. The smell of Tub and his dog hair permeated the thing, even with a blanket slung over it.

I made up my mind. Screw it. Enough was enough. Out on my balcony in my shorts I yelled across the way. "Hey guys! You across the way! It's almost one o'clock, would you mind turning off the lights? How about it? I'm trying to get some sleep over here!"

No answer. No response.

A minute or so later I tried again. "Hey, over there," I yelled. "This is your neighbor! Turn off the goddamn lights! Do you hear me?"

Across the way the sliding glass doors were closed but the dim living room lights were still on and I could hear faint music.

Then, beneath my balcony I heard a glass door slide open. "Hey," a man's voice yelled. "Over there! You're keeping me awake too! C'mon, give it up! Cut us all a break. Turn off the goddamn lights!"

I couldn't see the guy below but he called up to me. "Yo, howz it goin'? You're Ronny's new roommate, right?"

"Right," I said, "That's me. I'm the new designated doggy sitter."

"My name's Victor."

"Bruno," I said. "Hey, tell me something, Victor; does this shit go on night after night?"

"No, once in a while they turn 'em off. But they're dopers

or some damn thing. Don't know what to tell you. Sometimes those lights stay on for three or four days in a row."

"Yeah, well, I can't fucking sleep," I yelled. "I've been on the couch for the last few days but tonight I want to use my bed. I mean, this is bullshit. How 'bout this, Victor: Let's go over there and bang on the door?"

"Nah. No good," he called back. "That's a security building. I've tried it before. They never answer the freakin' buzzer anyway. Hey, you sound like you been celebrating, Bruno? You sound 'bout half in the bag, my man."

"I just set up my new bar. A move-in party kinda deal."

"Well, good luck to you, bro," Victor called. "Yo look, I'm done in, okay? I gets up early. I bought me some night blinders from the drugstore. Thatz what I use when this stuff happens. You should get you some too. Sorry I can't help you, man. Good night."

"Right," I called back. "Okay. See ya."

Then Victor was gone. I heard his balcony door slide closed.

Ten minutes later, still pissed off, after another tall whiskey, a solution came to me. Ronny LeCash, along with his granola and spinach leaves and microbiotic grains and health-food shit, was an audio buff. On either side of his living room's wall unit were powerful twelve-inch speakers that were hooked into the TV. All the apartment's electronic sound came through those speakers with annoying power.

It didn't take long for me to unplug his audio speakers and system, then drag the stuff into my room to do a quick reconnecting job with my penknife. The speaker wires were just long enough for me to remount the units on my balcony wall, facing out.

Back in the living room I looked through my roommate's stack of CDs. The rap disc I chose was by a *singer* named Sam'yall K. I'd never heard of the guy but I queued the disc up and pressed *play* on *low* to test my selection. Now satisfied of the desired effect, I re-queued the disc then cranked up the sound. *"Sha-baba-ah-babah uh uh uh! Sha-baba-ah-babah uh uh uh!!! You done know me butcha know me nowwww! I seen yo bitch at my back door . . . Sha-baba-ah-babah uh uh uh . . . Say she lookin' for sugar but I gah more . . ."*

It took less than a minute for the living room lights to go fully on in the apartment across the way. I had just lit a cigarette and was sipping my Schenley refill.

A tall guy in boxers appeared across the way. I couldn't see his face because it was obscured from me by his blasting wall lights. But I saw him scratch his head then squint out to locate the source of the noise. Finally, seeing me, he yelled out something that I couldn't hear. So I walked back into my room and faded the volume slightly, then returned to my balcony.

"How ya doin', asshole?" I yelled.

"Hey, man," he snarled, "what's your problem! You nuts or what?"

"Me? Nuts? Is trying to get some sleep an abnormal desire? Do you consider that nuts?"

"You've made your point, okay? Turn the sound down. We'll call it even."

"Fuck you," I yelled. "I'll let you know when we're even. This shit goes on every night. Now it's time for a free concert. I've got all the time in the world."

"Look, asshole, kill the noise before I come over there and *really* put you to sleep!"

"Suck my dick!"

"Okay, how 'bout this: no joke. If you make me come over there I'll take those speakers apart and shove them down your throat—one at a time!"

"How about this, Lucifer: Lick the shit off my dick after I fuck your mother up the ass."

"Whad'ya call me? Wha'd you say?"

"I said fuck you, moron!"

"You're making a mistake, my man. I don't like mama-rippin'."

"It was your mama that made the mistake. That mistake was not to flush you after she took the shit that made you."

"Okay, you got it! Stay right there. I'm on my way."

I hadn't factored in the other neighbor's reactions. Apartment lights in both buildings were now coming on. People began appearing at their windows. Balcony doors came open. But I was too crazy now and too filled with rage. It didn't matter. I didn't give a shit what happened now.

Captain Strobe appeared in the courtyard below wearing workout shorts and a cut-down college sweatshirt, carrying what looked like a pipe wrench in his fist. The sweatshirt was red. USC. Joshua, my ex–night dispatcher, had attended fucking USC! I'd flunked out of Santa Monica College and UCLA as a kid but I never would have attended that pissant school. Not on a bet. Dentists and engineers and wannabe psychiatrists. The offspring of the Los Angeles elite went to USC. Rich kids with family money. Those who considered themselves better than everybody else. Those who carried pipe wrenches in their hands to ensure their advantage.

• • •

He was standing directly beneath my balcony now, yelling up. For the first time I could see him and his face clearly. His round head and short, light hair and expression somehow looked familiar. Maybe I'd known him from a job somewhere, or a bar. Maybe we were once neighbors. Then it hit me. This asshole reminded me of myself.

I couldn't hear what he was yelling because of the angle and my blasting rap music, so I went in and lowered Sam'yall K a little more.

On my way back to the balcony I ripped my computer's monitor off the desk and brought it along.

"Hey!" I yelled down. "Lost your guts? You'll need more than that wrench to deal with me. I'm waiting, fucker!"

"C'mon down here you little shit," he bellowed, waving his pipe. "I'm going to adjust your speakers for ya."

In a single motion I raised my computer monitor and threw it down at him. The guy's reflexes were good and he ducked quickly. The thing missed him and crashed on the concrete patio, glass and plastic flying in all directions.

"You're dead," he raged. "You are a fucking dead man!"

"Maybe I am," I said. "But I'll take you with me. That's a promise. Now I'm coming down. Wait right there!"

It occurred to me then that I wanted to die. The idea came simply and clearly into my head. I was tired—exhausted by my own unending obsessions and my scalding brain and the pain and empty absurdness of my useless life. Death would be a relief. Today—now—was as good a time and place as any.

I still held the advantage over this asshole and I knew it. He was the one without the power. Beneath me three floors down, there on the ground with his big mouth and his weapon. I was up here.

So, instead of heading out my door and down the stairs, I decided to throw something else first.

The next closest thing in my room was my computer's CPU. I ripped it from the table.

The jerk was looking away when I threw it, waiting for me to come out the ground floor patio door.

The heavy metal unit caught him on the shoulder. He yelled out, then grabbed his arm and went down to one knee.

"Now I'm coming down!" I snarled. "Now *you're* the fucking dead man!"

On my way out, in LeCash's kitchen, on the counter in a wooden holder was a butcher's knife set. I grabbed the biggest one he had, then went to the door and started for the stairs.

But suddenly, as I stomped down the steps, on the landing below stood a big black dude blocking my way. He had his hand up like a traffic cop. "Hold it!" he ordered.

I was the one with the knife and nothing was going to stop me. "Move," I yelled. "Get out of my way. Don't fuck with me."

In a one-two motion the guy grabbed the knife from my hand and punched me. I second later I could feel my head strike the wall with a thud.

Looking up from the floor he was standing above me. "I'm Victor," he said, "your downstairs neighbor. You're Bruno, right? Remember me?"

"Yeah," I said. "Now I do."

"Time to call it a night, Bruno. You're in pretty deep as it is."

"That fuckshit is waiting downstairs. The prick's got a pipe in his hand."

"I know. I saw what happened. And you winged him pretty good with that amp."

"It was my computer's CPU. Just let me up, okay? Get out of my way."

"You gonna kill that fool or maybe get killed."

"That's right," I hissed. "One hundred percent. Someone's going to die tonight."

"Not here. Not now. I live here too, my man. This is my house too."

"Look, he started this."

Victor outweighed me by fifty pounds. He yanked me to my feet, then threw my knife up the steps to the third floor landing. He grabbed me by the back of my shirt and one arm and began pulling me down the stairs. I tried twisting myself free but it was useless.

When we got to the front door exit he reached into my pants pocket and pulled out my house keys. "Get going, Bruno," he said quietly. "If you come back here tonight you gonna be dealing with me. Juss go find a park somewhere and sleep it off."

thirty-two

The first couple of days at the beginning of my six-month stay at Charles Street Recovery House, near the beach in Costa Mesa, were the worst of my life. By calling in a favor from a probation judge, Attorney Busanzian had managed to wangle me a scholarship grant to the program. I was a charity case. Had he not done so I would have been on my way to Wayside jail for the full term. But I hated the place. It was a jail without bars.

My group was comprised of twelve guys. Most were crack-heads or tooth-rotted meth suckers. Only one or two were like me: drinkers. The current catchphrase in the recovery business is "dual-addiction." They tell you it's all the same disease, but that's crap. Alcohol and drugs are very different. They affect the brain differently. But *recovery* is a big, snowballing industry. They want your money—everybody's money—and they mix all species together in the same bubbling piss pot.

At first you sit in "group" three times a day and listen to the raging rock-heads scream and whine about their bizarre lives; this burglary or that carjacking or ripping off their parents' jewelry to get money. Confrontations and fights between the speed freaks are common in the first few days. Then, luckily, the staff physician, Dr. Fix-You-Up-Right-Away, prescribes load-levelers and downers for the rock-heads and they become more like amiable, distracted zombies. That's what you get for your 10K a month. And Charles Street was cheap by comparison.

But either way drunks simply don't fit in. Me and the other boozer, Paul, didn't relate to any of what was being said and our best conversations were between sessions when we talked about our favorite bars in L.A. and the nasty women we'd met. So, at least for me, "group" turned out to be a waste of time.

My counselor was a guy named Armondo, a former Mexican gang guy who'd done a dime at Pelican Bay and a nickel bit in "Q." He'd found God in recovery going to prison Alcoholics Anonymous meetings.

Mondo was huge. He had a shaved head and his body was knife-scarred and covered with prison tats. Sitting behind his desk, the guy's white, starched dress shirt and tie made me think of a chimp in a TV commercial trying to portray a human. I disliked the fat prick at first sight. His recovery philosophy could easily be summed up in a three sentences: *I'm the MAN* and you are shit. I hold all the cards and you are shit. *I've been through it all and you cannot con me because you are full of shit*. This attitude served only to cement my resistance.

I was in his office for our second scheduled session. My first mandatory one-on-one meeting had been aborted after a six-hour group session in which all new residents, me included, went through the first three AA steps. Mondo and I were supposed to hook up then but I'd gone back to my dorm room claiming sick. I was desperate to get out. The place was a hell.

The meeting with Mondo purportedly had to do with my past. My history. My written fourth step: "Made a searching and fearless moral inventory of ourselves."

"First off," Mondo said, "before we get down to it, what would you say is your main objective at Charles Street? What do you hope to gain from completing our program?"

"Release," I answered. "My hope is to return, in tact, to *living my dreams.*"

"Bullshit, Dante," he barked. "Let's end the babysnot right up front."

The office we sat in was small and un-air-conditioned and it has always been my observation that fat humans perspire a lot. And big Armondo was the emperor of flop sweat. His bald dome and face were covered with it, yet the sun was barely up.

He looked up from his photocopied form and glared. "Okay, let's try again," he said. "We're gonna do this every day at five forty-five a.m., so if I were you, bro, I'd juss get used to the process."

"I'm court-sentenced, man. I'd like to tell you what you want to hear but I'm fresh out of *fake it 'til you make it.*"

"Thaz good, my man," whispered Mondo, "because either I get full cooperation and participation or you get an X on this intake form and off and you go back to County. So, we got us a door number one or door number two scenario here. Pick one. Truth is, it's all the same to me. I cash my paycheck every Saturday."

It only took a second for me to respond. "Go ahead," I said,

staring at the floor, "I'm down. I've got zero interest in returning to jail. So let's do it. Ask your goddamn questions."

Mondo wiped his forehead with the sleeve of his size XXL
shirt then picked up a clipboard. "Question One: *When you
look back at your life, what memories are still uncomfortable or
painful? What incidents make you feel dirty?*"

"Okay, look," I said, my mind now on scream, "I just can't
do this. I can't do it right now."

Big Mondo got to his feet. "Well, I guess that's that. It's
your call, Dante."

"Okay, look, what about this: Can I take the thing back to
the dorm and do it there? In private."

Mondo wagged his neckless head then sank back into his
chair. "Yeah, okay, that's allowed."

Then, reaching down into a drawer he handed me a yellow
writing tablet, then a pen. "You got two hours, my man. Have
it back here by eight o'clock. Complete. Answer all the questions. Understood?"

"Okay," I said. "I understand."

Back in my room, ten minutes later, sipping a mug of caf-
feine-less tea, sitting at the writing desk in my beige-walled
dorm room, I made up my mind to complete the annoying
exercise. For me, Charles Street was the last house on the
block. Fuck it. I'd do what I had to do. I'd been eighty-sixed
for the last time.

Then, something startling happened: My hand began to
write. My brain switched gears and submitted. Words began
pouring out. They were mostly lies but that didn't matter. I
was doing it. Two pages later I was done with Question One.

Question Two was: *In what ways do you experience yourself
as inadequate?*

No problem. Two more written pages. Boom boom boom. Again, the stuff I wrote was mostly made up, things like being a molested child and being beaten as a kid, and going deaf. But so what. I'd be okay. I could hack it. No more County Jail.

Question Three: *What people do you resent, and why?*

I began with David Koffman and listed every employer that I could remember going back as far as I could, and the reason why I disliked the pricks. It was easy.

An hour and a half later I'd answered all ten questions and I was done. The relief was palpable.

In the cafeteria I congratulated myself with three un-sweetened jelly doughnuts and another cup of their best swill herbal tea. I could make it work. *One day at a time. Fake it 'til you make it.*

thirty-three

The death of my brain came two weeks later. By accident. There were only seven of us left from the original group and we were van-driven four hours north for a weekend retreat at a place called San Antonio Seminary in the hills, thirty miles inland from Santa Barbara. Rolling horse-ranch country.

What I learned about San Antonio was that for a long time it had been a training compound for novitiate Franciscan brothers in long brown robes. Polished concrete floors and twenty stark, single rooms, with Jesus photos and religious statues and God paraphernalia everywhere. The place turned into an AA retreat house by accident when one of the senior brothers needed help with his booze problem. The guy who drove up from L.A. to get him and deliver him to an inpatient treatment program in L.A., where he got sober, was looking for a weekend facility for himself and his AA buddies to go over the steps and talk about recovery and hang out. Now, ten years later, San Antonio had become an AA oasis for recovering drunks. Their only business now was holding retreats two weekends a month. A bare-bones staff of brothers remained to oversee the place.

The guy leading our thirty-man retreat was named Bob Anderson. He was seventy years old. A former biker and barroom pugilist with a huge belly and a bad temper, turned AA guru.

For the first two hours in front of the group that Friday afternoon, in the small library hall with folding chairs, old Bob talked only about himself and his alcohol history. He talked about what it was like to be his kind of drunk and juicehead. But he also talked about pulling guys out of their cars on the freeway, even after years sober, to punch them out. About his ex-wives and lost jobs and brutal life. Sober. I'd never heard this kind of AA recovery story before. The party line was, you get sober then tiptoe through the tulips for the rest of your days. This guy was very different.

In a way what Anderson said sounded like pretty standard stuff, but there was an honesty about him and a deliberate effort not to impress anyone. He wasn't ranting about higher powers or being saved by AA from booze and a past life of destruction. He was talking about something different. He was talking about his life sober, about still being crazy after years off booze. That got my attention.

But the other thing that impressed me about Anderson was what one of his friends—a guy named TJ—told me when we finally had a break: Seven years before Anderson had been given a death sentence from cancer after a five-hour surgery to remove his esophagus. He'd been told he had a 3 percent chance of living out the year with his stomach now attached to his throat. Time went by but Anderson didn't die. Instead, he began leading AA retreats and speaking at meetings all over L.A. He always talked about the same thing: how to apply the steps to treat what he called *the Disease of Alcoholism*.

He did this twice a month. The old guy stood in front of the room smiling and talking about himself while strapped with a chemo pack to his waist. The thing loudly hissed a dose of Drano into his system every two minutes, 24-7. And Anderson wasn't selling Jesus, he just talked about himself and how he had changed his life.

According to what TJ told me, Bob would speak on the AA steps, on his feet, for eight hours today, Friday, then twelve hours on Saturday, then another five on Sunday. The guy was such a medical oddity that a team of filmmakers had even done a TV documentary on him. There were only a half dozen people in the world who had survived his kind of cancer and surgery. And most of them were in hospitals, dying.

After the first four-hour session in the library, where old Bob never even sat down and answered written question that the guys passed forward, the group of us filed into dinner in the big retreat mess hall. A ninety-minute break.

More statues and Jesus stuff. A big woven banner above the tables on the wall depicted St. Francis feeding a sparrow. The words sewn into the cloth beneath it read: *You have not chosen me—I have chosen you.* All of us, including the three brothers in robes who ran the place, began our meal by joined hands and parroting the Lord's Prayer. But the food was okay.

After the meal, while a lot of the guys were outside smoking and petting the four adopted stray dogs that roamed the grounds, I pulled TJ aside to ask him if it'd be okay for me to speak with Anderson privately. He said, "Sure, Bruno, I'll talk to Bob and set it up."

Twenty minutes before the next session Anderson and I sat down in the library alone. The old man had been a line mechanic for Lincoln-Mercury for thirty years. I could tell by his manner that he wanted to be friendly, but he was an impatient-type person and his interpersonal skills weren't too good.

Bob was sitting on the corner of a table. He rocked forward then faced me. "TJ says you're sober a few weeks."

"Right," I said. "I've tried AA a few times, but it's never stuck. Something always happens and that's it."

"What happens?"

"I usually get depressed or pissed off. My brother also died recently. That did me in. And I was in a job that I hated. But look, I heard you talking about your thinking, about being sober a long time and your mind still killing you. That rang my bell. I'm like that."

"Look kid, I got alcoholism, see. My trouble with the law and all of that stopped when I quit the booze. Right? I mean, I thought I was okay. Right? I thought I was what in AA they call a *winner*. I mean I was sober, right? So how come my wife left me? How come I kept getting fired from jobs because of my bad temper? Here I was twenty years sober but I wasn't no *winner*. See what I'm saying?"

"I do. A few weeks ago I tried to kill a guy. So I know exactly what you're saying."

"I've worked with four men that died from suicide, sober. Four. They were like me. Just like me. So what's my problem? How come I'm a person who wants to do well—to do the right thing—but I can't? How come I'm always mad at my boss and I still terrorize my kids? How come years sober, I'm still pulling guys who cut me off on the freeway out of their cars and punching them out?"

"Right," I said. "How come?"

"Because I have to treat the mental part of my disease. Quitting booze is one thing. Living with my brain *sober* is another. But, see, today it's all different. I have been at peace with myself for a long long time. That's what I want you to hear. Not the war stories. We all got those. I want you to hear that today—right here, right now—I got a good life. My *living* ain't always so great. I mean, I got cancer and I take chemo all day and every time I see the doctor he shakes his head and tells me I might cash in anytime. But that's okay, see. Because, inside I'm okay. I'm at peace with myself. I got a good life. I'm not angry or pushin' and shovin' the way I used to. My brain's okay, right now. I'm alive and happy, right now. This minute. And right now is all I got. Can you hear that?"

I nodded.

Anderson was smiling for the first time. "Your name's Bono, right?"

"Bruno. Bruno Dante," I said.

"So here's the thing, Bono . . ."

"Bruno."

"Right. Okay. So, see, unless you change how you think you've got zero chance at this deal. Guys like us—you and me—have to apply this thing as a way to live, as a treatment for a broken brain. AA meetings are okay—they're good—but they don't treat *thinking*. Your brain will kill you sober, Bono. Mine almost did more than once."

"Bruno." I said.

"Right. *Bruno*."

"So what do I do? And I'm sick of all the slogans and recovery-ese. *Let us love you until you can love yourself. One day at a time*. That crap. Right now I'm in a six-month inpatient program and I hate it."

"What about a higher power? How you doin' there? What's your understanding in that way?"

I thought about it for a few seconds. "Not so good, I guess. It's pretty nebulous if you ask me."

Anderson was glaring at me. "What's nebulous? What's that word mean?"

"Well, I guess what I'm saying is that I ignore Him and He ignores me. I try to avoid getting zapped. My opinion is that God has zapped me a lot. God doesn't like me much. That's what I think."

"Listen to me. You and me got to live with the disease of alcoholism for our whole lives. But we don't have to die from it."

"Meaning what?" I said.

"Do you want to get this deal? Do you want a good life? Are you ready to start to turn this thing around?"

"I am. I mean, I've got nothing to lose. My life's morphed itself into a pile of dogshit. So sure. I'm ready."

Anderson stuck a craggy old finger into my chest. "Then will you do something for me?" he asked in a low voice. "Will you do what I ask you to do without any argument or back talk?"

"Okay. If you think it'll help. Sure."

"Go back to your room now. Get up and do it. Go in and close the door. I want you to get down on your knees and I want you to ask God—whatever you think that God is—for help. Will you do that? Just say *God please help me. I can't do this alone. I can't go on like this no more.*"

I had to take a deep breath. "Yeah, okay," I said. "I don't want to, but if you think it'll help, I will. I'll do it."

"When we get back to town I want you to call me every day. If you do what I tell you, you'll get what I got. I'll give you a guarantee and sign it if that's what you want. Fair enough?"

So I went back to my room and closed the door. I thought about what Anderson had said for a long time. Then the thought came: *fuckit. You've got nothing to lose.*

So I got down on my knees and I looked up. There on the wall was a picture of some medieval angel or saint with a halo painted around his holy head. I had to close my eyes to remove the image. Then I said the words. *Okay, God, it's me,*

Bruno. I've really screwed things up. If you're there, and can hear me, I need your help. I can't do this alone.

That was it.

When I opened my eyes nothing had changed. I felt the same. The saint was still there on the wall and I didn't feel any different.

Across the room in my suitcase was my cell phone. Before I went into the next meeting I wanted to make sure it was still working so I could call Anderson when I got back to Costa Mesa. So I went over to the chair and unzipped the side pocket of my bag, found the thing, then turned it on.

There were two more messages from Dav-Ko.

I was going to delete them but I decided to call back instead. I pressed *redial* and the number clicked in. Rosie Camacho answered on the first ring.

"Hi, Rosie," I said, "It's Bruno. You guys have left some messages for me."

"Hiya, honey. Howz it going?"

"It's going. What's up? Why the phone messages?"

"Hang on, Bruno bambino, lemme check something. There was some mail—a couple of things. I put 'em in a box under my desk. Stuff that wasn't a bill. They came three or four weeks ago. I left you those messages about it."

"Right. I know. I didn't listen to them. I just didn't feel like any more bad news. Sorry."

"Okay, here it is. Here's a letter. It's from—lemme see— Charter House Press."

"Open it for me, will you?" I asked. I could feel myself holding my breath.

Then I heard Rosie tearing open the envelope and pulling the letter from inside.

". . . Okay," she said. "I got it. I'll read it to you, okay?"
"Okay."

Dear Mister Dante.

Your manuscript was forwarded to us and submitted
for publication by Ms. J. C. Smart. Years ago Ms. Smart
was an editor for this firm and has remained one of our
consulting directors.

After reading your stories we have decided that we
would be delighted to publish your work. A contract will
follow.

Sincerely, Justine Quinn, Editor.

"So, thaz good news, right Bruno?"

It took me a few seconds be able to answer. "Yeah, Rosie,"
I said finally. "That's good news. That's damn good news."

"Oh good, Bruno. I'm really happy for you . . . Oh, hey,
there's another letter here too from them. Same place. A thick
one. Should I open it up too?"

"No, Rosie," I said. "That's okay. That's their contract. Just
do me a favor, will you?"

"Whatever I can, honey."

"I'll call you on Monday and give you the address of where
I'm staying now. Put both letters in another envelope and
send them to me, okay?"

"Sure will, Bruno."

"And thank you very much. I mean it. Thank you very very
much. For everything."

"My pleasure, honey. Hey, keep your phone on, okay? You
never know."

"You're right. I'll keep it on, Rosie. That's a promise."

• • •

I caught up with Anderson in the dining room a few minutes before the start of the next session. "Hey, Bob," I said, "can I talk to you a minute?"

"Okay, we're about to get going again but I got a minute. What's up?"

"I did what you said. I went back to my room and I got down on my knees. And then I said, *God, I need your help.* I prayed."

"Okay, good. That's good. That's a good start."

"Yeah, but nothing really happened. I mean I made a phone call but nothing, you know, *happened.*"

"What'd you expect?"

"I don't know," I said. "I don't know what to expect."

Old Bob was getting impatient. "Look, Bono, God ain't a desk clerk or a bellhop. He don't bring room service. It takes time—application. See what I mean? Steps and application."

"Okay, I guess so."

"You're wearing a watch. I see you got a watch on."

"Yes, I am. I've got a watch."

"Good. Take it off and give it to me."

I took off my twenty-nine-dollar Timex with the fake leather band and handed it to Anderson. He looked at it for a second then gave it back. "Put it on the other wrist—on your right wrist," he instructed.

I did what he said and strapped the watch on my other arm. "Okay. Now what?"

"Keep wearing it like that until I tell you to stop. Can you do that?"

"Sure I can do it. But what's the point? What's the motivation?"

Old Bob was smiling again. "Every time you look for the time and have to remember that you switched wrists, I want you to say, *Thank you, God. Thank you for my life.*"

"That's it?"

"That's it. Pretty soon you'll get it. After you've done it ten or twenty times a day you'll know what I'm talking about."

He reached into his pants pocket and then handed me a business card. I looked at it. The card read simply, *Bob A.* There was a phone number underneath.

"And call me tomorrow. At home. Like we said. You call me every day at seven a.m. We'll talk some more. Deal?"

"Okay, deal," I said. "So . . . what will we talk about?"

"The steps, Bono. We'll talk about how you're going to change your life. We'll start from Step One."

"Bruno. It's Bruno. And I've already done Step One. We did it and the other ones at Charles Street."

"Not with me. You didn't do no steps with me."

"But what's the point? I mean, if I already did it?"

"Are you arguing with me?"

"No, I'm not." I said.

"Good. Because I don't argue. I talk—you listen. I answer questions but I don't argue or debate. Understand?"

"Okay. I understand."

"Good. Look, the meeting's getting started. We gotta go here. Any more questions?"

"Yeah, about a hundred."

"Good. Call me tomorrow morning. Seven a.m. Every day—seven a.m. If you want to change your life I've got all the time in the world. And keep that watch on the other wrist."

The old guy patted me on the back. "Look, kid, you just do what I tell you and everything will start to change. See, if you want to, if you listen, one day at a time I'll show you how you'll never have to take a drink again."

"Okay," I said. "I'll give it a try."

"And Bruno?"

"Yeah."

"You made a good start. Keep going. Keep going for more. You've got nothing to lose."

"You've got that right. I have nothing and I have nothing to lose."

thirty-four

That Sunday in the early afternoon, after the retreat ended, and everybody had had a chance to stand at the podium and talk about their experience with sobriety, the seven of us from Charles Street were on our way toward Orange County in the van with Armondo driving. It was a quiet ride. Nobody said much.

About an hour down the freeway, in Ventura, Mondo decided to pull off so we could use the bathroom and all get sodas and he could get something more to eat.

We found a shopping center with a big, new Ralphs market and drove into the parking lot.

When it was my turn at the deli counter, I ordered an iced coffee. The girl behind the glass was pretty. Early thirties with big, bright eyes. A light-skinned black woman. Her name tag read "Maria." She was smiling. A pretty smile on a pretty face. "So how ya doin'?" she asked.

"I'm doing okay," I said. "Actually, I'm better than okay. I'm having a good day."

"You up here for the weekend?"

"Yeah. There's a group of us. We were at a place above Santa Barbara in the hills. Horse-ranch country. Nice. Very pretty."

Maria was still smiling. "So, you don't get up this way much?"

"Not much," I said. "But I want to come back."

She was looking down, her eyes fixed on the counter. "Well, here's your coffee," she said. "And next time you're up this way, stop in and say hi. Okay?"

"I'd like that. That's a grand idea."

"So what's your name?"

"Bruno. It's Bruno."

"I'll be right here, Bruno." Maria said, now looking at me.

Walking away from the counter with my coffee I realized that something was different. People looked the same. The guys from Charles Street looked the same and the people in the store looked like regular people and pretty Maria was probably the same, but I felt different. Then I noticed something—the voice in my head—*Jimmy*'s voice, was gone—or asleep.

Back in the van Mondo started the motor. We pulled out of the parking lot and back on to the freeway. To our right was a hundred miles of Pacific Ocean. There'd been a storm and the sea was choppy. I began counting the sets of waves as they crashed in on the shore. We headed south back toward Los Angeles.

Acknowledgments

Ayrin Leigh Fante, my wife, who from the day we first met, has kept the faith, stayed for the ride, never looked back, and managed to keep her seat belt strapped tight.

Bruce Fitzpatrick, my good friend, for his support, humor, and ownership of a cell phone.

Mark SaFranko, author, musician-performer, poet, songwriter, actor, fiction editor, astrologer, etc., and the goddamndest best example I know of a man who presses forward and refuses to quit—no matter what.

Tony O'Neill, without whose generosity of spirit this book may never have seen print.

Michele Weisler, for her swarming brilliance and friendship and her unapologetic devotion to my work.

John Fante, who missed the boat yet managed to land on top of the mountain, and continues to inspire and amaze me.

Amy Baker at Harper Perennial, for supporting and publishing my stuff and for her kindness.

Bettye LaVette, for changing my life with a single blues song.

About the author

Insights,
Interviews
& More . . .

About the book

Read on

Meet Dan Fante

About the author

DAN FANTE was born and raised in Los
Angeles. At twenty, he quit school and hit the
road, eventually ending up in New York City
for twelve years. Fante has worked at dozens
of crummy jobs, including: door-to-door
salesman, taxi driver, window washer,
telemarketer, private investigator, hotel
night manager, chauffeur, mailroom clerk,
deckhand, dishwasher, carnival barker,
envelope stuffer, dating service counselor,
furniture salesman, and parking attendant.
Fante is married and has a five-year-old son
named Michaelangelo Giovanni Fante. He
hopes to eventually learn how to play the
harmonica. ◠

Living in My Dreams

A Letter from Dan Fante to His Mom, Joyce, During a Serious Illness

May 12, 2002

SOMETIMES WITH MY WRITING, I spend time reflecting on my past and childhood, turning over stones, exposing some of the most slimy snakes and worms. I do this because I have to, because my feelings in my own history have become the source of a lot of my material. But lately, these last years, it turns out that the exercise is no longer uncomfortable for me. I have done it so much in my writing life that now I see myself merely as one or another of the characters in a piece rather than something decomposing or struggling against a madness that so often seemed to possess me when I was younger. I feel like a cameraman smudging the outside of his lens with Vaseline to soften the scene; the effect on me now brings a kind of ease to my thoughts. A peace, even.

And very often these days, writing poetry, I think of you and Dad. About the house on Cliffside Drive. About being a kid with all of us together. Nick and Vickie, and Jim. When I close my eyes I can return there effortlessly and find you cooking dinner and all of us just coming in from playing ball on the big lawn. And us all sitting on those terrible old couches in the TV room. And you coming in the room and shooing Rocco or some other flea-ridden monster from that corner cushion to claim your place. And Dad getting pissed off by a commercial or show and snarling at one of us . . . "Change the station, kid." ▶

> Very often these days, writing poetry, I think of you and Dad. About the house on Cliffside Drive. About being a kid with all of us together.

3

Living in My Dreams *(continued)*

Even the awful report cards I used to get. Once Dad called one of them an "abomination." I remember it was the first time I had ever heard the word, and I was pleased to have a father who could use such a word. "Abomination." Pretty cool. And I remember the time my junior high counselor told you, "Don't worry, Mrs. Fante, your son Daniel is an underachiever but someday he'll find his niche." How furious you were with that asshole. All this and reams more I can evoke effortlessly these days. Like flipping pages in a vacation photo album.

But never in those thoughts is there a time when you were not my friend, when you were not there to help me through all my confusions and catastrophes as a kid. I could always let Mom know what was going on.

So thanks, Mom. Now that this thing I do is a *living dream* for me, it is the sweetest one I have. Because, as it turns out, everything is good in my life today—the joy of doing the thing I always wanted to do, putting words on paper and giving them away, is something I got from you and your love of literature, and Yeats, and T. S. Eliot. And from Dad. I'm living that today. I haven't had a drink in years. Today things are possible for me that I never could have imagined.

It's a helluva great deal, Mom. So thanks. I love you. ❧

❝ I remember the time my junior high counselor told you, 'Don't worry, Mrs. Fante, your son Daniel is an underachiever but someday he'll find his niche.' ❞

Silencing the Noise in My Head

I HAVE BEEN ASKED by Harper Perennial to write about my relationship to Bruno Dante. So I will.

I began to think of myself as a writer after many years as a drunk. There were jails, a hundred jobs, train wrecks and off-the-wall, winner-take-all relationships. Somehow, up until then, most of my adult life had been spent being one kind of a pitchman or another. I've always found myself gravitating toward the jive and shuck: selling. This is strange to say because, by nature, I don't like people and I'm a loner.

After I stopped the booze and left New York City, boiler-room selling in Los Angeles came naturally, and I fell into the phone sales business. The fast buck made me feel good—like a success. After a year or so I got pretty good at it and began to do quite well. I bought stuff: clothes, a house at the beach. A fast, nifty, kick-ass sports car. And on came the women. I become desirable, taller, and better-looking. Success can do that.

But sober, my philosophy of life had now diminished to one line: *when in doubt, make more money.*

The problem was that I was pretty much the same defiant asshole I had been as a boozer. I'd done a lot of damage to others over the years and I was still doing damage. People, women, stuff, came in and out of my life like fast-forwarding through bad TV.

I still had a voice that talked to me continuously. It was judging and snarling. ▶

> **❝ I began to think of myself as a writer after many years as a drunk. ❞**

Silencing the Noise in My Head *(continued)*

I even named him and talked back to him in public. He hated me and made me crazy.

And I had ghosts too. The unfriendly, wake-your-ass-up-in-the-middle-of-the-night kind. This continued for a long time. I didn't drink and I went to AA meetings and I kept making money but I was still me—the same guy. Crown Prince Screwyou. Once, I remember complaining to an old AA guru-type guy named Ted Harbock in a coffee shop after a meeting. He'd listened to me spill my yarn then sucked back a deep drag on his Camel. "Look kid," he hissed, "if nothing changes, then nothing changes."

Swell. From then on I did my best to avoid Harbock.

Then it all when to hell. I had a beef with the owner of the company I was running and decided hey, if you don't *get* who I am and what I've done for you then, well, sayonara, shithead.

A couple of months later I was drunk again. I had money in the bank at the time. Quite a bit of money. But I owed the government too because I had worked as what the IRS calls an independent contractor. My best reasoning at the time was to spend it all. So I did. It didn't matter that the result of the decision would be years of tax problems.

Many months later I managed to put some sobriety together again and was living in a room at my mother's house, driving her hand-me-down *seven*-cylinder Chrysler, walking to local AA meetings. Mom wasn't delighted at the prospect of having a middle-aged bad-tempered roommate. My unemployment checks had just run out from the last job I'd been fired from: a hotel night manager gig.

One day in my parent's garage I discovered and dug out my father's old Smith Corona typewriter. There was half a ream of yellow legal typing paper there in the box too. Before he'd gone blind John Fante had written his last novel on that paper using that typewriter.

All my life I'd wanted to write but could never make it work. As a cabbie in New York City I'd scrawled hundreds of poems on my big lined notepad and thrown each one away at the end of the shift.

But now, back in my room, the tools were there in front of me. I'm pretty sure I was insane at the time and I could not read and/or watch the TV or concentrate on anything because I had endless swirling thoughts of vengeance and killing myself.

So I typed. I typed for hours and hours. I typed to shut my mind off. I typed to stay alive.

The stuff was crazy, meandering, styleless rage and bitterness and sadness. I wasn't much as a typist but I didn't care. The words just kept spilling out, single-spaced, mistakes and all.

A few weeks later, after a hundred pages or so, I reread the stuff I had written. It wasn't good but there was something there beneath the muck—the seed, a speck of an idea.

That idea was about my father. We had never really connected as people and never liked each other much. He was a drunk and a rager and a crazy, passionate artist. Pop had seen himself and his life as a failure. But somewhere in me I came to understand ▶

66 So I typed. I typed for hours and hours. I typed to shut my mind off. I typed to stay alive. 99

that I loved him deeply and unreasonably. I wanted to say something about that love.

So I started the story over trying to tell it in a way that no one I'd read had ever tried to tell it. My desire was to say something new. I didn't care about entertaining or impressing anyone. I wanted to grab the reader by the shirt and scream into his face.

In the book I called myself Bruno Dante and what I wrote compressed the last fifteen years of my life into three weeks. The literary term for that is "fiction." The title I finally chose for the manuscript was *Chump Change*.

When I was done with the book I realized I no longer wanted to die or hated my father. There was less noise in my head. It was like taking a deep breath for the first time. Another life had replaced the old one. Just like that. And Bruno Dante had became me—my voice on paper.

Maybe it was all an accident or maybe it was the act of a patient, tolerant God. What I can tell you now—for certain—is that I can't stop writing.

In the book I called myself Bruno Dante and what I wrote compressed the last fifteen years of my life into three weeks.

An Excerpt from Dan Fante's Upcoming Book, *Fante, a Memoir*

The following is from my upcoming book, Fante, a Memoir. *The book is about my literary heritage, my father, my family, and the first forty or so years of my life.*

WHEN MY GRANDFATHER, Nicola Fante, came to America at the turn of the nineteenth century he brought something priceless along that would not fit into his ratty, rope-tied suitcase, something that even the reprobate old shit could not desecrate. Those bitter winters in his hometown of Torricella Peligna in Italy, the thousand nights in saloons telling tall tales with his *paesanos,* had eventually produced a superb storyteller. Give the snarling old juicer a couple of glasses of rosé and he could go on for an hour or more, hypnotizing those before him with images of absurd bravery, of battles and blood vendettas where dozens met their end, of full-breasted maidens and swords of fire, of fearless Uncle Mingo with his long red mustache and wide, feathered white hat, leading his gang of thugs on to glory.

Over the years, with each rendering of an heroic account, Grandpa Nick's stories took on more color. His villains' villainy became more villainous and their treachery more diabolical. To kids like me and my older brother Nicky, the stuff was magical.

As boys in L.A. we would sit on the floor by our fireplace (a ten-foot wide stone monster that Grandpa had built himself to ▶

> 66 Over the years, with each rendering of an heroic account, Grandpa Nick's stories took on more color. His villains' villainy became more villainous and their treachery more diabolical. 99

replace the termite infested original) and listen to his fables, never missing a word. We would laugh and our mouths would fall open and allow our minds to float with him back to old Abruzzo in his homeland.

One of Grandpa's favorite targets for stories was aristocratic treachery. We were treated to evolving versions of one particular yarn. The original incident probably happened in the town of Roccascalegna, a two-hour walk from Torricella Peligna. There is a stone tower in Roccascalegna above a small castle, and for a long time a baron named de Corvis Corvo was the overlord. This knucklehead had a less than paternal way of exacting tribute from his subjects. Before giving his consent for maidens of the area to be taken in marriage, this *barone*'s price was to spend the wedding night with the bride to be. Nice, right?

This shittiness went on for years until one of the bridegrooms, after hearing the cost exacted for matrimony, decided that enough was enough.

Of course as Grandpa Nick's account evolved, the bride, Lucia, got more beautiful—a near princess—and young Giuseppe became more like Robin Hood than the stocky teenage son of a shoemaker. Eventually, Grandpa managed to endow the kid with a splendid black stallion and a silver-tipped stiletto.

Giuseppe and Lucia had traveled a full day to arrive at Roccascalegna to get hitched. In Giuseppe's wagon, in the wedding trunk, were two handmade dresses.

After several hours of celebrating in the town square, that evening, when Lucia was escorted to the tower to service her patron and dispense with her virginity prior to the wedding, she had a stand-in. The *barone*'s chickens had come home to roost. His royal chamber was candlelit and dim, and Giuseppe had on the second dress from the trunk and a head-covering veil, and the *barone* was probably drunk enough, so the impersonation worked.

Once in bed, Giuseppe slashed the baron's throat, then hung him out the tower window to allow his blood to flow down the rough castle stones to the street below.

Of course, according to Grandpa, the town was liberated from tyranny and years of injustice and everyone celebrated for days on end. That is, until the next hideous knucklehead of royal blood took his place. But Grandpa never got to that part.

Old Nick always acted out all the characters as he told his stories to us. He would move a step or two, then change his voice and facial expression so we would know which character he was playing. My favorites in his stories were always the bad guys, because Grandpa had a decided flair for villains and how their faces looked and how they spoke. He always wrung his hands and made a twisted face for the baron. The performance was pure theater and could last an hour or more as long as there was wine left in our kitchen.

"Danny-boy, you like how Grandpa tell you da *barone* storee?"

"Sure, Grandpa. I like that one a lot. But ▶

> 66 My favorites in his stories were always the bad guys, because Grandpa had a decided flair for villains and how their faces looked and how they spoke. 99

this Giuseppe guy, what happened to him? Did somebody kill him because he killed the baron?"

"I done kno. Too many questions for a kid. How 'bout Uncle Mingo? You wanna hear Uncle Mingo and da Bandits again?"

"Sure, Grandpa."

"Okay, go pour ol' Grandpa some vino. . . . You know, Danny, Uncle Mingo had one thousand cats."

"C'mon, Grandpa. A thousand cats?"

"Go get me da wine—I'll tell you wha happened. I tell you da whole store."

There is no doubt in my mind that my father's gift for writing, and eventually mine, were inherited from a superb storyteller named Nicola Fante, from a little town high in central Italy, beneath Mount Majella, called Torricella Peligna. This jewel of a place was mostly destroyed by the Germans during World War II, but one of the buildings the Krauts could not blow up still stands. It is a thick stone barn built by the hands of a hot-tempered little guy who eventually became a master stonemason. An artist. My grandfather, Nicola Fante. ∾

> " There is no doubt in my mind that my father's gift for writing, and eventually mine, were inherited from a superb storyteller named Nicola Fante. "

Three Poems by Dan Fante

In the Sunshine

I met the meanest bastard starving cat while
    sitting with a book
smoking half a pack of Luckies on a bench at
    Venice beach

He saw me and came up—white—with one
    green eye and one yellow eye
and a fresh slash on his scarred ear
angry as a wounded wolf he kept his distance
and his look said, "feed me or fuck off"
that bench you're on is my territory

    What he didn't know is that I know
desperate too—and crazy—and what
emptiness and aloneness and rage can do
to you when you've got nothing but pain in
your pockets and your home is a busted-out
twenty-year-old Pontiac stalled in an alley
in West L.A. and the voices in your head
are carving you up and killing more of you
off each day—and you wake up and drink
more rat-piss wine to keep you from instant
madness and God becomes a guy coming out
of the market handing you chump change
toward another fucking jug and fear is your
finest feeling and love is dead and all time is
dead and even your eyes stink and your gut
is bloated with the screaming voices of those
you hate and the only sanity can be found in
the small miracle of sucking back one more
drink—

That mean white cat didn't know that I've
    been cut too

Three Poems by Dan Fante *(continued)*

from the same cloth
The only difference between us is fifteen years
   and my typewriter

Asking
For years I thought that
talking to the Gods
was an exercise done privately under
   unforgiving
distant stars

Ridiculous unrequited prayer
evoked by staring at old, cold books—
   with mean small print

But then I discovered
that
just ain't it at all

God can be found in the "thank you" voice
   of the guy
at the counter in the supermarket or
the quietness of a stranger's parking lot smile
or
the rattle of weeds across a dry summer
   Mojave
or
watching my unfettered fingers jump jump
   jumping
across the computer keys
deep in the middle of typing three hours
   worth of unscrubbed truth

God, for me, has turned out to be a conscious
   choice—a self-evoked experience
just
like
love

For Mark

Walk with only words and books as your
    friend
Dream the dreams of deviant dead writer
    saints
Who coming before you
Drowned the pain of their purest hearts in
    vats of gin
Like a flailing, unloved cat

Embrace selfishness and joblessness
smoke millions of unfiltered cigarettes
and glue your ass hopelessly
to the evilest drunken crack-whore who'd
trade your balls in a New York instant
for the guy at the end of the bar
with the pitted face and a fifty-dollar bill

Do not be courageous
remember that all men are fools
and liars
soulless captives of their own blood-stained
    necessity

And forgive nothing

Then maybe one day
like me
your feet aching and your head still raw
    from last night's festivity
you'll kick over a box
or turn a page
and find yourself face-to-face
with the blurry eyes of God ∾

Favorite Writers and Their Works

Hubert Selby, Jr.: *Last Exit to Brooklyn*
Eugene O'Neill: *Long Day's Journey into Night, A Moon for the Misbegotten*
Edward Lewis Wallant: *The Pawnbroker, The Tenants of Moombloom*
Tennessee Williams: *A Streetcar Named Desire, The Glass Managerie*
Edna St. Vincent Millay: All poems
William Butler Yeats: All poems
Truman Capote: *In Cold Blood, Handcarved Coffins*
Knut Hamsun: *Pan, Hunger*
Charles Bukowski: All poems
John Fante: *Ask the Dust, Dreams from Bunker Hill*
William Shakespeare: "Romeo and Juliet," "Julius Ceasar," "Hamlet"
Lewis Carol: *Through the Looking-Glass*
Alfred Lord Tennyson: All Poems
Woody Allen: *The Complete Prose of Woody Allen*
Fyodor Dostoyevsky: *The Idiot, Crime and Punishment*
Albert Camus: *The Stranger, The Plague*
William Saroyan: *The Time of Your Life: A Comedy in Three Acts*
Franz Kafka: *The Metomorphosis*
Luigi Pirandello: Short stories

Have You Read?
More by Dan Fante

**Coming in Fall 2009 from
Harper Perennial, the Adventures
of Bruno Dante Continue . . .**

CHUMP CHANGE

Aspiring writer and part-time drunk
Bruno Dante returns to Los Angeles to face
his family in the wake of his father's illness.
The tension and stress drive him to dull the
pain the only way he knows how—with
alcohol. A couple days later he wakes up
naked in a stolen car with an underage
hooker whose pimp has stolen his wallet,
and this trip has just begun.

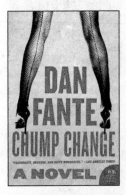

"Don't miss *Chump Change*. It is passionate,
obscene, and quite wonderful."

—*Los Angeles Times*

MOOCH

Bruno Dante is the best boiler-room
salesman in Los Angeles with one problem:
He can't keep a good thing going. When he
enters into a love-hate relationship with a
beautiful and dangerous coworker, his world
begins to spiral out of control.

"Breathtaking writing. . . . Angry, acerbic,
self-pitying, and often painfully funny. . . .
Read it at your peril."

—Anthony Bourdain

SPITTING OFF TALL BUILDINGS

Bruno Dante has fled Los Angeles for New York. The string of deadbeat temporary telemarketing gigs is getting to him and the steady work he can stand is hard to come by. But things get all the more complicated for Bruno as he endures a never-ending stream of drinking binges and blackouts.

"Evokes brutally and skillfully the violently numb condition of his alter ego."

—*The Times* (London)

Don't miss the next book by your favorite author. Sign up now for AuthorTracker by visiting www.AuthorTracker.com.